I0788459

"You should know that my blood is very powerful."

"As is mine," he replied, his accented voice a touch deeper now.

A predator about to strike, I thought, admiring the silver in his irises. It blended with the black edges, reminding me of a bursting star. *Alluring. Tempting. Sinful.*

"Are you accepting?" he asked, his English lilt more prominent now and giving away his anticipation.

Yes, he definitely wants to taste me as much as I want to taste him.

"I am, yes." *Bite me, if you dare, King of Gold and Garnet. Because your reaction to my blood will show me if you're really worthy of my time.*

Only the strongest could handle an essence as intense as mine. Hence my warning. But he'd responded confidently, as he had with everything else.

A true leader. A royal. A vampire king.

His expression shadowed, some intrinsic part of him understanding the challenge I'd just laid at his feet.

You're mine now, Goddess of Night, he seemed to say as he pulled me impossibly closer with his arm around my lower back. His hand remained against my nape, giving it a subtle squeeze as he lowered his lips to my neck.

USA TODAY BESTSELLING AUTHOR

LEXI C. FOSS

CRAVE ME

Immortal Vices & Virtues

This is a work of fiction. Names, characters, places, and incidents are either the product of the author's imagination or are used fictitiously, and any resemblance to actual persons, living or dead, business establishments, events, or locales is entirely coincidental.

Crave Me

Copyright © 2022 Lexi C. Foss

All rights reserved.

No part of this book may be reproduced in any form or by any electronic or mechanical means, including information storage and retrieval systems, without written permission from the author, except for the use of brief quotations in a book review. This book may not be redistributed to others for commercial or noncommercial purposes.

Editing by: Outthink Editing, LLC

Proofreading by: Katie Schmahl & Jean Bachen

Jacket Cover Design: Clarissa Yeo, Yocla Cover Designs

Book Cover Design: Manuela Serra

Interior Art: Manuela Serra

Cover Photography: CJC Photography

Cover Models: Peter Stelling & Jenna Elisabeth

Published by: Ninja Newt Publishing, LLC

Hardback Edition

ISBN: 978-1-68530-151-4

To Iceland, for continuing to inspire stories in my head. Your magical landscapes and stunning waterfalls (Fosses!) are among the most beautiful I've ever seen. I can't wait for us to meet again.

And to Kel, for creating this gorgeous world and allowing Nyx to crash-land on the shores of it. I hope she makes you laugh, my dude. Oh, and please send my love to Uriah. #SoulMate

CRAVE ME

An Immortal Vices and Virtues Novel

Once upon a time, a series of portals opened on Earth, allowing magic to spill into the human world.
Houses were created. Supernaturals were assigned. And a new balance was formed.
All new arrivals are required to join a House.
But this is the tale of a goddess who refused and the House King who brought her to heel.

Nyx.
Goddess of Night.
My newest obsession.

The daring female killed one of my men.
Which made it my job as the Gold and Garnet House King to make her pay.

Oh, there were so many things I wanted to do with that disobedient little mouth of hers. But she was much stronger than she led anyone to believe.
Now I'm left with a craving I can't quite sate.
Because one bite wasn't enough.

You may be the Goddess of Night, but I'm still your king.

You will kneel.
You will beg.
And most importantly, you will bleed.

Welcome to the House of Gold and Garnet, where power defines the monarchy and blood is a preferred currency.
Proceed at your own risk.

Author's Note: *Crave Me* is a dark standalone paranormal romance set in the Immortal Vices and Virtues Universe. Every book in this shared world is a guaranteed happily-ever-after with a satisfying ending and no cliffhangers.

For fans of the Blood Alliance series, this is the story of Nyx and Vesperus, the goddess and her vampire lover that started it all...

Hello and welcome to the chaos inside my head!

This was such a unique book to write. It's very much part of the Immortal Vices and Virtues world, but it also leads into another series of mine that some of you might have read—the Blood Alliance series.

However, the tone of *Crave Me* is just so much different as a result of the world rules and the voices I chose to explore.

Nyx is quite possibly one of the most powerful heroines I've ever written. But she's not over the top in her strength; she's… *quirky*. She's a goddess exploring a realm and the magic within it. And she's not letting anyone tell her what to do or where to go. Not even the vampire king who finds her.

Therefore, I would categorize this as a "lighter" read from me (if comparing it to the Blood Alliance world). But I still have my blood-play moments. Vesperus is a vampire, after all. So if biting isn't your thing, then… that might be a problem.

But if you're looking for a standalone read filled with humor, sensuality, a little blood play, and forbidden romance, then you've definitely chosen the right story.

Crave Me can be read without knowledge of any of my other books, and it's a complete standalone in the Immortal Vices and Virtues world.

It just also happens to be the origin story of how Nyx met Vesperus. And to my Blood Alliance fans, it'll tell you what led Nyx to create the Blessed Ones… ;)

PROLOGUE

NYX

Roughly Three Months Ago

Another realm.

Another failure.

I sighed and flipped the enchanted obsidian medallion through my fingers.

This was my seventeenth universe, and it was somehow even worse than the last sixteen. No magic. No supernatural presence. No excitement. And no moon.

I turned my gaze up to the smog-covered sky, my lips curling down. The mortals of this realm had polluted their atmosphere so spectacularly that there was no longer any light here. And most of the humans were dead as a result.

No sun meant no plants.

Which led to no animals.

The sense of starvation was so potent that I could almost taste it in the dirty air.

There wasn't even any water left, the sewage having tainted the streams and oceans and reducing it all to toxic waste.

Definitely not my ideal reality, I decided. *Again.*

The other realms had at least offered me a few months of intrigue. This one hadn't even lasted days.

"Right." My fingers stilled as I focused on the magic embedded inside the crescent-shaped medallion in my hand. "Shall we try again?"

No one could hear me.

But I was used to that.

I often existed in my own world of creation, which was what had inspired this hunt to begin with. I wanted a home. A partner. A fulfilling existence. *Friends.*

Alas, I was beginning to think that fate disagreed with my desires.

Well, too bad, Goddess Destiny. I want more than to just exist in the background of a world. I want a true purpose, whatever that may mean.

I closed my eyes and focused on the obsidian stone, words of the ancient tongue spilling from my lips as I ignited the enchantment that would help me traverse reality once more.

The magic hummed around me, stirring a flicker of light behind my closed eyelids that almost made me dizzy. It was a subtle warning that said I'd used the charm again too quickly, but I had no choice. This realm was uninhabitable.

Perhaps if you sent me somewhere more accommodating, I wouldn't have to do this, I thought at the stone. *However, you seem determined to—*

A blast of power shocked my system, lighting my veins on fire and eliciting a sharp gasp from my lips.

My eyes flew open, searching for the threat, only for my world to be flipped upside down as a whirlwind of dark energy caught me in its web.

I growled, my own energy flaring to life as I called upon the moon to light up this inky abyss.

A sprinkling of starlike orbs appeared in my peripheral vision, my magic flickering to life. But it wasn't fast enough.

The dark spiral swallowed me whole, sending me into a whirl of foreign energy that had me crashing into a wave of icy water.

I sputtered, my feet kicking on instinct as I forced myself to the surface.

Just to be sucked back down again and spun in a lethal circle that shoved me into a jagged wall of sharp rock.

I grasped at the wall, searching for something to grip to try to yank myself up out of the waves, but the water was too powerful, the moon controlling the tide.

Mine, I thought, lassoing the old magic I felt swirling around my birthright. *You are* mine *to command. Hear me!*

It took several tugs for the tide to settle, the moon shifting and allowing me to temporarily control the waves enough for me to break free. The whole world would feel it. But they wouldn't be able to explain the shift.

A majestic event, the humans would say. *A phenomenon that can't be described.*

Assuming the mortals of this world were like all the rest, anyway.

I spat out a mouthful of water as I used the tide to take me around the rock cliff and toward a nearby shore.

Then I collapsed against the dark sand and heaved a breath as I released my control over the moon.

Magic fizzled over my skin, the world righting itself again.

The ocean rebelled with a massive wave that nearly sucked me out to sea once more, but I pushed it back with a blast of energy, reminding the substance who the real master was here.

I'm the Goddess of Night. The Mistress of the Moon. A queen who will not bow.

I'd been called so many names throughout my existence, all of them accurate. But I usually just preferred *Nyx*.

I rolled to my back and admired the beautiful midnight sky above, noting the lack of clouds and inhaling the clean air.

Much better, I thought dreamily. *No smog. No pollution. Just an invisible layer of...* I frowned, my hands going to the earth as I tried to push myself upward. *Well, that's new.*

This world had magic.

A lot of it.

I could feel the energy pulsing all around me, the vivacious nature of it an intoxicating presence that sent blissful shocks through my veins.

My lips began to curl, my heart skipping a beat.

Have I finally done it? Have I finally found a proper—

A harsh zap rippled up my arm, making me drop my stone in the sand. "What—"

My eyes rounded as the obsidian medallion dissolved into ash.

No, not ash.

Sand.

Except... I ran my fingers through it, my brow furrowing. "That's impossible."

I could still feel the power shimmering in my spirit, the stone's magnetic energy having simply been transferred to something else.

My legs shook as I forced myself to stand, my gaze searching the beach and nearby rocks for the mystical source. *Where did you go?* I wondered, spinning around. *I can feel you. Why can't I see you?*

I glanced again at the tiny pile of sand that used to resemble my medallion, my lips curling downward. "Is this a punishment for using you again too soon?" I asked it.

The magic seemed to shimmer in response.

"I see." I narrowed my gaze. "So you've moved into a new object, and now you're going to make me work to find you."

A majestic game of hide-and-seek.

I pinched the bridge of my nose and shook my head. This was going to take a while. Because the magic could be anywhere.

I whispered an enchantment, one meant to make moon energy appear only to me. But other than the tide behind me, my senses picked up on nothing.

Which meant the magic had left this area for another. Fortunately, it still existed in this realm. If it didn't, I wouldn't even be able to feel it.

Fine, I thought at it. *I'll hunt you.*

And in the meantime, I would explore this magical world. See what it had to offer. Maybe even stay for—

A bullet cracked through the air, making me phase on instinct to about twenty yards to my left. The sound of a male cursing followed, with another yelling, "There!"

Two more shots fired, forcing me to wrap myself in shadows and phase again.

"What the fuck is that?" one of the men demanded.

"I don't know, but it isn't registered. Kill it."

My eyebrows lifted. "Excuse me?" I materialized beside the one demanding that the other *kill it.* "I'm not—"

His hand appeared with a blade, the metal sharp and nearly puncturing my chest as he lunged for me with a feral growl. Magic rippled around him, telling me he wasn't human. And neither was his friend.

Nor were the three others who had suddenly appeared with weapons, all aimed at me.

"Well, this is quite a primitive welcome," I muttered as I hit them all with a gust of energy.

The tide responded to my call, the water whirling in the air and slamming the five offenders against the beach.

I stood before them, hands on my hips, as they all grappled for their weapons. "I don't appreciate—"

Another bullet fired, this one nearly hitting me in the head, but I phased before it could meet its mark.

"*Rude,*" I growled, moving to the being in question who had just tried to shoot me between the eyes. I tsked. "You have very bad manners." I yanked his gun out of his hand and threw it into the sea.

Only to be tackled by a wolf.

Shifter, I realized immediately, my eyes narrowing as his teeth attempted to sink into my throat. That would *not* end well for him.

I shoved him off me with a harsh push that sent him back a good twenty feet, causing all the others to curse in his wake.

I'd clearly gotten off on the wrong foot with these inhabitants.

With a sigh, I attempted to brush the sand off my damp clothes and take on a regal position. "Now. If you would be so kind as to allow me—"

Magic hummed in the air, warning me of the incoming army of supernaturals. There were at least a dozen, all of their auras aggressive and filled with a mixture of energy.

My lips flattened.

I did not want my grand entrance to a potential new home to be defined by bloodshed. I was not Ares. He might have chosen war, but I preferred more amicable introductions.

I would deal with these beings after I had a proper shower, napped, and dried my clothes.

Then, if I was feeling better, I would make my presence known.

Or maybe I'd poke around a bit first. Learn the rules and laws of the place. Decide if I wanted to stay.

And search for my lost obsidian magic in the process.

Yes.

A sound plan.

"Enjoy your night," I told them as I pulled one last massive wave from the ocean. It was meant to be a distraction more than a retaliation, but the moon sensed my displeasure and reacted accordingly.

So the wave was more of a tsunami in size.

It wouldn't kill anyone. However, it would certainly send a message.

A goddess walks among you. Be respectful. And maybe, if she likes this realm, she'll choose to stay.

I smiled. *Time to explore.*

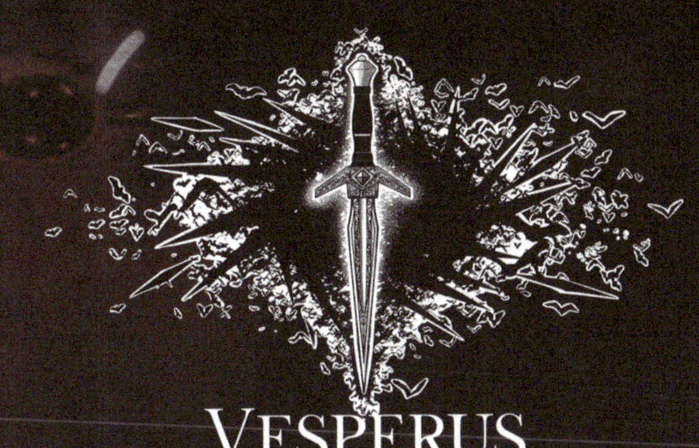

VESPERUS

THE HOUSE OF DEATH AND DIAMOND.

A fitting name, considering how I felt right now.

So. Many. Fucking. Emails.

And the paperwork. Fuck, I was drowning in it.

Sign this. Approve that. Review these.

I wanted to bang my head against the goddamn desk. This was the part of being a king that I strongly disliked.

It was something I also rarely had to do as King of the House of Gold and Garnet. Most of my paperwork involved signing death warrants or providing kill orders.

We were a House of mercenaries who dealt blood like currency.

Alas, the formation of a new House within my territory required a whole different realm of administrative bureaucracy.

Especially when it resulted in all my constituents needing to decide whether they wanted to move into an area within the new boundary lines, or shift allegiances.

Most had opted for the former, selecting new homes throughout Scandinavia and sending me the bills for their relocations.

But a handful had chosen to shift Houses, their notorious penchants for death arousing their interests in the new formation. Particularly as it was filled with the newest supernatural breed in existence—the phantoms. They were similar to ghosts, being able to shift between corporeal and ethereal states.

I would have felt a bit slighted by the choice, except two phantoms had opted to join Gold and Garnet. And I was very much looking forward to getting to know them.

Once I surfaced from this administrative hell.

"You're growling again," Cara said as she set a mug of blood-spiked coffee on my desk.

I grunted and picked up the much-needed refreshment to take a sip.

The warm substance resembled liquid heaven against my tongue.

"A-positive," I murmured, pleased with the offering. "Thank you."

Cara winked and plopped down on the couch beside Larus. He gave her a deadpan look and asked, "Where's my coffee?"

"Still at the coffee shop, I imagine," she replied in a succulent voice that she paired with a batting of her long blonde eyelashes.

"Hmm," he hummed, his silver-blue eyes lighting with a familiar fire. "Then perhaps I should be jealous?"

She smiled. "Maybe that's the point."

"Feeling bored, sweetheart?" he asked, his long, dark hair flickering with fae magic. "In need of a reminder regarding who you belong to?"

"Mmm, I do enjoy your reminders," she whispered.

These two fae were as bad as vampires, constantly baiting each other into fucking. And they were known to enjoy an audience, too.

I cleared my throat. "This paperwork is hell enough without you two throwing sex vibes all over my office. If you're not going to help, then get the fuck out."

"So grumpy," Cara teased.

"He prefers playing with knives over pens," Larus replied. "But as the Gold and Garnet King, he has to address all these concerns personally or risk dissension within the House."

"So you keep saying," I muttered. Larus often served as my political liaison, his ability to politely appease others far superior to my own. But as the head of the House, I had an image to maintain.

And he helped me accomplish that by advising me on appropriate responses.

Such as now with all these requests.

"It will mean more coming from you," he'd said as the requests had started pouring in. "Our people need to know you care."

Which I did. I cared about them more than they could even fathom. I just preferred showing it via protective measures, not politically correct ones.

It wasn't about power, although I did enjoy the benefits of being king. But it was more about duty for me. I was the strongest in our lands. Therefore, I led. If someone stronger surpassed me, I would consider relinquishing the role.

Alas, the only one close to me in strength had no desire to lead.

Kaspian, my second-in-command, much preferred playing in the shadows. He hid his power behind a mask of boredom, choosing to follow my command rather than create his own. But when needed, he showed up. And that, at the end of it all, was what would eventually push him into a leadership role.

"Here." Cara gestured with her elven-shaped chin toward the coffee table in front of them, and a muffin appeared. "Espresso chip with a few extra chocolate chips."

Some fae could conjure weapons. This one could conjure baked goods. Not exactly a helpful mercenary trait on the surface, but it didn't detract from her lethal nature. It simply made her that much more deadly.

A true black widow—sweet on the outside, absolutely deadly on the inside.

Larus grinned. "A woman after my own heart."

"No. I already own that." Her confident words had the male beside her humming in agreement. The mated duo shared the role as my third-in-command, the powerful fae couple being two of my best sharpshooters.

Only my second-in-command could best them.

My talent for guns paled in comparison to all three of them. Mostly because I preferred a good old-fashioned sword. Throwing knives worked, too.

Or simply fangs.

Alas, I was trapped in my office for the unforeseeable future.

I need a good fuck, I decided. *Or a fight.*

I'd have to arrange something for later. Or maybe both. Perhaps Jira would be up for some playtime. She always did fancy—

A stack of papers on my desk fluttered to the ground as my second-in-command appeared beside me, his vampiric speed rivaling my own.

I set my coffee mug down and eyed him. "Do you have any idea how long it took me to organize those?"

Kaspian glanced at the mess, then set his phone on the desk. "Slater just called."

That certainly wasn't an expression of regret. However, those three words made an apology moot.

Because there could be only one reason why Slater would have called my second.

I locked gazes with Kaspian. "He found it?"

It being the unknown magical entity causing issues all over the fucking country.

Gold and Garnet had taken responsibility for tracking *it* down nearly three months ago, and so far all my mercenaries had failed despite the hefty bounty hanging over the unknown entity's head.

I'd finally given the job to Slater, my best tracker, with the hopes of wrapping all this up. Because whatever this thing was, it was causing issues. All of vampire kind could feel the presence of the unwanted power. And many other supernaturals had sensed it, too.

Which had led to a myriad of messages and phone calls that I would prefer not to be taking on the issue.

"Yes. It's in a pub," Kaspian replied, his dark irises radiating savage excitement. "In Ireland."

"A pub?" I repeated. "Slater's sure?"

"He hasn't gone inside yet, but he says the magic he's been tracking leads to this location." Kaspian pulled up an old Dublin pub on the screen. "We still have several of our men in Ireland. I say we call a few in and end this game of cat and mouse."

I nodded. "Cheers to that." I was so beyond fed up with this mess. "Call Klas. He's eager to prove his worth. But call in Nolan, too. If they can't capture the being alive, they have permission to kill it."

Given how elusive this thing had been, I would not be surprised if this situation ended with the latter.

Regardless, removing this entity would be a weight off my shoulders.

I'd promised to handle it months ago, and, well, that hadn't happened. Something Volker and Elias had absolutely reminded me of on more than one occasion. Both monarchs had felt the entity's arrival and subsequent magical disturbances, and I'd volunteered my House for the task. It'd been an appropriate move, as I had all the resources required to track and remove the illegal being.

Except it kept escaping.

And no one could even tell me what it looked like. Female. Male. Vampire. Witch. God. Nothing. Because the few who had set eyes on it had referred to it as a shadowy figment.

Fucking useless border patrol. They hadn't been *my* House members, but ones who were part of Spirit and Sapphire. Odin and Lady Gabriella had waved it all off like the failure hadn't mattered.

"Whatever it is, it escaped," Lady Gabriella had said, her voice holding a note of disinterest. "But surely you have the resources to find it, right? That's the whole purpose of your House, is it not?"

The words had served as a taunt. A way to pique my interest and provide a challenge, all the while not taking responsibility for the initial fuckup.

"Oh, and be sure to keep Sky Serpell up to date," she'd added, referring to one of the high-ranking members of Spirit and Sapphire. "We'll await your report once you finish detaining the entity."

Political games.

Something that had only worsened over the years, despite the peaceful ambience all the Houses played at.

The Great Sacrifice twenty-four years ago had really only ended a physical war. The mental one had continued, every leader on the board moving pieces and parts to strengthen their territories and increase their power.

I loathed it all.

Alas, I was quite skilled at chess. So I kept playing. And winning, too.

However, had such a border failure occurred in my territory, it absolutely would have been dealt with swiftly. Gold and Garnet did not allow trespassers.

Although, apparently this infamous entity had decided to vacation on my former shores in Dublin.

I would need to have a conversation with Kieran and Sabrina, the new monarchs of Death and Diamond, about increasing security along their perimeters. Well, technically, Sabrina was the monarch and Kieran was her consort. But they were both very much in charge.

"Consider it done," Kaspian said, his phone in his hand as he carried out my orders regarding Klas and Nolan. "I'll tell Slater to hold until they arrive." He started toward the door, his focus on his screen. "I'll let you know when I learn more."

"I'll be here," I admitted, unable to hide my disappointment. I would much rather be Slater right now, in the field, tracking down a magical essence. And I probably would be if I didn't have this mountain of requests to sort through.

Fucking Kieran and his new House, I thought as I picked up the papers Kaspian had knocked onto the floor.

It wasn't technically Kieran's fault, or even his new mate's. I'd voted in favor of the House creation, mostly to clear an old debt. Or that was the excuse I'd provided.

What I would never admit to anyone other than Kaspian and the two fae in this room was that I'd recognized the difficulty of maintaining all of our island and land territories.

Gold and Garnet owned all of former-day Scandinavia, including Iceland—the home of our capital and my current home—along with the United Kingdom and Ireland. It was too much land when the majority of my people wanted to take bounty-hunting jobs around the world. I didn't want to stifle their desires by forcing half of them to remain home and guard our borders.

So giving up the isles would be beneficial in the long term.

But for now, it sucked.

I picked up my mug of coffee and went back to work, losing my mind to the menial requests before me.

These were the types of things I wanted to delegate, but Larus was right. My people needed to hear from me personally.

And while, in the past, an email might have been easy to spoof, the way magic worked to power technology in our world today made my participation mandatory. They would be able to feel the energy lingering in the message, which served as my personal signature—a signature no one else could replicate.

Hence, I had to respond.

To. Every. Single. Message.

Rather than voice another complaint, I buckled down and focused on the myriad of requests. There were a few I sent over to Kieran. He would either handle them or give them to Sabrina. If I knew the female phantom baroness—a title she preferred over *queen*—better, I'd have sent them to her. But it was Kieran I had owed a debt to, making him a more obvious recipient.

Larus and Cara worked silently with me, each of them taking over the responsibility of sending funds for relocation as I approved the requests.

There were a few we paused to discuss, but the majority of them were relatively straightforward.

We worked through most of the night, the moon still an orb in the sky when we finished. Of course, it was December in Iceland. So the sun barely existed during this time of year.

I lifted my arms, stretching out stiff muscles, and stood, ready to call it a night, when Kaspian entered.

His grim expression told me I wasn't going to like his report.

"Klas is dead," he said, wasting no time.

My eyebrows flew upward, my entire body rippling with shock. "*What?*" Klas was a vampire. Killing him would require a beheading or fire. "How?"

Kaspian shook his head. "I don't know yet. Nolan and Slater are both unconscious but said to be healing. Kieran sent a witch to help them along."

I blew out a breath. "Fuck."

Klas is dead?

He was a lower-level assassin, but a good one.

And Nolan was one of my best, with the others in this room being the only ones ranked above him.

Not to mention Slater's skills for not only tracking but also reading a room. He would be able to sense a threat from a mile away. And he knew how to avoid them.

If this thing managed to lure all my men into a trap, or worse, then it was clearly a lot larger than any of us had given it credit for.

So far, it hadn't caused any violent disturbances, just a few magical ones. Which was why we wanted it removed.

Now I had even more motivation to take it out.

It killed one of my men.

Gods damn it. I was going to need to get back on a plane, something I'd hoped not to have to do for a few weeks. I'd just returned from Scotland a few days ago after attending Sabrina and Kieran's mating ceremony.

"How pissed are they?" I asked, referring to the new territory owners of Ireland.

"Given the situation, not very," Kaspian replied. "It helps that I gave Kieran a heads-up prior to carrying out the mission."

I nodded. "Thank you." The last thing I wanted was to piss off the new Baroness and Her Consort of Death and Diamond. "I'll follow up with him on the plane."

"You're heading to Ireland?" Cara asked.

I met her pale green irises. "This thing has been wandering our world for three months. And I'm done playing games with it."

It'd just killed one of my mercenaries, after managing to dodge all my hunters for months.

And it'd taken down Slater and Nolan, two of my most talented House members.

This powerful being was clearly an even larger threat than any of us had originally anticipated. It'd obviously just been biding its time until the right moment. And who the fuck knew what it was planning to do next?

But one thing was certain—I would not be sacrificing any more of my people for this cause.

All the paperwork was going to have to wait because it was time for this entity to meet the Gold and Garnet King.

And die.

NYX

I tugged on my ruined dress, my lips curling down at the sides.

One minute, I'd been scouting the magical bar for my medallion, and the next, I'd woken up covered in dust and buried beneath a bunch of stones.

It'd taken a little finagling, but I'd managed to pull enough energy into my being to shadow myself out of the rubble. Then I'd realized there were others who had been caught up in the explosion. Rather than leave them, I'd helped unearth them.

Unfortunately, there'd been two who'd been too close to the blast. I'd tried to revive them, but I'd failed.

The others would survive, though.

Once they woke up.

My lips twisted to the side as I tried to find the source of the enchanted blast. I'd followed a strand of power to this place, hoping it would lead me to my lost medallion, but I no longer felt any trace of it or the energy source I'd been tracking.

Stars, I thought, blowing out a breath. As much as I liked this colorfully charmed realm, I really wanted my ticket out. Just in case I decided to leave.

While I enjoyed the magical sensations warming the air, I wasn't keen on the underlying tension from some of the regions. Especially the area known as Fire and Fluorite—a name I'd picked up through my travels.

It seemed the usual country names had been replaced in this realm with affiliations to certain "Houses." A unique way to govern the world, but of course, everything about this reality was unique.

There were portals in various areas that led to specific lands, too. I'd considered passing through one, just to see where it went, but the magical doorways were heavily guarded. And I wasn't quite ready to make my presence fully known.

Not after the warm welcome I'd received, anyway. I'd kept to myself since, trying to learn the rules and laws of the land. But some of these inhabitants were downright rude.

I'd been called several vulgar names, all of them linked to me being "Houseless." Which was how I'd learned about their various regions and the hierarchy within them. Apparently, it was considered unsavory not to join a House. They offered protection to those within their territory.

But I didn't need protection, something I'd tried to explain on countless occasions. Yet the beings who'd approached me had taken my words as a challenge more than a rule, and I'd been forced to defend myself.

Maybe if I found a House I liked, I would consider joining.

Alas, I hadn't been all that impressed yet.

Spirit and Sapphire was the House that had attacked me upon arrival, so no, thank you. I would not be staying with them.

Besides, they had an imposter calling himself Odin. As I knew the *real* Odin, I didn't have much of a desire to meet the fake version.

Fire and Fluorite was filled with deceitful leadership who continued to usurp one another. Not interested.

Air and Amethyst had just undergone some sort of political

upheaval that I wanted no part of, despite their king being a Moonlight Wraith.

Sea and Serpentine primarily existed in bodies of water, and I preferred land.

Blood and Beryl had intrigued me with its vampire king and hybrid wolf-vampire queen, but its close proximity to Fire and Fluorite left me uneasy.

But the vampire prospect had made me skip Earth and Emerald and come straight here to investigate Gold and Garnet.

Except this area had apparently just been claimed by a new House, Death and Diamond. And from what I understood, it'd been an amicable agreement.

A vampire king with a penchant for diplomacy? I'd thought. *Hmm.*

Except then I'd sensed a familiar surge of magic, and I'd come rushing here.

Only for the whole establishment to explode.

This game of hide-and-seek is growing tiresome, I thought at the wandering enchantment. *Maybe I'll just go to the portal nearby and learn how to manipulate that magic instead, hmm?*

It wouldn't be too hard. I'd just have to circumvent the portal guards, which I could do with a few well-placed shadows.

But I really needed to change into a more appropriate gown first.

Rather than shadow, I meandered around, searching for an open store. But the late hour left them all closed. Not that I had much in the terms of currency to barter with. The beings of this realm used strange things like blood and saliva instead of money.

Sighing, I opted to phase into a nearby store to shop after hours.

I'd leave some stardust behind to help boost the shopkeeper's sales. It would be akin to a bout of good luck that she or he wouldn't be able to explain. That should make up for stealing a garment from the shelves.

In other realms, they would see it as an honor just to have a goddess enter their store.

But not in this world. Not when supernatural energy was so openly used.

There were actually very few humans left, as the magic had essentially infected most of their kind. The remaining full humans had all been reduced to slaves, the supernaturals of the world being superior in every way. Some treated their mortals well. Others did not.

I hummed as I drew my fingers along the various fabrics, searching for the right texture. Not too heavy. Not too light. Something flexible.

This, I decided, pulling a pretty black gown off the shelf. No sleeves. Thin straps. Low back. Slits up to the thighs. *Perfect.*

I grabbed a bag at what I assumed was the checkout desk.

"Thank you so much for your hospitality," I said to the store and left a sprinkling of stardust behind for fortuitous prosperity.

Then I wrapped myself in shadows again to phase to a nearby hotel.

It took three tries to find a vacant room, but once I did, I shed my clothes and showered. They had complimentary bottles of shampoo, just like the last hotel I'd stayed at.

Or I assumed they were hotels.

They might have been random apartments.

But this place felt like a hotel with its sparse decorating and clean linens.

Regardless, I almost felt immortal again once I finished. But not quite.

I just need a short nap, I decided, the magic from the explosion earlier having left me a bit drained from all the cleanup. *Then I'll continue my journey.*

I hung my new dress up in the closet, pulled on a fluffy robe —*thank you, hotel*—and sprawled out on the bed.

Time to sleep with the moon, I thought dreamily, my night-driven power dwindling as the sun took over the sky. *See you in a few hours.*

A jolt of power stirred me from my rest, my eyes flying open to assess my unfamiliar surroundings.

Window. Light. Closet door. Dress. I blinked. *Hotel room.*

I pressed a palm to my head as the events of hours ago returned on a whoosh of energy, the explosion pulsating in my vision. Not my version of an ideal night.

And I still didn't have my medallion. Or whatever form the enchantment had chosen to take whilst in this realm.

I will find you, I promised it.

A shimmering energy responded, one that made me think the magic was laughing at me. Only it didn't dissipate. It remained. My lips curled down as I lifted my hand toward the humming substance.

Not a response, I realized. *But the power that disturbed my rest.*

I slowly pushed upward in bed, my focus on the alluring energy signature. *And who might you belong to?* I wondered, slipping out of the covers.

The magical essence seemed to kiss my cheek, luring me forward. *One moment, please,* I murmured. *I need to prepare for wandering outside.*

I found some essential items in the bathroom to use, including a brush for my hair. It took a few minutes to tame my long, dark strands, but I managed to work out the kinks. Then I used a little stardust to weave some gold leaves through my hair, the signature serving as my midnight crown.

The dress came next, the material touching the floor near my bare feet. I twirled in a nearby mirror, loving the way the obsidian fabric flowed sensuously over my curves.

Definitely the right choice, I mused.

It left my neckline free, allowing my gold necklace to shine. I murmured an enchantment to create some golden cuffs for my arms, my crescent moon marker decorating the metal and denoting my birthright.

With a nod, I found my flat sandals and laced the golden ribbon up my calves, then smiled at the swirling energy in the air. It wasn't exactly visible, more of a promise that lingered just out of reach. A complement to my moon magic, or that was how I chose to interpret it.

"Take me to your owner," I said, curious to meet the one who possessed such an enticing aura. He or she was clearly powerful. Dark. Potentially dangerous.

I was definitely intrigued.

The intangible shimmer led me down the hallway and outside into the warmly lit street. My senses greatly appreciated the overcast sky, as bright light severely diminished my ability to see.

I much preferred the night.

But I could live here, with the cobblestone streets and cute architecture. I'd always enjoyed Ireland, though. In every realm. The humans there often possessed an uncanny understanding of the supernatural. I supposed the fae were responsible for that.

The dancing figment of magic led me down one street and then another, the presence growing stronger with every step. Whoever owned this energy source was quite powerful. My stomach twisted with excitement, my heart skipping a beat at the prospect of meeting someone with such immense talent.

Another god or goddess, perhaps?

Whoever it was, he or she possessed ancient magic. I could taste it on my tongue, the decadent flavor making me crave *more*.

I'd never experienced this sort of pull before, this intrinsic need to know the entity behind the power. It left me feeling young. Innocent. Borderline inexperienced.

New sensations were rare. I found myself thrilled by the potential of whatever existed on the other end of this magical strand.

Who are you?

What are you?

Why am I so drawn to you?

The magic seemed to spin with excitement, the invisible strand a kiss to my senses that I could feel more than see. *This way, this way, this way*, it seemed to say, leading me toward the bar I'd been in last night.

I frowned but continued along the path, curious as to why it'd chosen this location.

Is your owner here investigating?

Is this some sort of lure to bring forth witnesses?

Perhaps someone had cast a spell meant to draw out those who'd been at the bar last night.

I didn't mind speaking about what I'd seen.

But I was far more interested in whoever possessed this alluring aura.

So sweet and seductive. Like a decadent dessert. *Mmm.* I inhaled, my blood heating at the prospect of indulging this immense craving.

It was as though this enchanted call touched my very soul, making my heart chant, *Mine, mine, mine.*

I'd never felt anything like it.

The magic curled around another bend before drawing an invisible arrow in the air that pointed directly at a powerful male standing near the wreckage from last night's explosion.

He held his hands loose at his sides, his stance comfortably confident as though he feared nothing. With all that magnetic energy swirling around him, I could understand why.

It didn't matter that the street was filled with supernatural beings, because this man's aura stood out among the rest.

A leader.

A powerful figure.

A sexy vampire with physical traits that were clearly blessed by the gods of this realm, I mused as I hid within the shadows to properly observe my prey.

He was tall with lean hips, a muscular back, and broad shoulders—the kind I would enjoy sinking my nails into.

And his hair was thick and tousled in dark waves atop his head, which had my fingers itching to pet and stroke and *fist.*

A being with this much power would definitely be fun in bed.

Maybe I would take a detour home with him before continuing the pursuit of my medallion.

Oh, yes, this male was worth the hunt indeed.

A thought that further strengthened as he finally turned.

Because his face resembled that of a fallen god, all sinful and wickedly crafted with sharp cheekbones, a chiseled jaw, and cruel silver eyes.

Those eyes were fixated on me, seeing right through my shadowy essence and drawing me from my not-so-subtle hiding place.

Power sees power, I thought, starting toward him and matching him in confidence.

Because I wasn't afraid of anyone here, not even him and his fiery aura of luscious energy.

I wanted to taste him, not fight him.

Bed him. Play with him. Mark him. *Bite* him.

His dark brow arched upward, giving his handsome features an arrogant twist that warmed my very being.

How godly, I thought, appraising him all over again. *Well, perhaps you'll appreciate my presence more than the others of your realm.*

He hadn't tried to shoot me yet, something I took as a good sign as I stopped only a few feet away from him.

Maybe this being would finally give me a second to introduce myself before trying to subdue me.

"Hello," I greeted, pausing to see how he would reply.

He merely cocked that brow a little higher.

So delicious, I thought, practically salivating for all that self-assured energy.

I smiled. Because it seemed he'd earned one from me with this silent show of dominance.

But he would kneel soon.

They all did.

"I'm Nyx," I introduced myself, waiting for a sign of recognition.

He gave me none.

Given the way magic worked in this realm, I wasn't too surprised by that. This reality didn't seem to value mythology in the same way as others did.

"I'm the Goddess of Night," I continued. "Or Mistress of the

Moon, as some have called me."

That eyebrow remained in place, his gaze surveying me in a manner similar to how I openly scrutinized him.

Except he still didn't speak.

He merely stared.

But the energy around him pulsed in welcome, the power seducing my heart and giving it a squeeze inside my chest.

Lick, my soul whispered. *Taste him.*

I took another step, feeling drawn to him in an almost enchanted manner.

He seemed equally transfixed, his gaze snapping to mine and holding me hostage before him.

"Your magic is breathtaking," I confided.

I knew what he was by his presence, his vampire soul speaking to mine on an intimate level. But something about him went so much deeper than a mere supernatural type.

I wanted to know this great being. To touch him. Kiss him. Pet him. Revel in his power. Anything he desired.

Just for a little while.

Then I'd resume my hunt for my lost magic.

Or maybe the medallion would simply reappear.

Enchantments were volatile in that way, always choosing their own paths and changing on a whim.

But this male oozed power that he seemed to control. No errant strands. Just the one that had coerced me into finding him, the one I could feel sliding through me to touch my very soul.

This magic was beautiful.

Hypnotic.

And left me sighing in this great man's presence.

He still hadn't spoken, but only a minute or so had passed since I'd approached.

While silence could be rude, his lack of a response simply felt contemplative. Like he was developing the right words to say.

That was fine. I'd wait for him to speak, and admire his physique in the interim.

So solid and firm.

Definitely a male of worth.

Mine, mine, mine, my heart continued to thud.

Touch, touch, touch, my fingertips urged.

Taste, taste, taste, my mouth whispered.

I swallowed, this foreign attraction leaving me a bit dizzy. *Is it an enchantment? A lust spell? Or just my reaction to his intensity?*

My eyes met his again, my throat dry. "Who are you?"

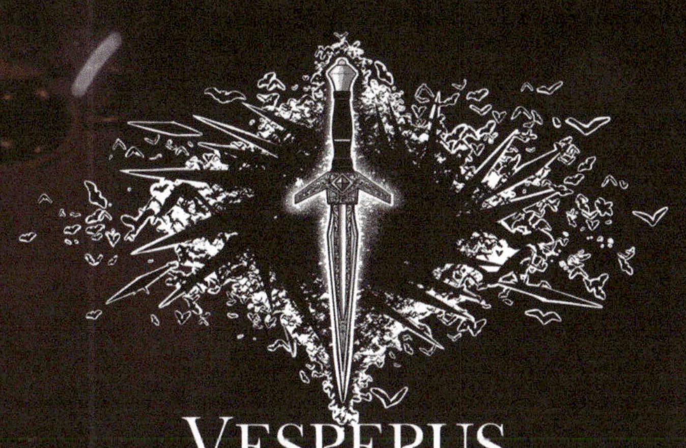

VESPERUS

THIS WAS THE ENTITY RESPONSIBLE FOR THE BAR EXPLOSION. THE being who had entered our realm illegally. The bounty my men had been searching for all these months.

The immortal I'd fully intended to hunt down and slay as a result of Klas's untimely demise.

A goddess.

Yeah, I believed that, with her hypnotic gold irises, thick dark lashes, softly curved chin, and full, fuckable lips. She certainly fit the part physically.

But also in power.

It rippled around her in tangible waves, making her long black hair flow with every movement. Even her dress—which was better suited for a beach in Greece than winter in Ireland—seemed to move as though energized by her very spirit.

Ethereal described her physical presence. *Stunning*, too.

And she was staring at me as though she wanted to devour me.

Not in a murderous way, but in a sensual manner.

The tightening in my chest urged me to let her do whatever she wanted to me, too.

Because this female—this being whom I'd fully intended to kill mere hours ago—was *mine*.

My fated mate.

My future.

I'd felt her presence like a knife through my heart. Her energy had warmed the air, insisting that I turn to face her and *claim* her.

Only, she'd been encased in shadows, hiding from everyone on this street except for me.

One look from me and she'd dispelled that magical cloak, allowing me to really see her.

And, fuck me, I liked what I saw. I liked it so much that I hadn't even reacted to her approach.

I'd just stood here like a lovestruck fool, allowing this ancient magic to take hold of me as it demanded that I accept my fate.

This isn't me, I thought, still speechless by this female's presence.

"Who are you?" she'd asked.

And I found myself wondering the same damn thing.

Because I didn't feel like an ancient vampire right now, or a powerful king.

Just a man entranced by a woman. *My woman.*

I could feel the pull wrapping around my heart and redirecting all of my instincts toward a primal need to possess her. To touch. To *bite*.

Not to kill or to capture or to punish.

But to *fuck*.

It left me feeling off-kilter. Punched in the chest. *Winded.*

Only for the sound of metal whizzing through the air to cut through the moment and ground me in reality once more.

My hand flew upward to catch the knife aimed at my fated mate's head. Her eyes widened, her focus going to my palm and the deadly blade embedded into my skin. I'd caught it by the sharp end.

Rather than pocket the item, I dropped it and looked at the source of the throw.

Kaspian. I growled at him.

"She's enchanting you," he warned, another knife already in his hand. "She's some sort of goddess-witch hybrid."

Nyx made a sound of protest, suggesting his terminology had insulted her.

I ignored her and stared calmly at my best friend. *She's my fated mate,* I told him. Not all vampires possessed the ability to speak into another's mind. But I did.

Kaspian couldn't reply that way. But his expression told me he'd heard me just fine.

Because his cheeks had gone white.

She's also the entity we've been hunting, I added, in case that wasn't clear. *So I'm not enthralled, just surprised.*

Each word spoken into my second's mind further cemented me in reality.

I could still feel the pull to *take,* but the overwhelming shock of the moment was slowly yielding to sense once more.

Kaspian's dark eyes rounded. "Fuck."

Yeah, I agreed. Though, I wasn't sure if it was because that was what I wanted to do—*fuck*—or because of the situation.

While Nyx certainly reminded me of a succubus, I wasn't under her thrall. I was just a slave to our joint fate.

A fate I could reject with a few carefully spoken words. They would free me instantly and give me back my steadfast control.

Except I found myself struggling to voice them.

Because I can use this, I thought to myself, my link to Kaspian having disappeared shortly after my last reply. *I can use this to make her explain herself. Then I can reject her.*

It would hurt. But I didn't want to be mated to this creature. She had no House affiliation. She shouldn't even be here. *And* she'd killed Klas.

I'd gather information, escort her to the appropriate portal, and then send her back to her realm of gods.

Or maybe I'd reject her and kill her.

Being here without an association to a House was a death sentence anyway.

Depending on how she answered my questions, maybe I'd make it quick.

Or prolong the agony if she showed no remorse.

My experience with gods fell firmly in the latter scenario—they very rarely seemed to regret their choices. They were all-knowing and arrogant as fuck as a result.

The ancient mate magic tying my soul to a goddess seemed appropriate, given my history with the gods.

And fate loved to test me.

Fortunately, I'd always enjoyed a good challenge.

This one just happened to be wrapped up in a sexy midnight dress that hugged her assets in a way that tempted me to admire and *touch*.

Instead, I returned my attention to the goddess's alluring golden irises and focused on my task.

Gather information. Then break her.

"Goddess Nyx?" I asked, tasting her name and finding that I rather liked it.

She stepped closer, her sensual form scant inches from mine. She seemed to be studying me again, her gaze leaving mine to stare at my mouth and then my shoulders before venturing lower.

"You can call me Nyx," she murmured. "I prefer to avoid titles. I've found that they don't mean much, and sometimes they provide a false context for one's true power in life."

A wise sentiment. However... "Titles can also demonstrate respect for a well-deserved position."

She shrugged. "There are better ways to show someone respect."

I tilted my head, curious. "Such as?"

"Such as not throwing knives at them," she replied with a pointed glance toward my second-in-command. "Or calling them a goddess-witch hybrid after already being given their title." She looked at me again. "But as I said, titles are a false context. I could demonstrate my power instead, if you'd like?"

"Like you did with the bar?" I gestured to the remains and arched a brow. "I think we all received that message loud and clear, *Goddess.*"

Her forehead crinkled a little as she glanced between me and the destruction she'd caused. "Are you referring to how I excavated everyone after the explosion?"

Now it was my turn to frown. "Excavated everyone?"

"Well, technically, I teleported them out from beneath the

rubble." Her gaze flickered over the crowd. "Like that one." She looked pointedly at Slater. "He was in pretty bad shape because of all the bricks holding him down, but he started to heal the moment I removed him from the rubble."

She continued surveying the scene, finding Nolan next.

"Him, too," she murmured. "But there were two I couldn't save in time. They were too close to the blast."

She shuddered, suggesting that the memory of the event irked her.

Which didn't make sense at all.

"Did your power call me out here to provide my statement?" she continued, her focus returning to me. "It's very impressive. I imagine you have a title to go with all that intoxicating energy."

Her palm went to my sternum, her nostrils flaring as she inhaled my scent.

"You smell like a decadent dessert." Her whisper was low, meant for my ears alone. "It makes me want to lick you from head to toe."

I caught her wrist before her hand could wander, but I didn't release her. I simply held her to me and said, "Three men."

Her brow furrowed. "What?"

"There were three men who didn't make it out alive, one of whom was a member of Gold and Garnet." Saying the words served as a reminder for my purpose—one this little vixen seemed intent on distracting me from.

Because that touch was burning a hole through my suit and scalding my skin beneath the layers of fabric.

I should push her away.

Except…

Keeping her close makes her easier to read, I reminded myself.

It was an excuse. A good one. But still an excuse just to continue touching her.

Recognizing that weakness, however, allowed me to maintain control of it.

And it had me locking in on my truth-seeking abilities, too. I always used them—they were second nature to me—but I wanted to be absolutely sure about her answers.

Which thus far had been truthful.

"From the explosion?" she asked, searching my gaze. "There were three who didn't make it?"

"Yes. Three died from your attack." Not two like she'd previously said.

Her eyebrows flew upward as she tried to take a step backward, but my grip on her wrist held her in place. "*My* attack? I tried to *help* them, not *attack* them."

"By blowing up the bar?"

"Why would I blow up the bar?" she demanded, her regal tone heating my blood. Because I'd always enjoyed a strong woman. And knowing this one was meant to be mine only increased my interest.

An interest I ignored in favor of seeking the truth.

"You blew up the bar because you knew my men were close to capturing you," I told her.

Or that had been my theory, anyway.

Until I'd met her.

Now I wasn't so sure.

Primarily because I hadn't scented a single lie on her yet. Every word she'd breathed thus far had been the truth.

Including her comment about wanting to *lick* me.

But I would handle that one later. In private.

"Capturing me?" She blinked a few times. "Why would they *capture* me?"

"Because you're in this realm illegally."

"Illegally?" She gaped at me. "How does one 'illegally' enter a realm?"

"As a goddess, you should have come through the portal in the Himalayas. That's where your realm seeks permission for entry." Something she should already know, as not only was it the first portal that had opened on this earth, but it'd also sprung to life several thousand years ago.

Yet her confused expression only deepened. "My world does not have a portal to yours."

"Yes, it does, Goddess. In the Himalayas."

"Nyx," she corrected. "And there is no portal between my realm and yours. I'm only here because of my medallion, which is also the reason I haven't left yet. Because it's…" She trailed off, frowning. "The magic decided to go on holiday in your world somewhere."

I stared at her. "The magic decided to go on holiday?" I repeated.

She blew out a breath, her frustration oddly kind of endearing. "It's mad at me for using it to realm-jump too quickly, so it's teaching me a lesson by taking me on a tour of your world. I thought I felt it here in Dublin, but…" Her lips twisted to the side. "It's gone now."

All truth, I discerned, both surprised and confused.

Either this being had figured out a way around my family's ancient talent for lie detection, or she'd meant every word.

Either way, it was interesting.

"I've done all I can," Trixie said, her exasperated tone pulling my focus away from Nyx and redirecting it at my second-in-command and the witch walking toward him.

Trixie was the one with healing powers that Kieran had found for us.

I didn't know her well, as I tended to avoid those affiliated with the House of Spirit and Sapphire—they were all as pretentious as their rulers.

But this witch had been helpful, so I owed her a debt of gratitude.

Hmm, I'd probably gift her some of my vampire venom.

Witches often used various supernatural essences for potions, or simply to trade. As an ancient of my kind, and the descendant of a powerful vampire family, the venom in my mouth would be worth more than most. She could use it to craft a truth serum or something similar.

It was a form of payment I didn't often provide, as it hinted at my inherited abilities, something most master vampires preferred to keep hidden.

But I could easily tell her I'd procured it from someone else, and she'd be none the wiser.

"I can't cure that kind of darkness," she went on, her vibrant blue eyes glowering up at Kaspian as he towered over her petite frame. "You'll need a coven of Triarchy-like power to accomplish that."

I looked around the witch to find Slater shaking his dark head a few feet away, his slate-gray eyes narrowed in annoyance.

"Darkness?" Kaspian repeated, his voice holding a dubious note to it. "He seems fine to me."

"Because I am fine," Slater insisted.

"You're not," the witch warned him. "You've lost all your light."

Slater glanced down at his tanned arms and back up at her. "I've always been this way. Comes with being a raven shifter, darling."

"Stubborn males," she muttered, turning away from them with a wave of her pale hand. "I don't have time for this."

She sauntered off to heal a vampire across the road, leaving us all to frown at her back.

Odd bird.

Slater looked well healed and as good as new.

Well, apart from a need to shave. His usual dusting of dark hair along his jaw had lengthened to an unkempt sort of look, one that I had no doubt he'd fix as soon as he returned home.

Which he could do now that we'd caught the errant supernatural wandering the globe.

The rest of this problem was officially mine, what with her being my fated mate and all.

Her comments regarding her realm not being attached to this one were also going to be a problem. A political one. Because I'd felt the truth in her words.

Which meant we had yet another realm of supernaturals accessing our world.

And this being was powerful. *Too* powerful. Hence the reason there was a bounty on her head. Everyone had felt her arrival, and she had more than a few kings—myself included—who wanted her gone.

Except she's apparently my mate, I thought, returning my attention to her.

Nyx was studying my neck, her pupils dilating as she licked her lips. It seemed her annoyance at my questions had disappeared, leaving only stark fascination behind.

I arched a brow. "Do goddesses bite?"

"This goddess does," she whispered, her hungry gaze lifting to mine. "Your power is a drug."

I nearly grunted. *I could say the same about you, sweetheart.*

"You must have a title." Her nails dug into my dress shirt, reminding me that I still had her wrist caught in my hand. "A powerful vampire." Her eyes searched mine. "A king."

"King of Gold and Garnet," I confirmed. "Vesperus."

"Vesperus." My name resembled a benediction on her lips, the sultry tone one I'd enjoy hearing her repeat in my bed.

Yeah, this is definitely a problem.

I knew fated bonds could tame even the most powerful of beings, but I'd walked this earth for over fifteen hundred years and I'd yet to feel a pull toward anyone.

Until her.

This otherworldly being spouting explanations that defied what I'd thought I knew about the situation.

It could all be a dangerous ruse, a way to usurp me. Or fate tying me to the most dangerous of complications.

"So if you didn't cause the explosion, what did?" I asked, needing to take control of the situation again.

"I don't know," she answered.

And again I tasted the truth.

"I was searching the bar for my missing magic when everything burst with light. Then I woke up covered in rubble." Her brow puckered. "I shadowed everyone out. But two of them were already dead."

The third must have died before Trixie had arrived on the scene.

But that detail wasn't important.

What mattered was the truth in Nyx's words. If she'd caused the explosion, it didn't appear to be intentional.

And considering she hadn't tried to hurt anyone else—that I knew of, anyway—it seemed in line with her behavior thus far.

Of course, this had been the first time my men had come close to capturing her.

"So you arrived in this realm via a magical medallion that you've since lost. And you've been, what, just wandering around searching for it all these months?"

"Yes." Her lips twisted again. "Well. I've also just been enjoying the world and deciding if I want to stay. That's the point of my journey—I'm looking for a new home."

My eyebrows lifted. "A new home?"

"I'm bored with creationism. I thought it could be fun to live in an existing reality, and this one has intrigued me the most so far." Her eyes went to Kaspian. "Except everyone here seems to want to kill me."

"Because you entered illegally and therefore have no ties to any of the Houses," I told her. "We don't tolerate outsiders here. Affiliating with a House is how we stay alive."

"I've stayed alive just fine on my own," she returned, her expression darkening as she met my gaze once more.

"Because you haven't crossed a being of equal or greater power yet." I tightened my grip on her wrist. "But now you have."

Her nostrils flared. "Don't make a mistake by underestimating me, *King*."

"I don't make a habit of underestimating anyone, *Goddess*. But the fact remains that you arrived via illegal channels. And you have no House affiliation. That's why there's a bounty on your head, one my House has personally been overseeing."

She frowned. "So you all want to kill me?"

"Yes." A blunt response, but I believed in the truth. Which was why I added, "But I'm willing to grant you temporary asylum with the House of Gold and Garnet."

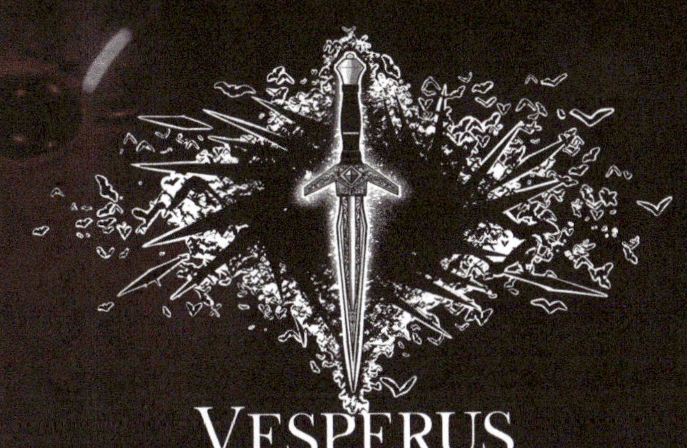

VESPERUS

I didn't need to look at Kaspian to know he disapproved of my rash decision.

But he wouldn't fight me on it.

She was my fated mate. And I was the Gold and Garnet House King.

I'd also said *temporary*, which was a key phrase in my proposal. Because I couldn't offer her anything permanent.

The other House rulers would immediately object to this deal. Nyx was too powerful. And having her under my House would give me an advantage the others would not be keen on allowing to exist.

However, some of my allies would begrudgingly agree to my temporary terms. Primarily as they all owed me some manner of a favor.

Elias, King of Blood and Beryl, had gone rogue when he'd taken a wolf shifter as his mate, thus changing the landscape of his battle with Fire and Fluorite.

I'd forgiven him because the end result had worked in all our favors.

And I'd known better than to get between a powerful vampire and his fated mate.

Volker, King of Air and Amethyst, technically owed me for granting two of his lieutenants asylum in my territory after his… *disappearance.* I'd also recently returned said lieutenants to his care.

Something I'd remind him of, as I suspected he would be the first one to call and protest my offer. His susceptibility to moon magic made him eager to be rid of Nyx. Something about her fucking up his powers even more during his revolution.

Whatever. He had his mate now, and she balanced him. He'd be fine. Or at the very least, he'd trust me to handle it my way. We shared similar methodologies in our political approaches, which made him more likely to trust my reasoning.

And then there was the new House of Death and Diamond.

Baroness Sabrina might not be thrilled, but I suspected she valued our relationship enough to give me a chance here.

All the other monarchs would be more difficult to convince of this path.

Especially Odin and Lady Gabriella. But they were the ones who'd lost Nyx upon her arrival. So they'd lost their chance to deal with her as a result.

She was mine now. I'd determine her fate here.

And maybe I'll find a way to keep her, I mused.

A powerful queen could make Gold and Garnet formidable.

Or make it a constant target for invasion and war.

Regardless, the potential outcomes would be moot if she declined my offer.

Her eyes swirled with a mixture of knowledge and intrigue.

"What would your temporary offer require of me?" she asked, intelligently having picked up on that key word.

No wonder fate paired us together.

"You will live with me," I said, voicing the terms as I thought of them. "And we'll work together to determine your future path."

Because if she was truly innocent, then I couldn't kill her. But it sounded like dropping her off in the Himalayas wasn't an option either.

So I needed to keep her close while I decided what to do with her. It was my responsibility as her fated mate, in addition to my role in this world.

I was the king of all the mercenaries for a reason. We valued glory, gold, and blood.

And I'd taken on the task of finding this foreign entity. The bounty hadn't actually dictated her death, just her capture. So by those rules, I'd done my job.

Now I just had to figure out what to do with her.

Because she definitely wouldn't be able to stay long-term.

Which led me to my final condition. "You'll need to limit your power in this realm. It's causing disturbances, which is what inspired the original bounty."

"Live with you, limit my powers, and work with you on my future path," she summarized. "Hmm. Or… I could remain Houseless, use my powers as desired, and determine my own way. Which would be how I've always lived."

She tapped her jaw with her free hand, her other still captured by mine.

"You said you were bored with creationism and looking for a new reality to live in. I'm giving you an opportunity to fully understand our world, which would help you decide your fate," I pointed out.

Her decision would lead her to leave, of course. But at least this would be an amicable solution to both our problems.

The flash in her golden irises suggested she was listening and considering my words.

"If you deny my offer," I added softly. "You'll continue to be hunted and attacked and never truly given the opportunity to see what our world has to offer you aside from death."

And that was assuming I let her leave Dublin without a fight.

It would be better for us both if she agreed.

It may just be pleasurable, too, I thought, my gaze dropping to her mouth.

Of course, if I fucked her, I would no longer be able to break our bond with a rejection.

However, there were other things we could do. Things I should absolutely not think about or entertain in any way.

But she wasn't the only one drawn to the power thriving between us.

A taste won't kill anyone, I mused. And I'd always been a risk-taker. Why stop now?

"My experiences so far haven't made me feel very welcomed here," she finally replied, her dilating pupils telling me she was fully aware of the lust firing between us. But I wasn't sure if she understood the fated connection or not.

Do goddesses even have fated mates?

Her reactions to me proved it wasn't a one-way connection. But that didn't mean she felt eternally bound to me.

"Perhaps I've already seen enough and don't wish to stay," she added.

I smiled. "Trust me, Nyx." I stroked my thumb in a slow circle against her inner wrist. "You haven't truly seen or experienced this realm yet. I can change that."

"Can you?"

"I can," I promised, fully confident in my ability to ensure a proper welcome to this realm.

Or, more accurately, my bed.

"And if I say no?" she pressed. "Then I continue this fight on my own and battle you?"

Yes, I thought. *That's exactly what happens.*

I let her see the answer in my eyes.

But rather than confirm it out loud, I said, "You're hunting for your missing medallion. Why not take advantage of my offer and use my resources to help search for it?"

"You're volunteering to help me find my missing magic?" The note of intrigue in her question told me this had been the appropriate avenue to take for her to truly consider my proposition.

"Yes."

"Why?" she pressed. "Why give me temporary sanctuary at all? What's in it for you?"

"The bounty is for your capture, not your death," I told her. "By granting you asylum and restricting your power, I'm technically following the rules."

"That doesn't tell me what you get from keeping me as a willing hostage," she replied.

"The bounty carries a heavy reward," I murmured.

She seemed disappointed in that. "This is about money?"

I shook my head. "Spells. Fae hair. Various other precious items from all the different Houses. Everyone wanted you caught, Nyx. And they've ensured the bounty is appealing to anyone and everyone who chooses to take it on."

She still didn't appear all that impressed. "So you'll win a wealthy prize in exchange for me accepting your asylum."

"No, sweetheart. My House will receive the wealth." I stepped closer to her. "*I* win a chance to play with you."

I hadn't realized until I'd said it how much truth existed in that confession.

But it was a motivating factor.

Because this female had piqued my interest. Which I knew was a result of the fated-mate bond throbbing in my chest.

But her energy appealed to me, too. And the potential role she could play in my House.

The more I thought about what it would mean to possess such a powerful player, the more I wanted to keep her.

I hadn't been lying when I'd told her the values of my House—valor, wealth, *prestige*. We valued it all.

And this female was built to be a queen of that sort of empire.

Which is precisely why the others will never allow this, I thought, thinking back to The Great Sacrifice. Just twenty-four years ago, the Houses battled one another for power. Many people had lost their lives. And a tenuous truce had been formed.

But the political rivalries remained. They were just quieter now, the movements on the chessboard much less obvious than before.

However, I saw many of those moves throughout the Houses.

Perhaps Nyx would become my powerful move.

She was my fated mate. Could I use that point as an argument for her staying in my House? Or would they all vote to have her removed?

I would have to see how my allies reacted first to know the answer to that.

Which required this beautiful being to accept my proposal. It might be a rash decision on my part, but I'd given myself a way out with the word *temporary*.

Just as I'd technically provided her with an escape, too.

"What do you have to lose?" I asked her. "Take the free trip to Reykjavik, see if my resources can help, and we'll go from there."

"While also promising to minimize my power and live with you," she reminded me.

I grinned, my thumb circling her wrist again. "I thought you wanted to lick me, Nyx."

Her gaze narrowed. "Maybe I would rather test your power first."

I arched a brow. "Does that mean you're rejecting my offer?"

"Hmm." She considered me for a moment. "No."

Fuck. My grip tightened on her wrist. "Nyx—"

"No, I'm not rejecting your offer," she clarified, her smile telling me that she'd been testing my reaction. "But it's good to know you want to taste me as badly as I want to taste you."

She drew her free hand up my arm and grasped my shoulder.

I held her gaze as she went up onto her tiptoes.

Then she pressed her lips to my ear. "Which, by the way, is the only reason I'm accepting your *temporary* asylum."

My lips twitched at her seductive tactics. I wrapped my palm around her nape and held her in place as I whispered, "I think we'll be doing a lot more than *tasting* one another."

She shivered against me, her arousal a sweet perfume to my senses.

My gaze went to Kaspian and Slater on the side of the road, their matching expressions telling me they weren't thrilled by this development. I was definitely going to receive an earful from my second later. Probably from my thirds-in-command, too.

Which made this next part necessary.

There were too many witnesses on this street. I couldn't risk any of them thinking I'd gone weak for this woman, even if she was my mate.

Making this public would also serve as a message of sorts to the other Houses. One that would likely earn me a few angry calls.

But I would handle them as they arrived.

This is temporary, I reminded myself. *A temporary offer of asylum while I figure out how to move forward with this development.*

I used my grip on her neck to pull her back, my gaze capturing hers. "House affiliations are often displayed with jewelry, or in some cases…"

I finally released her wrist, content with my other hand holding her neck.

Then I lifted my now free hand to show her my palm and the beginning of my bloodline tattoo that crawled up the underside of my forearm.

She couldn't see it all because of my suit, but the flare of her nostrils told me she wanted to explore it later. Probably with her tongue.

"Other Houses prefer jewelry, but tattoos are the tradition in the House of Gold and Garnet," I told her. "Blood fealty."

However, a tattoo was permanent, making it not a good option for Nyx.

But jewelry can be temporary.

"To finalize our agreement, you'll need a marking," I continued softly, aware of our growing audience. Some of them could hear our conversation because of their supernatural hearing. Those who couldn't hear us were being told in low whispers what was happening.

"The king is giving her sanctuary with Gold and Garnet."

"He's going to mark her."

"This is unexpected."

"She's powerful. A good addition."

"But she killed Klas and the others."

"She says she didn't kill them, and it looks like King Vesperus believes her."

"Truth serum," one of them murmured.

"Exactly."

No one was questioning my decision, just whispering about it. I took that as a good sign that most of the members of my House would accept this change.

The few who didn't would approach me directly for a frank discussion.

Such as Kaspian, I thought, meeting his narrowed gaze again. It was his job to question me. He often helped me see reason, and perhaps he would do that with this as well.

But for today, I'd made my decision. *She's mine. I'm keeping her… for now.*

"A marking," Nyx said, repeating part of my last comment. "What kind of marking?"

I returned my focus to her and admired the low cut of her black dress before noting the jewelry painting her skin. *I'm starting to see why fate sent her my way.* "You're already wearing gold. You just need a little garnet."

Her nose crinkled. "Garnet's not really my color."

I smiled. "It's about to be."

She frowned. "What?"

"Blood, darling." My thumb brushed the pulse point of her slender neck. "It's how we give fealty to Gold and Garnet—blood loyalty."

I'd bled with my tattoo.

And now this beautiful creature would bleed for me.

Her eyes narrowed. "You said there were no other stipulations."

"This isn't an additional stipulation. I already told you—my prize is the chance to play with you. And in my world, that equates to blood play." I wrapped my arm around her lower back, my hand still on her nape.

Her nails dug into my shoulders in response, her irises reminding me of liquid gold.

"You're not the only one who bites, Goddess," I told her, my lips curling to reveal my fangs. "So what's it going to be? Will you accept my offer and bleed for me? Or would you rather test my power first?"

NYX

This male.

This sensual, intelligent, calculative being.

Mmm. The energy around him pulsed in expectation, ready to strike at any moment.

"Because you haven't crossed a being of equal or greater power yet. But now you have."

Some supernaturals boasted their skills unnecessarily, entirely underestimating their contenders. However, this man—this *king*—wasn't overconfident in his assessment. Simply self-aware of his prowess and abilities.

It would be a decent fight.

One I would win, but not without effort. *And pain.* Not to me, but to the others around us.

Two powerful beings attacking each other in the street would not end well. And I really didn't want to take this man away from his role. The air of reverence here wasn't directed at me, but at him—the Gold and Garnet House King.

No one had interrupted our conversation. No one had attacked me after Vesperus had caught the single knife aimed at my head. No one had questioned him offering me temporary asylum either.

They'd all just accepted his word as law.

Not because he was a tyrant, but because they respected him.

This was the kind of male I wanted to know, and not just as a consequence of his intoxicating magic. Even now, I could feel it thrumming in my chest, beating a rhythm that begged me to take him, to accept him, to *worship* him.

No one had ever cast such a magnetic energy over me before.

And I desperately wanted to learn more about this foreign sensation. It was so new and addictive, leaving me really with only one option.

Accept his offer.

Which I'd already planned to do. I could easily play along and escape later, hopefully without causing too much damage to his kingdom in the process. Because I really didn't want to battle him or the others. I just wanted to exist in peace.

And find my errant magic.

He'd offered me his resources. Why not see what that meant? Why not explore? Why not indulge in this attraction just a little bit more?

I tilted my head to the side, my gaze on him. "You should know that my blood is very powerful."

"As is mine," he replied, his accented voice a touch deeper now.

A predator about to strike, I thought, admiring the silver in his irises. It blended with the black edges, reminding me of a bursting star. *Alluring. Tempting. Sinful.*

"Are you accepting?" he asked, his English lilt more prominent now and giving away his anticipation.

Yes, he definitely wants to taste me as much as I want to taste him.

"I am, yes." *Bite me, if you dare, King of Gold and Garnet. Because your reaction to my blood will show me if you're really worthy of my time.*

Only the strongest could handle an essence as intense as mine. Hence my warning. But he'd responded confidently, as he had with everything else.

A true leader. A royal. A vampire king.

His expression shadowed, some intrinsic part of him understanding the challenge I'd just laid at his feet.

You're mine now, Goddess of Night, he seemed to say as he pulled me impossibly closer with his arm around my lower back. His hand remained against my nape, giving it a subtle squeeze as he lowered his lips to my neck.

His fangs brushed my skin, stirring a trail of goose bumps along my arms.

Yes…

So much power.

So much dominance.

A worthy counterpart, my soul whispered, causing my heart to skip several beats.

Vesperus released a low growl against my skin, the predator within him sensing my excitement. I wasn't going to hide from him. If anything, I wanted to invite him to act faster.

His tongue circled my pulse, drawing out the moment, making me pant for it. I clung to his shoulders, my eyes falling closed.

The auras around us all pulsed with interest, heightening my expectation.

This… this is so unlike anything—

My lips parted as Vesperus bit down, his fangs unleashing some sort of euphoric venom into my bloodstream that had me clutching him harshly.

Oh, stars… I wanted to rip off our clothes and *fuck him* in front of all these supernaturals. Allow our power to truly mingle. To test his full potential, see exactly what this heated enchantment inside me meant.

Does he feel it, too? This strand of energy tying us together? Is it real? A figment? My own magic playing tricks on me?

I shivered, losing myself to the intensity of his mouth, the powerful tug of his essence on mine as he swallowed my blood.

He didn't convulse. He didn't react as though I'd poisoned him.

No, he drank from me as though I had just redefined his meaning of life.

But all too soon, he stopped, his tongue tracing the mark on my neck to gather some of the blood.

Which he brought down to the crescent moon hanging between my breasts.

Power hummed along my skin as he painted the golden surface with my blood.

My thighs clenched at the intimacy of the act, his eyes on mine the whole time.

Eclipse, I breathed, noting the inverting color of his irises. They'd been silver surrounded by black before. But now they were black and edged with sparks of silver, reminding me of that majestic moment when the moon covered the sun.

Striking.

Enigmatic.

Rare.

His lips returned to my neck to seal the wound with his venom, his essence making me tremble with intrigue and need.

I wanted to bite him.

Kiss him.

Mount him.

What is this insanity?

He pulled away to look at me again, his mutual interest a hot promise that had me nearly stripping out of my dress with the demand to *take me.*

I'd experienced attraction before. But nothing on this level.

Is it the magic of this plane? The rules of this world? Something he's doing? Should I—

"My liege," a deep voice interrupted. I recognized it as belonging to the vampire who had tried to throw a knife at my head. "Kieran has arrived, and he's brought a few phantoms with him who are interested in Gold and Garnet."

Vesperus said nothing for a moment, his gaze still holding mine. Then he finally glanced at the male beside us. "Is it something you can handle? Or would it be prudent of me to attend the meeting?"

I followed his stare to study the dark-haired male with the penchant for throwing daggers first and asking questions later.

Dark, soulful eyes.

Athletic form.

Deadly.

The latter I assessed as a result of his powerful aura, the energy around him almost as intense as the one holding me.

Yet I didn't feel any sort of pull toward him. No squeezing of my chest or invisible strands of alluring magic. Nothing.

Just a frank assessment of power.

What makes this one different? I wondered, my gaze returning to Vesperus as he and the deadly vampire spoke about *Kieran* and his *phantom*s.

I ignored their idle chitchat, instead choosing to focus on the pulsing energy encircling Vesperus's spirit. It was so warm and intoxicating, making me want to lick him all over again.

Bite. Suck. Taste.

This attraction was borderline toxic, like an enchanting spell that had woven our souls together in an unbreakable embrace.

What is this magic? I marveled, my gaze on his neck.

More words thudded in my chest, a chant demanding that I *take, take, take.*

But when I leaned forward to kiss his throat, his hand on my nape pulled me back. "Not yet," he said, his tone a command I longed to disobey.

I'd never been one for orders.

Obedience had to be earned. And in my very long existence, there were few who had ever come close to making me want to submit.

You bit me. I'm going to bite you.

I used my shadowing ability to break free from his hold and appeared behind him, my mouth a scant inch from his neck.

Only to find my back slammed against a nearby brick wall with a heated Vesperus pressed up against me. "Patience," he said quietly. "Or has no one taught you that virtue?"

My lips curled. "I live by a very different set of *virtues*, King."

I phased out of his grip again but found myself right back in the same position as he shifted with me.

My eyes widened at the display of power, stunned by his ability to keep pace with me. *That… that shouldn't be possible.*

And his expression told me he agreed.

But a sense of understanding seemed to overtake his features as his gaze went to my neck.

My powers.

He… he imbibed them…

Well, that's new.

He wasn't the first to have ever bitten me, but everyone else had been almost repelled by the intensity of my essence. He'd not only swallowed it without issue, but he'd also absorbed some of my power with it.

"Oh," I breathed. "That…"

"Is impressive," a new voice said, the dark quality of the male tone underlined with sardonic intrigue. "It seems I've missed some sort of party. Care to enlighten me on what's happened in Death and Diamond's territory?"

Vesperus slowly looked at the newcomer, his irises still resembling that of an eclipse. "You mean the territory that used to be Gold and Garnet's up until fourteen days ago? *That* territory?"

I evaluated the man beside us, noting his mixed-magic aura. *A vampire-fae hybrid. One with death magic. That's interesting.*

"Yes, the territory that now belongs to my mate, Baroness Sabrina," the male replied. "The same territory that I kindly allowed you to enter in pursuit of…" He trailed off, his piercing gray eyes meeting mine. "*Her.*"

"Hello," I greeted, feeling the need to speak so these males remembered that I was a living, breathing being with a brain, not a conversation piece. "*Her* name is Nyx, Goddess of Night."

The male arched a black brow, the color matching his long hair. "Hello, Nyx. I'm Kieran. No title. Well, not one I care to use, anyway. Just Kieran will do."

"Owner of the ouchie-maker," Vesperus murmured. "Seems a fancy enough title to me."

Kieran startled at that, his eyes flashing to Vesperus. "Did you just make a joke?"

"I don't lack humor," the vampire king deadpanned. "And I would still like to know what the fuck it is."

"I can give you a hands-on demonstration, if you'd like," Kieran offered, the words somewhat resembling a threat. "Is there any information you need gathered from Nyx? I've never tested the device on a god or a goddess before."

Vesperus growled, the sound low and vibrating against my chest. "*No.*"

Kieran shrugged. "Another time, then."

"No," Vesperus repeated, that menacing note still in his tone. "No one touches Nyx apart from me."

"Nyx is right here and capable of issuing her own requests," I interjected.

"Understood?" Vesperus added, ignoring me.

I rolled my eyes. "Men."

"I see." Kieran glanced at me before returning his focus to Vesperus. "This may cause some discussion amongst the Houses."

"I'm counting on it," Vesperus replied.

"Hmm," Kieran hummed, then looked at the two men behind him. "Then you may want to interview these two faster than anticipated. They might be able to help you."

Help what? I wondered, glancing over their strange mystical auras. *Ohhh, they're phantoms!* "I'm intrigued by your kind," I murmured, admiring their ethereal energy. "*Very* intrigued." But not in the same way that Vesperus piqued my interest. Only his power seemed to have this magical hold on my being.

Hence the reason I hadn't tried to shove him away from me yet. I rather liked the way he felt pressed up against me.

"I'll be with you in a moment," Vesperus told Kieran. "Kaspian will fill you in."

The vampire-fae dipped his head. "I can take a hint."

"Good. Respecting your elders is rule number one for surviving in this political arena," Vesperus replied.

"And there you go giving me advice again," Kieran drawled. "Don't make a habit of it, or I'll think you have a crush on me."

Vesperus smiled, but it didn't appear all that friendly. "I just want to make sure my former territory thrives in your care."

Kieran rolled his eyes, then led the two phantoms at his back down the alleyway toward the street beyond, leaving me alone with Vesperus once more. "You and I need to have a conversation on manners," he informed me.

I smiled. "Is this where you tell me that I need to bow to you as king?"

"Yes."

My lips curled even more. "Goddesses don't bow."

"If you want to survive, you will." The severity in his tone matched the narrowing of his gaze. "Gold and Garnet thrives on respecting the hierarchy. You are a *temporary* member, which means you need to behave. Or I will be forced to exile you."

His hand went to my throat before I could speak, his power forming a noose around my neck.

No, not his power.

My power.

The power he'd inherited via his bite.

"I'm not the kneeling type," I promised him, ensuring he felt the push of my energy against his. He might have imbibed my strength, but I'd lived with it my entire existence. I knew how easily it could overwhelm someone else.

Although, he was admirably in control, something I respected on a deep level.

He wasn't threatening me right now, just holding me in place.

"Nyx, I offered you a temporary reprieve. I need you to honor that gift by following my lead. At least while I handle this situation. Because everyone out there, including the essential monarch that you just met, all feel *you* are responsible."

"I'm not," I said immediately.

"I believe you," he replied, shocking me a little. "But they're not going to listen unless they see you being respectful. So I need you to keep that seductive mouth of yours away from me while I work through the political bullshit."

"Seductive mouth?" That had me smiling again. "Tell me more."

"Nyx."

"Vesperus." He really did have a sexy name.

He sighed, the sound exasperated. "I have a job to do. If you want me to help you, you'll let me do that job."

"And then?" I prompted, arching a brow.

His gaze went to my lips before slowly tracking back upward, that eclipse still shining brightly in his alluring orbs. "And then we'll have a further conversation about that seductive mouth and what you can make it do."

He released my throat and took a step backward, but the heat in his gaze left behind a brand that seared my entire being.

Yes, this male had certainly been worth meeting, I decided, evaluating his towering frame and sensuous features.

It was a risk dancing with this powerful being. But it also offered something *new.*

Which was the only reason I slightly lowered my head in a respectful gesture. I'd never truly bowed for anyone, and I wouldn't be starting now. However, I could feign reverence for an immortal of worth.

"I'll behave," I promised him. "But only to clear my name." Not that I should really care what these supernaturals thought of me. They hadn't been all that welcoming, and I wasn't even sure I wanted to stay.

Alas, it seemed I might be here for a while if my magic continued to defy me.

Is this what you want? I thought at it. *For me to give a realm a proper chance?*

Maybe that would provoke the mischievous enchantment into returning to my palm.

I could test that possibility and play with Vesperus in the interim.

The magic in my chest pulsed at the thought, approving of the notion.

Yes. Play with Vesperus. And continue hunting for the magic.

"Lead the way, *my king*," I said, doing my best to appear *obedient*.

The dark glitter along the edges of his silver irises told me he saw right through the act.

But he silently offered me his hand anyway.

I accepted it, more than happy to resume touching him again.

Is this how he behaves with all his new House members? I wondered as we started walking, my lips curling down. *I certainly hope not.*

Which was a strange thought.

Why should I care how he interacted with others?

A weird vibration shook my chest, the sensation reminding me of a growl. *Strange.* But the idea of him touching anyone else suddenly had me wanting to commit murder.

I blinked, startled by the foreign inclination.

This magic is… dangerous.

Yet I couldn't seem to dismiss it. I didn't *want* to ignore it. Or reject it. I wanted to embrace it. To revel in it. *Thrive.*

Vesperus gave my hand a squeeze. "I'll do the talking."

Like you did with Kieran? I thought, snorting.

"Nyx."

I glanced at him, arching a brow.

"Respect," he mouthed at me.

Respect is earned, I thought. *So we'll see.*

But I didn't say that aloud.

Instead, I smiled and gave him my best obedient tone as I replied, "Of course, *my king*."

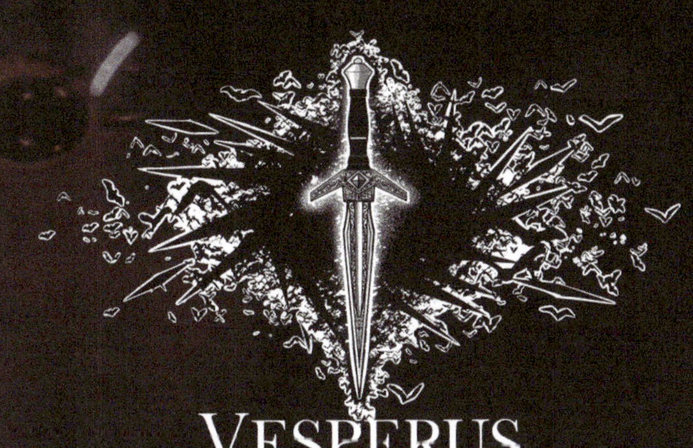

VESPERUS

If Nyx referred to me as *My King* one more time, I was going to rip that dress off her and fuck her up against the first surface I could find.

Yes, I'd told her to be respectful.

But she was doing it in the most seductive way possible.

And it was distracting the hell out of me.

Something I could not afford to feel as I sat at the table with Kaspian, Kieran, Slater, Nolan, and the two phantoms Kieran had brought with him.

Nyx had been offered a chair, but she'd opted to float around the room after saying a polite "No, thank you, *my king*."

She didn't seem to be one who could sit still for long, and now she was busy evaluating every corner of the old restaurant. Every now and then, she'd giggle at a portrait on the wall before moving on to the next.

Kaspian kept glancing at her, his lips curling down. "She's easily amused."

"She said she's been here before, but in another realm," I replied, the words ones she'd whispered to me upon entering the building. *Oh, I love this restaurant. Excellent choice,* my king. "She's… reminiscing," I added, my gaze narrowing in her direction.

"Another realm?" he repeated.

I considered how to reply, as there were several of us at the table, but I decided to go with the truth. "She's been traveling realities with a medallion that she says she's lost. That's how she arrived here."

"And you believe her?" Kieran asked, his tone emotionless.

My dealings with the vampire-fae hybrid were limited, but he'd impressed me a few weeks ago during the meeting with the other Houses, and my opinion of him had continued to evolve in a positive manner throughout this whole division of territory.

And now he was earning my respect for an entirely new reason —his ability to discuss business without giving anything away.

That trait would serve him well in his new role.

"I do," I finally answered him. "Because I can taste the truth on her."

I didn't elaborate on what that meant, and the fact that he didn't ask told me he already knew about my ability. Perhaps his step-uncle, Elias, had told him.

I didn't widely publicize my talent, but a close few knew about it. Particularly those who had ever possessed a need for my ability.

And anyone I'd ever lent it to—typically via a truth serum created with my venom—kept the trait a secret. Because they were allies.

It seemed Kieran might become one of those.

"I also believe that she didn't cause the explosion," I continued. "She pulled everyone out of the rubble."

Which had explained how all the bodies had been left haphazardly on the street rather than buried beneath the building's remains.

She hadn't exactly left them in the most comfortable of positions, suggesting she'd been in a hurry to save them all.

That behavior didn't add up with also being the one who had caused the initial destruction. Just like her showing up at the scene didn't strike me as the behavior of a guilty person.

Unless she was after something and using her powers to trick me in some way.

In which case, I'd kill her.

But I couldn't imagine what she'd want from me.

"Then who blew up the bar?" Kieran asked, his voice still lacking in emotion.

"A question that still needs to be answered." Because if it wasn't Nyx, then someone had attacked that pub for unknown reasons.

Magic gone bad?

A bar fight that had ended in an explosion?

Something else entirely?

I wasn't sure, and so far none of the witnesses could tell me anything about what had actually happened. Even Nyx had seemed unclear on the details, saying something about searching for her magic when everything exploded.

She'd woken up before everyone else—as evidenced by her painting the streets with survivors afterward—but she hadn't given me anything useful.

Yet, I thought.

It just served as another reason to give her temporary asylum. I could keep an eye on her while also questioning her for more details. Perhaps she'd remember something useful later.

Or maybe I'm just coming up with excuses because she's my fated mate.

I glanced at where she stood swaying her hips to the beat of the music. She was in her own little world on the other side of the restaurant, enjoying the soft tones playing from the sound system.

"The last thing I remember is walking toward the bar," Slater said, his voice low. "I can picture my hand on the door, and then everything goes black. My next memory is of Trixie waking me up." The way his tone darkened at the end told us all how he felt about that.

"I remember walking inside," Nolan added, his multicolored eyes reminding me of his shiny, diamond-like wings. They were hidden right now—a trait that seemed to come from his familial line of archangel warriors.

Or perhaps it was something others of his kind could do. Not many of them resided in this realm, despite the portal in the

Amazon. Probably because they were too busy fighting a war with demons in their home world—Celestia.

Nolan joining my House had been a complete happenstance of fate.

One inspired by Kaspian saving his life many decades ago.

"Then everything went white for me, not black," Nolan continued. "And I later woke up with that witch in my face."

I was sensing a theme here.

"She helped you both heal," I pointed out.

Both men grunted in response, clearly not pleased with having Trixie's healing magic touch them.

Typical. My men all preferred to wear their battle wounds with pride. And the witch had taken that away from them.

"I needed you alive and well," I added. "I'd thought we would be going on a hunt." My eyes traced back to Nyx. "But the prey came to me."

"And you gave her clemency," Kieran mused.

"Temporarily," I corrected him. "Until we can get to the bottom of this."

He arched a brow. "So you think there's at least some possibility that she's lying?"

"That's not what I said."

"No, it's not," he agreed, his arrogance reminding me of my own.

My jaw ticked as I considered how to shift the conversation. I fully expected him to report this conversation to Elias, which meant I needed to give him a little more to go on. Something to help pacify the Blood and Beryl King, while keeping my new Death and Diamond neighbors content.

"She poses a threat to our realm," I admitted slowly. "Granting her *temporary* refuge within my House allows me to keep an eye on her while I figure out what happened in the bar."

"I'm sure that's the *only* reason," Kieran remarked, obviously aware there was more to this situation than I was saying.

Since I'd damn near taken his head off for suggesting that I allow him to torture Nyx earlier, it seemed pretty evident that I wasn't in my right frame of mind as far as the female was concerned.

"It's the only reason that counts," I told him, fully aware that he could see through me.

But I wasn't ready to announce my connection to her yet.

At least not formally.

I'd let the others infer what they wanted about the situation.

"She'll remain with me until I determine the cause of the explosion. And also until I can help her find her missing medallion, as it seems the portals don't reach her world." I held Kieran's gaze. "Perhaps she's the first of her kind and a new species in our realm. I imagine that would be something you and Sabrina can relate to?"

Not Kieran personally, but his mate.

And the two phantoms seated near him.

They were a new species in this realm that had caused a bit of a stir. But we'd sorted it with the new House, which I'd voted in favor of.

Something Kieran knew and should respect, considering I'd also given them all a place to live.

Although, he was the only known vampire-fae hybrid in existence. So perhaps he could personally relate to Nyx's situation as well.

He nodded now, obviously reading the words I wasn't saying aloud. *We're engaged in a game of debt, one where I felt indebted to you, so I voted in your baroness's favor. Now you're going to work with me because it'll likely place me in your debt again, which you now know can be beneficial.*

His expression remained unreadable, his political poker face well crafted indeed. I imagined his familial relation to Elias had something to do with that.

"So you'll be taking over the investigation of the pub?" Kieran asked.

"I believe that's a given, yes. However, I'm happy to collaborate on the investigation." It was an offer I wouldn't usually make, but it seemed prudent to do so in this case. What with our amicable territory agreements and all.

Kieran shrugged as though it made no difference to him. "Sabrina will just want to be kept in the loop."

"I can continue to convey updates through you," Kaspian offered. "And if there becomes a need for collaboration on the issue again, we'll reach out."

Careful, Kas. Your diplomacy skills are showing again, I taunted him, ensuring he could hear me via my telepathic link to his mind.

He ignored me, used to my random commentary during meetings like this.

I would be receiving an earful from him later, though.

Kieran nodded. "Or perhaps you can take Nox and Bane on board, and they could serve as liaisons back to the House."

"With allegiance to Death and Diamond or to Gold and Garnet?" I asked.

"Death and Diamond for now," Kieran said. "Until they prove their worth to join your ranks." He glanced at them. "Yes?"

The one with darker features nodded. "Yes. I want to join Gold and Garnet, but I'm aware of the trials required."

Meaning they didn't just want to join my House for safety reasons, they wanted positions within my House.

I had to fight the urge to smile. Because this was exactly what I'd hoped for. And the slight glint in Kieran's gaze told me he'd known that, too.

Another way to put me in your debt, I thought, holding his gaze. *Clever.*

It seemed I'd underestimated this being's chess strategy. He always came off as flippant and arrogant. But there was a lot more to his persona than met the eye.

Or perhaps this was Sabrina's influence.

I would have to more carefully evaluate them later.

"Gold and Garnet accepts your candidacy," I told the dark-haired male. "Kaspian will tell you more about the trials required."

The phantom bowed his head. "Thank you, King Vesperus."

I looked at the other male, his features a lighter shade of brown. "And you?"

His piercing blue eyes met mine without wavering. "I, too, would like to join your mercenaries." His lips curled a little. "Death is a favorite pastime of mine. To make a job of it would literally be doing what I love."

Well, this one certainly had more personality than the other. "I thought phantoms were supposed to be pacifists."

"We are," he replied. "And I've spent a very long time living that life. But now that we're… exposed… I would like to pursue alternatives. Ones that aren't possible in Death and Diamond, considering recent events there."

"I see." I shared a glance with Kieran. It seemed he'd more than upheld his promise to find a phantom or two who might be interested in Gold and Garnet.

"They used to work for Max," Kieran said by way of explanation.

I had no idea who or what Max was, but I nodded anyway and refocused on the one who claimed to love death. "Bane?" I guessed.

"Nox," he corrected, his lips twisting into a sardonic smile. "It's short for Noxious. A chosen name, not my birth name."

I arched a brow. "Is that *chosen name* related to an ability I should know about?"

"I have a thing for toxins." He glanced at Bane. "He's better with traditional weaponry. But I usually enhance them with… chemicals."

"Yes, our former supervisor had a thing for experiments," Bane added. "And Nox enjoyed playing in the labs."

Interesting. I shared a look with Kaspian. "Sounds like you just made two new friends."

"We'll see if they can keep up," my second drawled.

Nyx twirled across the room, catching my gaze again. She appeared to be humming to some tune that only she could hear since the music had stopped playing.

"Anything else?" Kieran asked, sounding bored.

"Not unless you want to protest Vesperus's decision," Kaspian replied.

I studied the male, curious to read his reaction.

But he simply shrugged again. "It'll create an interesting

conversation, and my uncle isn't going to approve. However, I imagine you have a plan to deal with that."

I neither confirmed nor denied that assumption.

Which caused Kieran to smile as he pushed away from the table. "I believe my count is at two favors now, King Vesperus." He glanced at Nyx and then the phantoms. "Technically three."

"Noted," I replied dryly.

The cocky vampire-fae's smile grew. "Then I think our alliance is off to a fantastic beginning." He started toward the door, only to pause and add, "But my offer for a demonstration still stands. Let me know when you're ready or in need."

With that, he gave a slight bow to Nyx, one she returned with a full curtsy, and headed out the door.

I stared after him, amused.

"Demonstration?" Kaspian repeated.

"Of his ouchie-maker," I replied.

Kaspian's brow crinkled. "What the fuck is an ouchie-maker?"

"My question precisely." And why I very much wanted to know what torture device he'd named as such.

"It sounds like a kids' toy," Kaspian muttered.

"It does," I agreed. "But I highly doubt he uses it on children." Kieran struck me as having some morals, just like Elias and Volker.

Hence the reason I'd allied with them.

Empress Asbesta was another I often saw eye to eye with. But not always.

Regardless, none of us would fuck with kids.

Which, perhaps, might be the reason I'm protecting Nyx, I thought as she continued to dance with a childlike energy around the restaurant.

I pushed away from the table, more than curious to hear whatever tune she'd started humming, and left Kaspian to talk to the others. He would handle the investigation details, as well as assign trial-like tasks to Nox and Bane. They would all be trust-based and a way for us to decide their worthiness within our ranks.

Meanwhile, I'd handle the whirling goddess.

I caught her by the hip as she twisted right in front of me, then I dipped her down to the floor, my eyes on hers as she continued to hum an old Irish tune.

It was one I recognized as being at least a thousand years old.

I whispered some of the lyrics to her before pulling her back up into my arms. "How do you know that song?" I asked her.

"I heard it in one of the alternate realities," she murmured, falling easily into a dance with me. "Just like I heard every word spoken at that table over there mere moments ago. You're keeping me until you find the culprit behind the explosion."

Not a question, but a statement.

"I also said I would help you find your medallion."

She nodded. "And that you trust my truth because you're a lie detector."

"I didn't voice that part."

"No, I just inferred it." She rotated her hips, trying to take the lead of this dance.

I yanked her back to me, my hand tight on her hip while my opposite one found her palm. Then I led her around the room, my movements purposeful and commanding.

If we were going to dance, then I sure as fuck was going to lead.

She smiled as though indulging in my fun, her long black hair touching the ground when I dipped her again. The crescent moon between her breasts glistened, the hint of blood on the center giving it a brownish-red glow that resembled garnet.

Mine, a primal part of me thought. *This enchantress is mine.*

It came from the fated bond pulsing in my chest, the magic one I really should just break with a simple rejection.

Yet I wanted to entertain this risk just a little longer. Push the limits a little further. See what destiny lay on the other side.

Just for a minute.

Then I'd regain control of the situation and send her back to her realm.

Unless I find a way to keep her.

Because there was no denying how powerful she would make our House.

Decisions, decisions. None of which I was going to make right here and now.

Which left me with only one thing to say to her. "Are you ready to see what Iceland looks like in this realm?"

She stopped dancing, her eyes sparkling. "In winter? When the moon shines almost all day and night?" Her excitement was palpable. "Yes. Yes, I would like that very much."

Nyx

I couldn't remember the last time I'd flown anywhere. I typically traveled by phasing, but there had been a few moments in my past when I'd opted to take a plane.

Mostly to fit in.

And to see what it was like.

This experience was a bit more lavish than my previous ones. Primarily because we were on a jet powered by magic instead of fuel.

Fascinating.

I admired the sky as it shifted from lukewarm light to pitch-black darkness, my soul rejoicing at the renewed connection to the moon. It didn't matter what realm I ventured to; the orbiting satellite always refueled my energy and called upon my spirit to create.

Stardust tickled my palm, my skin humming with revitalized energy and strength.

I inhaled deeply, reveling in the sensations, and smiled at the glittering gems on the horizon.

Flying certainly had its perks, and the view was one of them.

Vesperus and Kaspian didn't seem to agree, though. They were seated near the front of the luxurious space, their heads close together as they conversed in low tones.

"Are you sure about this?" Kaspian asked, his question drifting easily to my ears as I shamelessly eavesdropped. Just like I'd done in the restaurant. "The bond could be clouding your judgment."

"I'm aware." Vesperus sounded tired. "Her powers also might make her impossible to read, but I haven't sensed any lies on her, Kas. Not even an inkling of untruth."

Because I've told you the truth, I thought at him. *What do I gain by lying?*

"So you're going to keep her until you decide otherwise," Kaspian translated.

"I'm granting her clemency until she gives me a reason to do otherwise," Vesperus corrected, his statement appealing to me far more than Kaspian's word choice of *keep.*

No one could *keep* me. I was a goddess. I would simply vanish if one tried to imprison me.

"She could prove to be a powerful ally for Gold and Garnet," Vesperus continued. "She could make a powerful queen, too."

I blinked. *Queen?*

"It would be her role as my fated mate," he went on. "And together we would be two of the strongest monarchs in the world."

"Odin and Lady Gabriella may have a few things to say about that," Kaspian said dryly.

"Their loss is our gain," Vesperus replied.

But I was still thinking about his term—*fated mate.* What did he mean I was his *fated mate?* Goddesses didn't have fated mates. We had consorts. Lovers. The occasional hookup with a fellow god for procreation purposes.

Not that I'd ever done the latter.

I hadn't found the right partner yet. I also hadn't decided what reality I wanted to settle in to raise a youngling, or if I even wanted a youngling.

"What happens if she doesn't want to be our Queen of Gold and Garnet?" Kaspian asked, piquing my interest again.

"If she doesn't want to be our queen, then we'll reject the magic tying us together and move on," Vesperus replied, making me frown.

Reject the magic?

What mag—

I blinked, my palm going to my chest. *This magic? The pulsing in my heart? Is that what it is, a fated-mate bond?*

"That requires you to keep your hands to yourself, then," Kaspian mused. "Otherwise, fate won't give you a choice."

"That's only if I fuck her." Vesperus's English accent seemed to caress that term—*fuck*—making my pulse heat in expectation.

Fuck. Yes, I would like that, please.

Except his words had implied hesitation, causing me to repeat each of their statements in sequence, my focus on the meaning rather than the potential action.

Vesperus had said we could reject the bonds.

But Kaspian had pointed out that Vesperus would need to keep his hands to himself in order for that to remain possible. *"Otherwise, fate won't give you a choice."*

Which meant Vesperus couldn't fuck me or we'd be tied together in this weird magic.

My lips curled down. *What sort of enchantment is this that can so severely dictate my future? Is it the same magic that drew me toward Vesperus to begin with? That invisible arrow that had essentially pointed right at him?*

"You think you can manage it?" Kaspian pressed. "I saw the way you danced with her."

Vesperus snorted. "That's just seductive foreplay. You should try it sometime."

"I often do, but only when I intend to fuck my partner."

"Then perhaps your imagination needs to be broadened, old friend. There's a lot more that can be done with hands and mouths, something you should probably learn before you find your future mate."

Kaspian barked a laugh at that. "Oh, I'm fully aware of how to use my mouth and hands, mate. But I'm not sure you can resist doing more."

"So you're questioning my control?" The warning note in Vesperus's tone didn't seem to have any impact on his friend because the other man merely chuckled again.

"Not exactly. I simply think you're severely underestimating the power of fate."

"I never underestimate anything."

"There's always a first time for everything, Ves," his friend drawled. "Case in point, your goddess mate staring wistfully out the window of your jet."

And listening to every word you're saying, I added, my gaze still on the stars while I continued to think through their commentary.

"She certainly caught me off guard," Vesperus admitted.

"Understatement. I thought you were going to let her eat you alive."

"I might have if my second hadn't thrown a knife at her head," my *fated mate* replied.

"I won't apologize."

"I know."

"You would have done the same for me," Kaspian added.

"I know," Vesperus repeated. "But if Nyx decides she wants to throw a knife at you in retaliation, I'm not going to stop her."

Hmm. A tempting notion, but I prefer not to start fights, simply finish them. However, Vesperus had halted that fight before it'd even begun by catching that blade by the sharp end.

An instinct to save me—his fated mate.

What amazing magic, I marveled. He'd protected me without even knowing me because of a bond he'd felt radiating in his chest.

That same pull had urged me to find him.

And it makes me want to lick him.

Would this magic remain with me if I left this realm? Would my heart break without Vesperus?

He'd mentioned rejecting the magic, though. So it seemed we had an option for breaking this spell.

My heart panged at the notion, denying my ability to fracture such a beautiful strand. So light and warm, filled with an energy my soul rejoiced within.

It made me feel full.

Happy.

Revived.

Like I suddenly had a new purpose in life—to be mated to Vesperus.

Is this all part of the spell? Or a side effect of it?

I could reject it to find out, but I wasn't quite ready for that. I wanted to experience some of it first, see what kind of enchantments our bodies could weave together.

Except he'd implied that fucking would cement our bond.

I'm a goddess. Nothing is ever finite.

But as his friend had said, there was a first time for everything.

Decisions, decisions, I mused, my skin humming with moon magic.

The two males continued their conversation, shifting their discussion to the bar explosion and my perceived innocence. From there, they went into a strategic discussion on how to determine the culprit. Apparently, the magic had knocked out all the cameras and security feeds in the area, leaving them without a trace. And Trixie, their healing witch, had said she didn't recognize the magic.

However, the Gold and Garnet raven shifter—*Slater*, as I'd later learned—had seemed somewhat familiar with it.

"It wasn't her, Your Majesty," he'd said to Vesperus before we'd left the restaurant.

Vesperus had left me near the door before stepping back to have a private word with his raven shifter.

Which I'd naturally listened to. I hadn't survived this long by ignoring private conversations, especially ones that were clearly related to me.

"Elaborate," Vesperus had said.

"I can sense the explosive energy," the raven shifter had murmured, his gray eyes flashing with power. "And it doesn't match the goddess's essence."

Vesperus had nodded, the two of them discussing the signature source for a few more minutes. It seemed the raven shifter had quite a talent for tracking. Hence, he had remained behind to see what he could find in Dublin. And the archangel had stayed with him.

The show of camaraderie was appealing and clearly a Gold and Garnet trait. It seemed the mercenaries weren't all lone wolves, that many of them worked well as a unit, too.

I suspected their leader was responsible for some of that, as he appeared to work closely with Kaspian. The two of them began strategizing for how Vesperus would respond to the other House leaders regarding my temporary asylum.

"Will you tell them about the fated-mate bond?" Kaspian asked.

"Not yet."

Kaspian considered him for a moment. "What about our House members? I noticed you failed to mention it to Slater and Nolan, but I think they suspected it. Just like Kieran, and likely the phantoms."

"Is that your way of saying I didn't hide it well?"

"You protected her against me, and again against Kieran. And you were... *touchy*. You don't usually do *touchy*."

Vesperus ran his fingers through his thick, dark hair, causing my gaze to drift away from the stars to admire his fingers in my peripheral vision. *Strong. Masculine. Perfect hands.*

"She's mine," he answered simply. "And she wasn't exactly keeping her hands to herself either."

"Which you normally wouldn't allow," Kaspian pointed out, his words intriguing me. Because it sounded like Vesperus didn't often take his lovers public, which made me unique to him.

I rather liked that.

Of course, it was probably related to this fated-mate nonsense, but a foreign part of me enjoyed knowing that this was a first for him.

"I won't go public with the information yet, but I won't explain it yet either," Vesperus told his friend. "Not until I figure out the best way to proceed."

Kaspian nodded. "And in the interim, it'll give us a good idea of how the other Houses will react to her becoming a member of Gold and Garnet."

"Exactly." He sounded amused by the prospect. "I'm surprised Elias hasn't called me yet."

"Perhaps Kieran is giving you some time to convey the update yourself."

Vesperus made a sound that suggested he disagreed, his palm going to the back of his neck to squeeze. "I'll start making calls tomorrow. I want to sleep first."

"No, you want to play first," Kaspian corrected him. "You might be my king, Ves. But you were my best friend long before receiving that title. I know you better than anyone."

How long before? I wondered. The magic coming off of them tasted old, suggesting at least a thousand years, perhaps two. Had they known each other growing up?

I nearly asked, my desire to know more about Vesperus overwhelming my thoughts. *This is the fated-mate bond,* I recognized. *Shall I reject it to turn it off, or allow it to consume me a little more?*

The former felt so boring and dull, as it would simply return me to my previous existence—assuming I'd understood Vesperus correctly.

While the latter option of indulging in this a little more had my heart racing with excitement. I rather enjoyed the concept of experiencing this a bit longer.

A fated mate.

Why not?

It sounds fun.

Maybe after I indulged for a bit, my magic would return.

Or perhaps the whole point of this was to ensure I met my fate.

Perhaps… I was meant to be here all along with Vesperus and *that* was why my medallion had crumbled.

I considered that train of thought as the jet began to descend, the familiar hum of night energy roaming over me in a kiss of tantalizing power.

Winter in Iceland was a treat, the moon almost always in the sky.

I sighed, content and pleased with this decision.

For now, I would indulge Vesperus and our *fated* magic while reveling in the dark skies and enchanted night.

You win, I told my medallion. *We'll stay a little longer.*

The energy hummed around me, the taunt reminding me of a happy giggle. Or perhaps a pleasing vibration. It was hard to say, as the magic seemed to have its own will and imagination.

But once I'm done with this realm, I expect you to return to me, I thought at it.

A soft hush fell over me, the magic neither agreeing nor disagreeing with my statement.

Perhaps it felt I would never be finished with this realm because it wanted me to stay.

I allowed that thought to follow us all the way to the ground.

Then I met Vesperus's expectant gaze as he stood.

And I accompanied him off the jet.

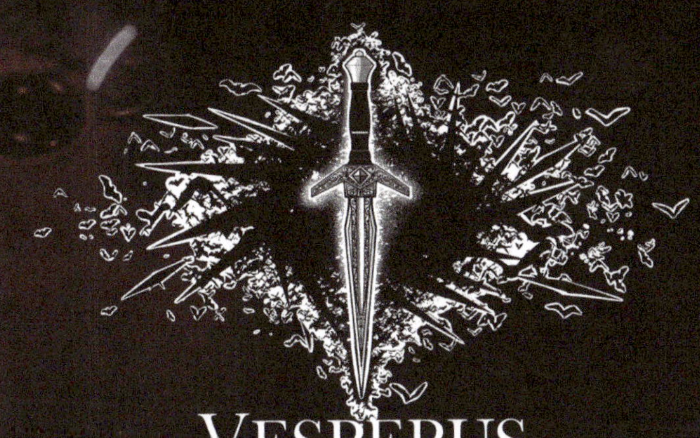

VESPERUS

Nyx said nothing as she followed us. She kept tilting her head back to take in the sky instead, her pale skin practically glowing beneath the moonlight.

There seemed to be a light sheen of golden magic covering her arms, making her appear even more majestic than she had earlier today.

Goddess of Night. Mistress of the Moon.

Sounds about right.

She looked so regal and untouchable right now. At least until I caught her eyes.

The fire burning in those golden orbs called to me on a base level, urging me to forgo my forward path and move sideways toward her instead.

I swallowed, fighting the inclination, and forced myself to continue onward to the parking lot.

Kaspian tossed me a set of keys as we approached the line of cars, then he twirled a second pair with his finger. "I'll wait for Manuela and Pam," he said, referring to our pilots.

I bet you will, I replied to him mentally.

He simply smiled, his lustful intentions clear in his dark eyes.

I suggest practicing your hand and mouth game, I added as I reached the passenger side of my SUV. *You know, to prepare for that future mate of yours.*

He snorted in reply, making Nyx look at him.

"Is your telepathy one-way or two-way?" she asked conversationally, her gaze flickering between us. "Hmm, one-way or you wouldn't have needed to speak out loud on the plane." Those stunning irises met mine. "You don't need to hide your comments from me, *my king*. I'm not easily offended."

With that, she teleported herself into the passenger seat and smiled at me through the glass window.

I narrowed my gaze. *My king.* It wasn't the phrase that heated my blood, but the way she kept saying it. Like she was trying to provoke me by mocking my title in the most polite manner possible.

It was a bratty move that struck me as disobedient.

And it made me want to do something to correct her behavior.

"I suggest you take her back to your place before you eat her, *my king*," Kaspian suggested, his open amusement curling around those final two words.

"I'm going to do a lot more than eat her," I muttered, using my vampiric speed to reach the other side of the SUV.

Nyx was already looking my way, almost as though I hadn't moved in a blink of time.

Perhaps to her, I hadn't.

I'd experienced a glimpse of her powers earlier after tasting her blood. It'd been heady and intoxicating, making me want to drain her and imbibe every ounce of her energy. But I'd forced myself to stop to remain in control.

"Don't do too much," Kaspian cautioned, the teasing gone from his voice.

"I don't need a reminder, Kas."

"Better to offer one than to regret not doing so later," he returned.

I ignored him and settled in the driver's seat. Kaspian's chuckle met my ears through the door, the sound a rumble that reminded me of the engine as I powered up the car.

Nyx remained silent while I navigated us out of the parking lot, Kaspian's midnight gaze following us the whole way. I'd heed and remember his warning because it was the same one rolling around on repeat in my mind.

"My realm doesn't have fated mates," Nyx said, startling me from my thoughts. "But I feel the magic in my chest. It's… it's not unpleasant."

No, I mused to myself. *It's certainly not unpleasant.*

"Your conversation on the jet suggested I'm your first," she continued, confirming what I'd already suspected—she'd overheard every word of our conversation. Just like in the pub. "Can you have multiple mates?"

I considered that for a moment, trying to find the best way to explain this concept. Everyone in my world grew up understanding fated mates, but she hadn't been born here.

"If you reject a mating bond, you can sometimes find a second-chance mate. But it's not common or guaranteed." As for having multiple mates, it wasn't something I'd ever heard of, but with the way magic shifted in this realm, anything was possible.

"So if we reject each other, you may find a second mate?"

I shrugged. "Possibly. But it took me over fifteen hundred years to find you, so I doubt it would happen anytime soon."

"Would you want to find a second mate?" Her tone suggested genuine curiosity rather than any potential for jealousy.

And a glance in her direction showed that her expression matched her voice. "As in a second mate with you still being my first? Or is this a hypothetical question that assumes we mutually rejected each other?"

She shifted her focus away from the window and toward me. "Would we need to mutually reject each other?"

"Yes." Otherwise, it could cause pain in the rejected mate.

"Oh." Her nose crinkled, the movement one I caught in my periphery.

"Some Houses have archaic rules that force a rejected pairing to fight to the death. Gold and Garnet has no such practice in place, but a non-mutual rejection can create a distraction. And my mercenaries don't tolerate distractions in the field."

"I see. So anyone who has been rejected without accepting it... is removed?"

"Removed from duty," I clarified. "Not killed." We weren't heartless, just practical. "And I can't afford to be *removed* from my position."

She considered that for a moment. "So we would need to mutually reject each other."

"Yes." I tightened my grip on the steering wheel, not liking the idea of rejecting this potential connection. So I focused on her original question. "And no, I would not pursue a second mate. Especially if we were still mated."

I wasn't even sure the scenario was possible, but it didn't matter.

"I prefer monogamous arrangements," I told her.

"Monogamous," she repeated as though tasting the word.

"Yes," I confirmed. "I don't share." And I would expect my mate to feel the same about me.

She stayed quiet for another few seconds, her hands still in her lap as she continued to study my side profile. "Gods and goddesses in my world often share freely."

My jaw clenched. "This isn't your world."

"No, it's not," she agreed quietly. "Which I suppose explains why I dislike the notion of you taking a second mate. It... it makes me feel angry." She sounded a little confused by her possessive instinct.

I understood her feelings to an extent. While I'd always chosen monogamy over casual experiences, I'd never felt the urge to mark one of those lovers as mine. Nor had any of them ever made me react possessively or protectively in front of others.

Which I'd done today with Nyx.

"The idea of you taking another mate angers me, too," I confided, enjoying this conversation. There were no games. No lies. No placative statements. Just blunt honesty.

It was... refreshing.

"This magic is intense," she mused, her palm coming up to rest over her heart. "I like it."

"Does that mean you don't want to reject it?"

"Hmm," she hummed, her gaze returning to the window. "No, not yet. It's new and different. A rarity for my existence."

"So this is more of an experiment for you?" I translated, uncertain of how I felt about that. Partly amused, but also irritated?

"Not an experiment," she murmured. "An *experience*. A magical one filled with foreign enchantment." She looked at me once more. "I've been traversing realms to find a new home, a new purpose. This is the first reality to offer me anything of intrigue."

My lips threatened to curl. "So I intrigue you?"

"Yes," she replied, her answer immediate. "Your magic is quite alluring, *my king*."

I growled, that phrase of hers erasing my amusement in favor of stark arousal. "Stop saying that."

"Why?" she asked, and I swear there was a hint of a purr in that single word. "Didn't you tell me to behave earlier? To show you respect?"

"For the meeting, yes. But we're alone now. No more titles." According to her, they didn't mean much anyway.

"So we have different rules between us when we're alone?"

"Yes." I slowed the car at a stop sign, then continued onward toward Reykjavik, or what used to be Iceland's capital, anyway. It was now Gold and Garnet's headquarters, and the city had been restructured as such.

"Then tell me the new rules." Her voice told me she was teasing, the goddess having no desire to bow to me whatsoever. I'd have to earn that kind of respect from her.

A challenge I fully accepted.

Because I very much wanted to see her on her knees. Particularly in my bedroom.

"There are no rules when we're alone," I decided, wanting to feel free with her. It was a risky proclamation, but why not test some boundaries? Being open would allow me to truly know her, and I would quickly discern whether or not she would be a good fit for my kingdom.

Besides, we'd established an unspoken expectation of truth

between us. I'd rather not fracture that tenuous foundation by layering it with rules.

"That seems rather trusting," she murmured.

"It does, doesn't it?" I made another stop, then turned onto the road that would finally lead us into the city.

The airport was a good forty miles from my house.

But magic allowed me to speed across the snow-covered roads. There were enchantments woven into the tires that essentially melted everything in its path, guaranteeing a safe drive despite the harsh climate.

"You can sense the truth and communicate telepathically," she said, telling me how well she'd read my abilities. "Can you read minds, too?"

No, I replied via a mental link to her thoughts. *I can only speak into the minds of others, not read them.*

She remained quiet for a beat. "So it's definitely one-way, then."

"It is," I replied. "But now I want to know what you said." Because she'd obviously tried to think something back at me.

"I was wondering if we'll be able to communicate back and forth once I taste your blood." The warm promise in her words had my blood heating in expectation.

"Only one way to find out," I replied, catching her wrist as her hand went to my thigh. I placed her palm back in her lap. "But not until we're in my house."

"Hmm, that sounds like a rule." Her comment wasn't a pout so much as a taunt.

"More of a precaution. I don't know how I'll react to your bite or how you'll respond to my blood." And I would prefer not to be driving when she put her mouth on me.

"So what does 'no fucking' qualify as?" she asked, her abrupt question almost causing me to veer off the road. "A rule or a *precaution?*"

I swallowed, my dick suddenly hard as a fucking rock.

Partly from her blood-play taunt, then the wandering hand I'd just caught.

And now fully from her saying the word *fucking.*

This female is going to test my control more than anything and anyone else has in my life.

"Because fucking each other makes rejecting the bond impossible, right?" she continued, that damn word igniting an inferno inside me. "Or that's what I inferred from your conversation with Kaspian."

I cleared my throat, my mind whirring with a dark hunger I needed to ignore. Otherwise, I might pull the SUV over and introduce her to the back seat.

"Mates can reject the bond," I said, my words gravelly to my ears. "But sex overpowers the rejection. So once you…*fuck*… there's no going back."

"Even for us?" she asked. "I'm not a being of this reality. Maybe the rules for us are different?"

As much as I wanted to test that theory… "I think that assumption is one we shouldn't consider. Because once fate's magic has secured two souls, it's impossible to break."

"Not even with death?"

"Are you saying you want to fuck me and kill me?" I countered, not appreciating the direction our conversation had taken.

She laughed, the sound unexpected and making me frown.

"No. I'm just curious as to how the bonds work when one dies. I have no desire to kill you. Only a desire to taste you." Her hand went to my thigh again, and this time I didn't stop her. "And fuck you."

Yes. Definitely a threat to my control. Because I could smell the desire she'd mentioned, that intoxicating arousal weaving a web around my senses that begged me to take her. To pull this SUV over, strip her, and lick every inch of her godly form.

Some women were over the top in their seduction, blatantly throwing themselves at me and making it clear they would do *anything* I demanded.

However, Nyx's approach was different. She was confident and forward, but not in an overly easy kind of way. She made her interest known while also telling me I'd have to work for her pleasure.

And if I didn't meet her expectations, she surely would not see to mine. Because she demanded to be worshipped before she agreed to reciprocate.

A very different experience for me, one that had me placing my hand over hers and bringing her wrist up to my mouth. I nibbled her pulse, my predatory instinct to bite a throbbing reality in my fangs.

"If a mated half dies, it can drive the other person to insanity," I said against her skin, responding to her question about how death played a role in the fated bonds. "The souls connect, almost thriving as one. So wounding a half damages the whole."

I pressed a kiss to her wrist, then placed her hand back in her lap again.

"So I suppose 'no fucking' is our only rule, as it's more than a precaution; it's potentially life-changing. Because while you might be from another realm, our souls will forever be linked. If we fully bond and you leave, it will likely feel as though you've died, and I rather like my sanity."

NYX

Vesperus's comments regarding the fated-mate bond swirled around in my mind for several minutes while he drove in silence.

I didn't like the notion of being his downfall. From the short amount of time we'd spent together, I could tell he was a decent ruler. Which matched what I'd heard about him while wandering Ireland prior to meeting him.

If we allowed this mating bond to thrive, and I eventually decided to move on to a new reality, it might destroy him.

Unless I took him with me.

But then he'd be leaving his kingdom behind for a woman he hardly knew, all because of some fated magic that said we should be together.

I frowned. "Maybe we need to reject it," I said, thinking aloud. "Before it… before it clouds our judgment and makes things irreversible." The latter part of that statement came out far less confident from where I'd started. It almost physically hurt to say.

Strange. I pressed my palm to my breastbone, attempting to massage away the dull ache that had formed inside me with my statement.

Vesperus remained silent for a long moment, the hum of the engine purring with this world's strange magic the only sound between us.

"It would be the practical decision," I continued. "To… to reject the bond, I mean." I massaged my breastbone a little harder, trying to erase the ache as I pushed my words forward. "This enchantment is unlike any I've ever experienced. And while I enjoy the sensation of it, I'm… I'm not sure the benefits are worth the risk."

Particularly as it seemed clear that this bond could dismantle his throne.

He was a king. He needed a mate who could rule at his side, and I likely wasn't the right candidate for that role. "I'm here to explore the realm and to potentially call it home. And while you are the best experience I've had thus far, I don't want a spell to taint my choice to stay."

"Spells often do taint our choices," he murmured. "Or magic, anyway. It's created chaos numerous times in this world, the last of which being a bit over twenty-four years ago—The Great Sacrifice."

"What happened?"

He shook his head, his expression revealing sadness. "Genocide, really. A mass extermination driven by a conflict between the Houses. It ended in a truce of sorts, but it's heavily strained. You being my mate… could disrupt the tenuous balance."

"Why?"

"Power," he replied simply. "Our mating will grant Gold and Garnet a superior position, one that many will not accept or appreciate. On one hand, it might add certain protections to my territory and chase off potential intruders. On the other…"

"It might start a war," I finished for him.

He nodded.

"That's what you meant about feeling out their reactions to my temporary asylum," I replied.

He cast me a sidelong glance, his lips quirking a little. "You really shouldn't listen to other people's conversations."

I could lecture him on the importance of finding more secure locations for private discussions, but I could read the humor in his expression. He'd likely known I was listening, as I hadn't bothered to hide it from him at the pub. "Information is valuable in all situations."

"It is," he agreed as he pulled over to the side of the road.

He didn't cut the engine, allowing the warmth to continue to filter in through the vents. Given the chilly air, I appreciated it. While I could regulate my inner temperatures with my magic, it made it easier to accept heat from another source.

His silver eyes met mine, the eclipse from earlier having reverted back to his normal color. That told me his access to my powers had been temporary, likely because he hadn't imbibed much of my essence.

"What if we rejected the bond and didn't tell anyone?" he suggested. "You'll still be given refuge in Gold and Garnet, and you'll stay with me. But we'll secretly deny the magic, to help us keep our heads clear, while we evaluate the acceptance of your presence in my territory."

"So we'll pretend that we're still fated…"

"It won't technically be pretend," he clarified. "The bond will be broken, but if we ever have sex, the mating will snap back into place. Which means our souls are still fated, but we're just not under the spell, as you call it."

I removed my palm from my chest. "Meaning this pull inside me will be gone, but if we *choose* to be together, it'll return?"

He nodded. "Unless our second fated mate somehow disrupts things, but as I said, those are rare. And that mate can be rejected, too."

"Would you reject yours?"

He stared at me. "That depends on where we are in our process. We might reject the magic and feel nothing for each other. Or we could feel exactly the same, just without…" He trailed off, his gaze going to where I'd been massaging my chest.

"There's really only one way for us to know," I said slowly.

"Then if… if I decided to stay… I would know it's for the right reasons."

"And we'll have had time to evaluate everyone's reactions to it."

"Except you weren't planning to tell anyone, right?" I reminded him, thinking about his conversation with Kaspian again.

"I wasn't planning to confirm or deny anything because that's the best way to let rumors do their job. I'll listen to what everyone is saying and use those reactions and stories to devise my next move."

My lips curled. "You're a very strategic king." Which added even more reason to why I needed to reject him. Because I couldn't risk his sanity for a decision that was driven by a spell, not logic.

While I enjoyed the sensation of being mated to him, I wasn't sure I wanted to keep it forever. Eternity with one person was a very long time.

Just as eternity of commitment to one reality seemed a bit daunting.

"I think we should do it," I said, feeling a bit more resolved on the issue now. My heart still hurt, but knowing there might be something else waiting for us on the outside of this spell drove my decision.

Maybe his magic wasn't like chocolate.

Maybe his aura didn't truly call to mine.

Maybe he was a troll, not a sexy-as-sin vampire.

I had no idea. This enchantment could be distorting everything in my mind, making me see a man who wasn't truly my type at all. Just a soul I was meant to meet and potentially marry to mine.

"It is the most pragmatic decision," he replied, his gaze roaming over me. "You'll still need to keep your power in check. And you can't cause problems in my territory, or I'll be forced to exile you… which means the Houses are likely going to demand your death this time."

My lips twisted. "Then they'll be very disappointed to learn that I can't die. I'm a creation goddess. If you somehow manage to destroy my corporeal form, my spirit will just go back to Khaos to be reborn again. And I would not be pleased."

His silver irises flickered with amusement. "No, I imagine you would not. But I suppose you would be in your home realm again."

I narrowed my gaze. "Where I can find another medallion and come right back here to return the favor, *King Vesperus.*"

His amusement only seemed to grow. "If there comes a time and a place where I need to kill you, Goddess of Night, then I will fully expect you to return and annihilate me." He didn't say it as a joke, but as a full truth. Which placated me only a little.

"Don't underestimate me, King," I warned him, not for the first time today.

"I wouldn't dream of it, Goddess," he returned, a little more seriously now. "But I need you to understand that it will be out of my hands if this truce between us goes sour. The Houses will demand that I hunt you, and you should not underestimate my ability to do so."

The warning in his tone sent a shiver down my spine, not of fear but of excitement.

And I suddenly understood his amusement from my threats.

They're arousing him.

Because his threat had me wanting to tempt him into a chase, to see how well he moved, to test his abilities, and fuck him as a reward —*if* he caught me.

I swallowed. "We need to reject this magic." It came out choked, my heart skipping several beats in my chest. "I don't like how it's… seducing me."

He cocked his head, the action all arrogance and sensual masculinity. "Is it the magic, or is it us?" he asked softly. "I suppose we'll find out. Because, Nyx, Goddess of Night, Mistress of the Moon, I reject you."

I gasped, my chest cracking wide open beneath his words and leaving me breathless beside him. I clutched at my dress, nearly ripping the gown off me in an attempt to reach my fracturing heart. But his hands caught my wrists, holding them down.

"Say it back to me," he said, his voice reminding me of a whirlwind of harshness, each word a barb to my senses.

He rejected me.

He rejected us.

He... he...

I shuddered, my mind splintering as my body shook with an agony unlike any I'd ever experienced.

Had this been a mistake? Should I not have suggested this? *Why did I suggest it? Why would I allow this? He's supposed to be mine... my fated... my soul...*

"*Nyx,*" his voice cut through my thoughts, eliciting a whimper from my throat.

I felt so weak. So cold. So alone. *Withering. Dying. A goddess without a home or a realm or a soul.*

I'd ventured to so many places, not once feeling right about any single aspect of those realities.

Until Vesperus. Until that tendril of magic that took me to him... whispering his power... his magnitude...

But he rejected it. He—

I jolted as his fangs cut into my neck, my eyes flying open as a scream left my mouth. "*How dare you!*" *How dare he reject me and then bite me!* "I'm not yours. You... you..."

His palms grasped my face, his irises bursting with eclipses once more. "Say, 'Vesperus Veritas, I reject you.'"

Reject him?

He rejected me...

"You promised to return the favor," he continued, his gaze burning into mine. "Don't get weak on me now."

I growled. *I am a goddess. I am not weak. He just... he just...* I swallowed, unable to finish the sentence. I felt so dizzy. So broken. So... so... *rejected.*

And I wanted him to feel the same way.

To experience this loss, to realize how much it hurt. This might have been my idea, but I hadn't expected this pain!

I growled at him.

Which made the bastard *smile.*

"There's my goddess," he said. "Come on. Reject me."

"Your goddess?" I repeated. "*Your* goddess?" This asshole thought to call me his after driving this bolt of invisible energy into my chest? *No.* No, that was not okay. Nor was I accepting it. Because… because… "Vesperus Veritas… I reject you."

Energy cackled in the air between us, causing all the hairs along my arms to stand on end.

I closed my eyes, my lungs fighting to breathe, my heart ceasing to beat.

Until…

Until it all cleared.

In a blink of time, everything shifted and a weight on my spirit lifted, freeing me from the agony of being rejected.

My lips parted, my insides in shambles over being shredded by a foreign spell. The moon kissed my senses, rejuvenating my spirit and sprinkling stardust all over my skin.

I sighed, relaxing into the leather behind me, and slowly opened my eyes.

Vesperus had released me, his expression giving nothing away as he sat silently beside me.

"You're definitely not a troll," I murmured, pleased to see that the deliciousness that was Vesperus still existed.

And, mmm, he still smelled like chocolate.

A glorious sundae with hot fudge and warm nuts. Yes, please.

"I don't think that worked," I said, leaning toward him. "Because I still very much want to lick you."

He arched a brow. "Do you?"

"I do." I ran my gaze over his delectable form. "So I guess the 'no fucking' rule needs to remain."

"It does," he said, his tone and expression still unreadable.

I pulled back a little to study him, slightly annoyed by his ability to turn himself off completely. "Do you still want to lick me?"

He ran those beautiful irises—still glittering like eclipses—over me in a slow, sensuous path. "We'll see," he replied, his hand going to the shifter between us as he pulled back out onto the street.

I frowned. *We'll see? What kind of answer is that? Does he no longer feel attracted to me like I do to him?*

My stomach churned in response.

Had cutting off the enchantment made him immune to me? Or was he playing coy? A king protecting his heart and throne?

Hmm.

I would just have to… test some barriers. See how he reacted. And go from there.

Perhaps he hasn't decided how he feels yet, I thought.

Well, if that was the case, I'd just have to help him along.

My gaze returned to the night outside, the moon calming my spirit and reminding me of my true path in life.

I came here to determine if this realm could be my home. Now I would also need to decide if Vesperus could be a future mate.

Or just a passing fancy.

Regardless of our fate, I planned to lick him.

Because chocolate was my favorite food.

And I fully intended to devour the treat beside me.

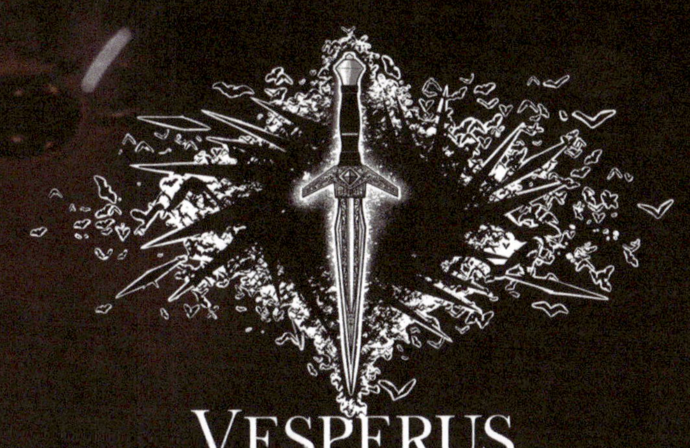

VESPERUS

Breaking the bond had been a sound idea. A practical choice. The right path.

And yet, I couldn't shake this feeling of wrongness.

Nor could I seem to handle my attraction to Nyx.

She hummed to herself as I showed her around my home, her gorgeous eyes flitting to the windows as often as she could to admire the sky outside.

Which was why I chose to show her the roof second to last.

We'd already been through the living area, the kitchens—where I'd introduced her to some of the staff members—and the three different dining rooms.

I'd also shown her the various quarters where everyone slept on the other floors and taken her through the library, into the adjoining conference hall, and by the second-floor seating area.

Then I'd bypassed the third floor with a soft "We'll come back down here in a minute."

And now I stood at the top of the stairs that led to my favorite sanctuary.

"This is a section of my home that is off-limits to everyone. But as my… *guest*… you may visit it anytime." It would serve as a way to inspire rumors regarding our mating. Only a future queen would be given access to my private sanctuary. Not even Kaspian was invited up here.

Of course, he would break that rule in the case of an emergency.

But that had never happened before.

My grounds were well protected, the manor—which was really more like a palace—had been built along the central harbor in old-town Reykjavik.

Water lined one edge of the property, and a thick park area framed the other three sides.

I'd forgone the park tour. I figured Nyx could explore those after a full night's rest. She'd be able to see it all in a moment.

My fingers swept over the keypad to unlock the door. "I'll have your biometrics added to the system later." It would essentially take a digital imprint of her magical essence and grant her access to everywhere in my palace.

Perhaps that was a lot of trust for someone I'd just met, but I was following my instincts about her.

Which hadn't changed in the slightest since our rejections in the SUV.

I still wanted her as badly as before, making me question if we'd even severed our bond. However, I couldn't feel the pulse of it any longer in my chest, so we must have succeeded. And this was just residual attraction.

Intense, insane, overwhelming attraction.

Fuck.

I'd thought rejecting her would dampen my interest. Yet it was almost as though it'd had the opposite impact, thus making me want to claim her that much more.

Swallowing, I forced myself to focus on the task of showing her my favorite space.

Her humming faltered as she took in the roof's landscape, the picturesque scene accentuated by the starry night sky.

"Oh," she breathed, her arms fluttering at her sides as she executed a twirl along the marble walkway. "Oh, this is perfect."

She continued forward to explore the benches built into the wall of one side. Then she took in the dark park beyond it before making her way to my favorite attribute—the pool.

It wasn't large, but big enough to swim laps in. However, that wasn't the point of it.

She knelt to skim her fingers along the surface. "It's so warm."

I smiled. "It's heated by magic." I'd wanted my own version of an Icelandic hot spring, so I'd used an enchantment to heat the water here. "It never cools."

Which was what made it more of a lounging pool than an athletic one.

Whenever I needed to think through a problem, I came up here and allowed the water to chase away my stress. Hence the reason I considered this my sanctuary.

I wasn't sure why I'd felt compelled to show her this. Perhaps because I'd wanted to give her an incentive to stay awhile, which went far deeper than simply inspiring the rumors to fly.

Even without the magic tying us together, I felt entranced by her presence. She was gorgeous. Powerful. Forward. Truthful. She didn't play games, just reveled in life and spoke her mind.

The mate bond might have been what forced me to see her, but my interest in her felt real.

Or it might have been a residual effect of the magic, a subtle enchantment trying to pull me back to her.

What I needed was some space to think, and I'd naïvely given her access to my favorite place for that.

Sighing, I settled onto one of the benches and watched her float around my private space. Her skin seemed to shimmer beneath the moon, the golden sheen drawing my gaze over every inch of exposed skin.

You're definitely not a troll either, sweetheart, I thought, admiring the view. *More like a seductive nymph dancing in the night.*

My blood heated as she moved gracefully around the pool, her dress flowing around her in regal waves of temptation. I wanted to wrap the fabric around my fist and yank it off her, expose all that creamy skin to my view, and see if the shimmer of magic spread to other parts of her.

Parts I wanted to explore with my tongue.

Because yes, I very much wanted to lick her, too.

But I wasn't going to tell her that. Not yet. Not until I was certain I could control this need. Otherwise, we would have rejected each other for naught.

And Nyx had been right—it was better that we not let the magic of our bond interfere with our decisions. I needed a clear head to make appropriate choices.

Yet my mind is utterly consumed by this enchanting being, I marveled as she whirled around, her steps that of a dancer more than anything else.

She spread her arms outward and laughed as she spun again, more of that gold magic appearing all over her skin.

"What is that?" I asked, my voice betraying my intrigue. "The glitter on your arms."

She glided toward me, her steps light as she moved to whatever song she heard humming in her head. "Stardust." Her delicate fingers flittered over me, sprinkling me with her glimmering substance. "It brings good fortune."

I arched a brow. "Does it?" I cocked my head. "And how do I know you haven't just enchanted me, Goddess?"

"You can taste lies, King." Her golden irises matched the shimmer on her arms. "Am I lying?"

"You're not," I confirmed, leaning forward. *About anything,* I added to myself. Including her comment about still wanting to lick me.

It would be so easy to strip her down here and fuck her beneath the moon. I could scent her arousal, see the taunt of it in her gaze.

But I couldn't give in.

Not yet.

Not until I knew exactly what this would do to my House.

"We should retire for the evening," I said, standing abruptly. Bringing her up here had been a bad idea. She was probably about to strip and swim naked, something I would love to see, and yet hate at the same time.

Because I shouldn't—*couldn't*—touch her.

Fuck.

I didn't look to see if she was following me. I just walked toward the exit, opened the door, and started down the stairs.

She sighed in my wake, the sound wistful, as though she were saying goodbye to an old friend.

I almost turned to look at her, but I didn't trust my reactions. This woman was under my skin, her soul having penetrated mine beyond the damn bond.

She's dangerous, I told myself. *More dangerous than any of us could have realized.*

Except Kaspian hadn't reacted to her like this, which meant my response was definitely tied to the fated-mate spell.

Only, we broke it, I thought, entering the third floor again and heading straight for my wing. *I felt it snap.*

My teeth ground together, my insides a hot pool of lust that longed to be sated by the being humming along behind me.

Is she even aware that she's singing? I wondered. *Or is this something she just does?*

And why the fuck is that so alluring?

I wasn't one for childlike wonder or sweet songs. Yet this being enchanted me with her music. The way she danced and hummed and lived in such a happy state of existence was enthralling.

I just need some sleep, I decided. *It's been a while since my last rest, and it's also been a very long fucking day.*

Pushing through the double doors at the end of the hall, I led Nyx into my private wing. "Seating area," I said, gesturing to the couches. "Bar." I pointed to the glass wall and counter affixed to it. "There's blood in the fridge…" I trailed off and glanced at her. "Do you need blood?" I imagined she didn't, but she'd mentioned a penchant for biting.

"Only yours," she purred, her sensual expression one that was going to haunt my dreams tonight.

Pure seduction.

I forced my gaze away from her and continued my tour. Which, of course, concluded with the bedroom. I didn't have a guest area attached to my suite, making the four-poster bed at the center the one we would share tonight.

Why did I decide she needed to stay with me, again?
Oh, right. Because I'm supposed to be watching her.
As my mate.
And I can't really do that if she's in the guest wing.
Awesome.

"The windows there lead to a balcony, if you want to indulge in your moon a little more," I told her, gesturing to the curtains covering the floor-to-ceiling glass wall. "Over here is the bathroom."

It had a tub built for six because I liked my space, and a walk-in shower beside it.

My closet was at the end of the large space, mostly filled with suits like the one I had on now.

"We'll need to arrange for you to have a wardrobe since you didn't bring anything here with you." I'd probably need to ask Cara to give her a tour of the town. Or maybe one of my other generals. Whoever was free to—

The water sprang to life in the shower, causing Nyx to clap in delight.

I gaped at her. "What are you…?"

Her dress hit the floor, causing me to lose my voice and whatever words I'd been about to say.

Then she bent to unlace her sandals.

Slowly.

So. Fucking. Slowly.

Providing me with ample time to study every damn inch of her.

This was absolutely a purposeful taunt, one meant to lure me into action. But I refused to take the bait. *I have more control than this, Goddess.*

When Nyx finally stood up again, her expression was so incredibly innocent that I couldn't tell if she was just an amazing actress or genuinely unaware of what she was doing to me.

"This is so much nicer than the shower at the hotel," she mused as she stepped into the glass enclosure and faced me. "May I borrow your shampoo and other essentials?"

My throat felt tight as I tried to answer her. Instead, I ended up giving her a tight nod.

Because fuck.

Fuck.

She was naked. In my room. In the shower.

And yes… yes, the gold shimmer did reach all areas of her body. Including her rosy nipples, which were more of a dusky brown from the gold.

Yet turning rosy again because of the water… washing away the shimmer… in alluring rivets that I want to chase with my tongue.

I cleared my throat and pivoted away from her, needing to regain my sense of control. It wasn't easy, and the image of her bathing behind me was firmly ingrained in my imagination.

Definitely going to haunt my dreams.

I grabbed some towels for the bathing goddess and set them on the bench near the shower. Then I selected an undershirt and boxers for her to put on once she finished… *dancing in my shower.*

Because that was exactly what she'd started doing, that hum of hers echoing enchantingly around her as mist began circling her gyrating form.

"I…" I trailed off, my throat tight again.

"Hmm?" She faced me, her hands in her glorious hair as she massaged some of my shampoo into it.

Now she's going to smell like me, too.

Damn it.

"I'm going to bed." My voice was harsher than I'd intended, but fuck, I had a fucking goddess naked and singing in my shower. "We'll talk about your clothes in the morning."

I didn't wait for her to agree, instead closing the door to my bathroom behind me and leaning back against it with a low growl.

This was a very bad plan. One I clearly did not think through.

I should just go sleep on the couch.

Instead, I opted for the bed.

I'll just pretend to be asleep when she's done. At best, it would give me a private chance to evaluate her—a moment of her not being aware of me observing her. At worst, she'd try to seduce me while I slept.

And then I'd introduce that disobedient mouth of hers to my cock.

If she wanted to taste me so bad, she could swallow.

I stripped out of my suit, leaving it on a nearby chair beside my kicked-off shoes. Normally, I'd sleep in the nude. But I kept my boxers on and slid under the covers.

My daily nightcap of blood would have to wait until tomorrow.

Besides, I had some of the goddess's essence running through me, which I suspected would keep me rejuvenated until breakfast.

I closed my eyes just as the water shut off in the other room.

Let's see what you decide to do, shall we?

NYX

Vesperus's home was everything I desired and more. Palatial in presence, elegant, filled with character and charm.

And that roof…

Oh, it was *divine*.

I almost phased up there to sleep on one of the benches. But his scent lured me back into his bedroom, where I found him already lying in bed.

I wandered over to him.

"Thank you for your hospitality, King," I whispered, aware that he wasn't really asleep.

But his lack of a response told me that he desired rest more than he wanted to play with me.

Fine, fine, I thought at him. *We can delay our dance.*

His response to my nudity had told me everything I needed to know about his attraction to me.

We'll see, indeed, I mused. *I certainly saw your reaction, Vesperus Veritas, King of Gold and Garnet. You want me. And I want you.*

However, I'd allow this attraction to thrive between us, *see* where it went, and go from there.

I meandered to the other side of the bed and removed my towel to wrap my hair up with it instead. It was easier than applying magic to dry the long, damp strands.

I was also admittedly quite tired.

It had been an eventful day, after all. I might as well indulge in a little rest.

Then tomorrow, I would explore my potential home.

And seduce its king.

I woke up alone with Vesperus's side of the bed cold to the touch.

Did you even sleep? I wondered, surveying the neatly tucked covers. *Or did I sleep too long?*

I slipped out of the sheets and wandered to the curtains he'd gestured to on the brief tour of his quarters. Peeking through them, I noted the sun's low position in the sky.

It was maybe two o'clock local time, then?

I wasn't certain, but the sun being out indicated it was afternoon for winter in Iceland.

Regardless of the physical clock, it was clearly time for me to explore.

Smiling, I retrieved my dress from the bathroom and laced up my shoes. A little stardust helped me fix my hair, and I was ready to go.

Where shall I go first? I tapped my chin and shrugged. *Anywhere.*

Vesperus had mentioned the need for a wardrobe, so perhaps I would seek that out during my tour.

I wrapped myself in shadows and phased to the park I'd seen from his roof. It placed me behind his estate on a snowy landscape littered with smaller trees.

The sidewalk was plowed, the lingering energy telling me it'd been done by magic and not a person. Similar to whatever enchantment had swept across the roads last night.

Exceptionally intriguing, I marveled, loving the kiss of vitality in the air. *This really could be an ideal home.*

I skipped along the path, enthused by the prospect of staying here. Would I keep Vesperus as a mate? Stay with him forever? Serve this territory as a queen?

How would that look in the long term?

So many questions. Rather than dwell on the answers, I chose to revel in the moment and continued my journey through the park.

It eventually ended at a fence that I phased through to reach the street on the other side.

Left or right? Left or right?

I spun instead and walked in the direction my spinning ended on—which happened to be right.

And a natural choice, too. Because it led me directly into the heart of town.

It seemed my wardrobe task would be successful after all.

Hmm. I perused the shop windows until I found one that appealed to me, and I stepped inside.

Fortunately, it was during working hours, so I would be able to properly pay for my clothes.

Well, sort of. That part needed to be negotiated.

"Hello?" I called out to the shop owner as I wandered through the clothing racks.

"Yes?" The female voice came from behind me, causing me to whirl and face a tall female with bright orange hair.

A shifter of some kind, I sensed. *But not a wolf. A large cat, perhaps?* I nearly asked but didn't want to appear rude, so I kept my conversation professional.

"Hello, I'm Nyx. I'm a new member of Gold and Garnet." I gestured to my crescent necklace. "And King Vesperus says I need a wardrobe. May I shop here for one?"

She blinked at me, the yellow slits of her irises confirming my guess about her being a cat shifter. "King Vesperus is paying for your new clothes?"

"Er, no. I can pay for that. You accept supernatural elements as currency in this realm, yes?"

She blinked again, her lids double-layered and making her eyes appear white before flickering back to her yellow coloring. "Blood is our form of currency in Gold and Garnet, but yes, we accept other forms as well." She looked me over. "What are you?"

Oh. Apparently, she didn't mind personal questions. "A goddess. You?"

"A tiger shifter." She folded her arms, appearing unimpressed by my presence. "What can you offer me? I don't see a purse or a bag, and that dress isn't hiding anything of value either."

I smiled. "I don't require a bag." Rather than elaborate, I held out my palm to display a small pile of stardust. "I have this."

She eyed my hand with distrust evident in her expression. "And what's that?"

"Stardust."

Her brow furrowed. "I've never heard of it."

"No, I imagine not. It's quite rare." I closed my hand, hiding the magic. "How about a demonstration? That will help you determine the worth, and then you can tell me what I'm allowed to buy. Fair?"

That distrustful glint didn't leave her features. "I don't know…"

"I promise you'll be pleased. We'll just do a tiny wish, something tangible."

"A wish?"

"Yes. That's how my stardust works. You wish for something as you sprinkle the powder, and the wish comes true." Like wishing upon a star, which was popular among humans in other realms. But I wasn't sure she would understand that here.

"A wish," she said again. "Like, I can wish for anything, and you'll give it to me as if you're some kind of genie?"

"Not me, but the stars. And there are limits to what a wish can become." Mostly because I controlled how much stardust I shared. "Here." I held my hand out toward her. "Wish for something tangible. Something you want to appear in the store. That'll help you see how this works."

She still didn't appear very believing, her arms remaining

crossed as she stared at my hand. "And you'll, what, sprinkle that over me?"

"No, I'll place it in your hand for you to sprinkle on the ground in front of you while you make your wish."

"Out loud?" she asked.

"In your mind is fine," I murmured. "Just make sure it starts with the words 'I wish.' Then the stardust will do the rest."

She studied me for a long moment before finally shrugging. "All right, then. Something tangible? Like a thing I want right now to appear before me?"

I nodded in encouragement. "Yes."

She looked at my hand, her nose twitching as though to scent out the magic. When she couldn't sense anything—because stardust had no fragrance—she held out her palm for me.

I released enough dust for her to create something special and took a step back to let her work.

Her expression told me she felt this was a waste of time, but she finally closed her eyes, and eventually she opened her hand to release the magic.

The store owner in Dublin wouldn't have known any of this, which was why I'd left the stardust on her counter with a wish of prosperity. She would likely experience a boom in sales as a result. Maybe a little more luck. And not much else.

But this shopkeeper was in for a real treat because she'd just used the stardust to create, which was my true form of power as a creation goddess.

As evidenced by the swirling magic dancing through the air between us.

She jumped back as it reached over six feet in height, making me wonder just what she'd wished into existence.

Then my lips parted as a bare, masculine back appeared before me.

Oh. Ohhhh. She'd… she'd created… *a man.*

And not just any man. He appeared to be a fae with pointy ears and long blond hair.

"Oh my Gods," the shopkeeper breathed. "Is it…? Is it real?"

"Erm, yes," I said, my lips twisting to the side as I moved around the fine male specimen to stand beside her. "*Very* real." And well-endowed, too. "You wished for a naked fae?"

"Technically, an elf," she whispered, her eyes wide as she stared up at the handsome male. "From… from an old movie…"

The creature before us blinked a few times. "Hello," he greeted. "Where am I?"

"Iceland," I replied. "Um. Hmm." I wasn't sure what to say. My stardust could create anything, even this. "I thought you would wish for a jacket or a necklace or something."

Not a naked… elf… with abs. And very muscular thighs…

"Is he going to disappear?" she asked, her eyes on his groin. "Or do I get to keep him?"

"I… I don't think it's wise to keep a living being. But no, he won't disappear. He's alive and—"

A blast of power shook through the store, sending me several paces backward as a shot rang through the air.

My eyes widened as the elf crashed to the floor.

With a bullet lodged in his forehead.

Dead.

I gaped at him, stunned, my stardust immediately building a shield around me and the shopkeeper as the dark energy shifted closer to us.

"What the fuck, Raymond?" the shopkeeper shouted, jumping forward to throw open the door to her shop. "You owe me a new window! And a new elf!"

I blinked several times. *What?*

"A new elf?" a deep voice repeated. "You can't just conjure creatures with spells, Lissa. You know the rules."

"Technically, I didn't conjure anything. I wished for it."

I crept forward to see her staring down a male nearly twice her size on the street.

"You wished for it?" he deadpanned. "Sure. With what?"

"Stardust," she replied, pointing at me. "From *her*."

The big man's eyebrows shot upward, his gun immediately

raising in my direction. "Who the fuck are you?" he demanded. "And where's your marker? What House are you aligned with?"

"Why is everything about Houses with you people?" I muttered, flicking a clump of stardust off my dress. "And why do you all feel the need to point weapons at me?"

It was truly starting to grate on my nerves. I'd thought this territory would be different. Alas, no. They still wanted to shoot first and ask questions later.

"She's a goddess, and her crescent is marked with blood," the shopkeeper—Lissa—told him. "She said King Vesperus sent her here to buy a wardrobe, and she offered me stardust as payment."

Not exactly the sequence of my statements, but her explanation was close enough.

"And you believed it?" Raymond snarled. "I could smell her power a block away. She's not one of ours. And you let her make you a bloody elf?"

Lissa rolled her eyes. "Don't get jealous, Ray Ray. I just wanted to play a little."

"*Play a little?*" he repeated. "With a sexy, naked elf?"

She blew out a breath, causing her orange hair to flutter over her forehead. "I wasn't going to touch it."

No, she just wanted to keep *it.*

"I'll deal with you in a minute," Raymond growled, his focus returning to me. "Let me see your marker."

I narrowed my gaze. "Why?"

"To see if you're legit."

"Why don't you ask your king?" I countered, arching a brow.

He huffed a laugh. "Because I'm not going to bother him with this nonsense. And your reluctance is all the proof I need, sweet cheeks."

The bullet cracked through the air, hitting my stardust shield and rebounding toward the moron who had tried to shoot me.

Lissa screamed, falling to the man's side as he crashed against the icy ground. The shot had ricocheted into his shoulder, the force of it taking him down. He'd live.

But Lissa's fury came out on a loud roar, telling me our brief friendship had probably just come to an end.

I retracted my magic from her and took several steps backward. "I don't mean any harm," I promised her. "I just wanted some clothes."

Her snarling reply was unintelligible yet conveyed everything I needed to know.

As did the flurry of shouts in the street that soon ended in a blaring alert that had me clutching my ears.

I stand corrected—this territory is not an ideal home. It's chaotic violence and unwelcoming and—

I phased as a fiery substance shot through the air toward my head.

And downright rude! I finished, irritated with these hostile beings who continued to try to kill me without preamble.

I'm done.

I called a wall of stardust to my aid and used it to shove everyone away from me.

Only for a trickle of magic to sneak through the wall and slam right into my chest.

I stumbled backward, confused by the familiar touch. *Why?* I thought at it. *Why would you do that?*

Because it was my medallion enchantment that had knocked me down.

I shook my head and tried to clear it.

And realized I was now the focus of at least a dozen pissed-off supernaturals.

Ugh. Here we go.

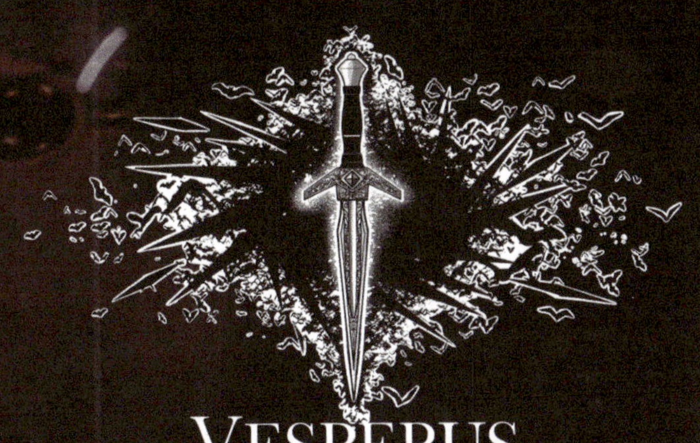

VESPERUS

A Few Minutes Earlier

My wrist buzzed with an incoming call, one I'd been expecting and dreading all day.

King Volker, House of Air and Amethyst.

We'd spoken a few times since he'd reclaimed his throne, mostly about his two loyal aids—Feyre and Lady Oleander Price.

I'd given them clemency after Volker's perceived demise, mainly because I'd known how valuable they'd been to him during his reign. And I'd known what the imposter on his throne would have done to the two female assassins in his absence. They were loyal to Volker, not to the new monarch.

So I'd offered them a safe haven in exchange for a handful of jobs.

And when Volker had miraculously risen from the grave—one he'd never actually been buried in—I'd allowed his two loyal subjects to return to him. They were blood-pledged to him anyway. It'd made sense to let them honor their bonds.

But that didn't mean Volker and I were friends.

Something that proved accurate as I pulled up a screen to reveal his stoic features. "Vesperus," he said.

"Volker," I returned.

A beat of silence followed, the recently restored king wishing to prolong the suspense in an admirable attempt to gain the upper hand.

But he should know by now that silence never unnerved me.

We were both from an era of honor that very few these days seemed to understand. It was why we tended to tolerate each other and often voted in favor of the other.

When he'd taken back his crown and throne with Air and Amethyst, I hadn't batted an eye.

But had he requested my assistance, I would have told him an honorable king handled his own business.

However, he'd never asked me for a damn thing. Because he already knew the unspoken rules of leadership and he honored them as I did.

"So you've heard about the bounty," I finally said, deciding to play the first hand. "I found her."

He arched a brow. "And you've decided to keep her." Not a question, but a statement.

"For now," I confided. "She can't leave through a portal. So I'm evaluating the situation."

"Why not just kill her?" he asked, his gray irises flickering with power even through the screen.

"Because she's done nothing wrong other than enter our world illegally." Which wasn't the full truth, but it wasn't a lie either. "She's trying to find some medallion that'll let her return to her reality."

"Return to her reality?" he repeated. "What is she?"

"A goddess. Specifically, the Goddess of—"

Power hummed over my skin, silencing my words. I glanced out the windows of my study, half expecting to see Nyx standing on the patio.

But she wasn't there.

However, I felt her like she was right next to me, her essence a beacon in the air that had me breathing heavily in response.

What are you doing? I wondered, my instinct to connect to her mentally almost driving those words to her mind. But I held back as I felt another jolt of power.

"What is that?" Volker demanded, obviously feeling it, too.

Which didn't bode well since he was in another area of the world. "What's she the goddess of, Vesperus?"

"The night," I said slowly as the room seemed to shift around me. "I need to go."

"You need to kill it," he corrected. "*Now.*"

"I don't answer to you, Volker," I replied, standing. "I'll call you back later."

I hung up before he could counter my previous statement.

Not that there was anything he could truly say. Volker and I lived by a similar code. He would understand that I only listened to two entities in life—myself and my people.

And right now, the intruder alarms were blaring outside. Which meant my people needed me.

Except I suspected it was a result of something Nyx had done.

Fuck. I shouldn't have left her alone, but I hadn't been able to sleep with her luscious, naked body only scant inches from my own. And I'd needed some space to think.

Which fully defied the purpose of keeping her in my room— where I could *watch* her. However, she'd been asleep, and I'd expected her to come find me whenever she woke up. I'd shown her where my study was last night, so she knew where to look.

But clearly, she'd had another agenda on her mind.

One I should have anticipated rather than leaving her to her own devices.

Fool, I chastised myself. This was obviously a result of not sleeping well enough to think through my ideas. Because an alert version of me would *never* have left a goddess alone in my palace without a guard.

I headed toward my patio door and called up Kaspian from my wrist. It was like a phone, only enchanted by magic, like everything else in this world.

"I thought you were babysitting your mate" was Kaspian's greeting as he picked up. "But I see she's causing problems over at Lissa's shop."

"Lissa's shop?" I repeated incredulously. "Why the hell would she…?" I trailed off as I recalled our conversation before she'd lost her dress. "Right. She went shopping."

I pinched the bridge of my nose and blew out a breath.

"You let her go shopping? *Alone?*"

"I didn't *let her* do anything. I left her asleep in my bed while I worked. Apparently, she's awake now." And I didn't quite care for his *babysitting* terminology. She was a goddess. I couldn't exactly *babysit* her.

"Apparently," he echoed.

"I'll meet you there," I said, hanging up and stepping out onto my patio.

The shop was only a mile or so from my grounds. Driving would take longer than running, so I engaged my vampiric speed instead.

Only to freeze upon finding Nyx behind a wall of swirling energy.

Her golden eyes were on the crowd of supernaturals behind it, her anger a palpable wave that prickled along my senses and caused every hair to stand on end.

It took me a blink to understand her fury—they were all blasting her with varying degrees of magic and weapons, the shield the only thing standing between them.

What the fuck?

"Stop!" I shouted, my command for those beyond the barrier.

"They're attacking me," she spat back. "I will not stop defending myself!"

"I'm not talking to you," I told her. "I'm talking to *them.*"

Several of my men immediately dropped to one knee, their expression of respect duly noted.

It took the others a few seconds to realize who had spoken, their eyes widening with fear as they fell to the ground in a display of obedience.

And the last among them—a bear shifter named Raymond— finally stopped trying to claw at Nyx's magic and sat on his rump with a loud huff.

"What the fuck just happened here?" I demanded.

Nyx didn't drop her barrier, her golden irises flaring with power.

I must have felt her calling on the moon to bolster her in some way because her shield was made of the same substance that had coated her arms last night.

Stardust.

"Um." A female cleared her throat. *Lissa.* "The goddess gave me some stardust to make a wish. And… and I wished for a character from an old movie. An elf. And it worked."

Raymond growled at that, causing my eyebrow to twitch upward.

"You created an elf?" I asked, glancing at Nyx.

"No, the stars did from her wish." The irritation in her tone was not lost on me. "I was trying to offer her stardust for payment of clothing, but that shifter"—she pointed at Raymond—"shot my gift in the head. And then he tried to shoot me after I told him to ask you about my clemency."

My other eyebrow lifted. "You tried to shoot my fated mate?" It wasn't what I should have said or what I'd even meant to say, but the shock pulled the words from my throat in a low, lethal tone, forcing me to voice them aloud.

This male dared to hurt what's mine?

We might have rejected our bond.

But we were still linked in a way, one I couldn't quite define.

And that made her mine to protect. Mine to court. Mine to potentially mate for life.

Yet this male had tried to take her from me? To ruin that opportunity before it had even begun?

I took a step forward, ignoring the gasps from the crowd. "*Face me*," I demanded.

He shifted back to human form, leaving him naked and kneeling on the other side of Nyx's barrier, his head bent in a show of supplication. "I… I didn't realize…"

"You didn't realize she was my fated mate?" I asked him. "Perhaps because you didn't deign to ask me about her presence?"

"N-no, Your Majesty. I… I thought she was lying… She's not marked. I didn't want t-to bother you," he stammered, sounding a lot less grizzly than usual.

I narrowed my gaze. "Perhaps you should have asked." I pulled a knife from my pocket and twirled it between my fingers, debating my next move.

The predator within me desired blood. But it appeared the male was already bleeding.

"Did you stab him?" I asked Nyx.

"No, the bullet bounced off my shield and went into his shoulder." Her gaze went to Lissa. "Which is when she started screaming, and then the alarms went off."

"I see." I continued twirling the blade between my fingers, my gaze not leaving Raymond.

If I punished him, I would have to punish them all. Because every single one of the kneeling beings on this street had tried to attack my mate.

Not my mate, I reminded myself. *Just… potentially my mate.*

And they hadn't known who she was, just saw her as someone new who had… *created an elf?* What a bizarre thing to start a fight over. "Was it her magic that caused your reaction?" I asked Raymond.

"Y-yes," he whispered. "And… and the naked blond."

"Naked blond?" I repeated as Kaspian arrived at my side.

"What?" he asked, glancing around the crowd.

"The elf," Nyx clarified. "He was blond."

"And naked," the bear shifter growled. "*In my mate's shop.*"

"Oh, it was harmless fun," Lissa retorted. "I wasn't going to do anything."

"Ugh, I just wanted some clothes," Nyx muttered, clearly exasperated.

"What the fuck did I miss?" Kaspian asked, his bewildered tone matching how I felt.

Nyx repeated the whole story for him, including the stardust, how it granted desires, and that Lissa had created a naked blond elf from some movie with her wish.

"Well, shit," Kaspian breathed. "Can I have some stardust?"

I growled at him and he grinned.

"Come on, mate. It could be fun," he offered, making me

wonder why I'd chosen him as my second-in-command if he couldn't remain serious in such a moronic situation.

The blade in my hand stilled as I considered stabbing him instead of Raymond.

"This is all clearly a misunderstanding," Kaspian continued, making me narrow my gaze. "How about everyone head on home while I have a word with our king and our goddess guest, yeah?"

I arched a brow, wondering what had given him the audacity to take charge of *my* people.

Yet they all miraculously listened to him, taking the first opportunity available to flee.

My jaw ticked. *Yes, I'm definitely going to stab Kaspian.*

"Stop looking at me like you want to murder me, and meet me back at your place." He engaged his vampiric speed before I could respond, making me growl in his wake.

It was a quiet sound, one no one heard apart from Nyx.

Because everyone else had fled back to their homes, leaving me alone on the street with my fated mate.

I looked at her.

And she stared back at me. "I thought we weren't going to tell anyone," she commented after a beat.

"I changed my mind," I told her. "Let's go."

I had a best friend to kill.

NYX

"Look, I just wanted some clothes," I explained again. "Your realm trades magic like currency, so I was offering some of mine for a new wardrobe—which you told me to acquire, I might add."

"I believe I said *we* would work on your wardrobe," he replied, his jaw clenching around each word. "You weren't supposed to wander off alone."

My eyebrows lifted. "First of all, I can handle my own clothes shopping—"

"Can you?" he interjected, pointing at the road behind us. Because for some reason, we'd decided to walk back instead of phase or run or whatever would have been faster. "You just created a shield of stardust from your moon magic, something that could likely be felt all over the damn world."

He lifted his wrist as though to prove a point.

"I've already missed three calls from King Laskaris and two from King Volker. I'm sure Empress Asbesta is next since your moon magic is impacting the oceans, too." As he spoke, his watch lit up and he growled, hitting *Decline*. "Make that four missed calls from King Laskaris."

"So it's my fault the shop owner's mate decided to kill my gift? And then tried to kill me?" I demanded, irritated by his dressing-down. "I'm a goddess, *King Veritas*. I should be able to go shopping as I want."

"Not without a proper introduction, *Goddess Nyx*," he bit back. "My people don't know who you are yet, and you didn't give me a moment to tell them."

"Because we had decided not to tell anyone, until you *changed your mind*." Which had been my second point of discussion.

Well, no, my *third* topic.

I'd wanted to address his new rule first, as I'd thought *no fucking* was our only stipulation.

However, now he'd added *no wandering* to the list, and I was vetoing that rule immediately.

He stopped near the gate to his park—something I hadn't seen before because I'd just phased through his fence—and faced me.

"I've explained to you how the Houses work in regard to affiliation. Your mark isn't as clear as most of those in Gold and Garnet, something I'd intended to address by bringing together my advisors and introducing you to them as my *guest*. But this afternoon's events have changed our path."

His tone was less hostile now and more tired, his eyes telling me that he hadn't slept much last night, or perhaps for several nights.

I frowned at him. "You need more rest."

He laughed humorlessly at that and opened the gate to wave me through. "Tell me something I don't know."

I considered his statement as I obeyed his unspoken request to enter his lands. "The blond elf was very well hung." There, that was something he didn't know, right?

"*Excuse me?*"

I glanced over my shoulder at him. "He was a well-endowed elf," I clarified. "Cute, too."

"Are you trying to piss me off?"

"No, I'm telling you something you didn't know. Now you do."

He gaped at me as the gate shut behind him. "In what world or reality do I want to know about another man's cock?"

I considered him. "Well, I imagine you would be interested if you preferred men in bed." I knew several gods that did, so it wouldn't be all that surprising. But Vesperus's infuriated expression now told me that didn't suit his interest at all.

"It was a turn of phrase, Nyx. Not a request." He prowled toward me, making me walk backward quickly until I hit a tree trunk. His palms slammed against the bark, blocking me in as he towered over me.

I could phase, but something about his simmering expression held me captive.

"I'm starting to understand why Raymond shot the elf," he said, his voice low as he leaned into me. "If I caught you in a situation with a *well-endowed* blond male, I'd shoot him, too."

I gaped at him. "*What?*"

"I told you, Nyx. I don't fucking share. And you're *mine.*"

My palms met his chest, my nails digging into his dress shirt. "We rejected the bonds."

"We did," he agreed, his muscles clenching beneath my hands.

"Then I'm not yours and you are not mine."

"That's not what we agreed to, Goddess. We agreed to remove the magic to clear our minds. And see how we felt *after* the spell broke."

"Right. And you said, 'We'll see,' when I asked how you felt about me," I countered.

"Yes, because it's not a simple response. I have to consider my House, my throne, and the future of my people, too." His wrist began to buzz again, making him growl. "Your power is a threat to the tenuous balance in this realm, Nyx. And you…"

I arched a brow. "I…?" I prompted.

"And you…" he repeated, his palm leaving the tree behind me to cup my face, his gaze going to my mouth. "You are an even bigger threat to me." His words were soft yet underlined in a dark emotion, one that had my heart skipping several beats.

I swallowed. "I'm not trying to be a threat to anyone. I just want a new home." And while this reality appealed to me in a lot of ways, it seemed clear that the occupants of this world weren't going to accept me very easily.

But then again, nothing worth having in life was ever meant to be easy. Happiness often required work. As did success and achieving goals and other joys in one's existence.

Like love, I thought. *And relationships.*

Two experiences I'd never thought to desire, yet being here made me wonder if I should strive for more. If I should *try*.

Is that why you shoved me earlier? I thought at my errant strand of magic. *Were you keeping me from hurting the people I'm meant to one day lead? Forcing me to see this chance for what it truly means?*

The enchantment didn't reply, but I swore I saw the answers in Vesperus's gaze as he lifted his eyes to mine. Answers that I couldn't decipher because they were too complex to understand. Answers that both of us sought and yearned for yet could only attain together.

Perhaps it was a trick of the light.

Or a strand of fate ensuring we shifted back onto our original track.

I really wasn't sure.

But in that moment, all I wanted was for him to kiss me. To let me taste him for the first time. To give me a glimpse of the power he held deep within.

The power I'd felt humming around him on the street moments ago.

The power that had attracted me to him in Dublin.

The power that I could sense now, swarming around us, and covering me in that delectable fragrance.

I want to devour you, I thought, my nails digging even more into his shirt. *Kiss me.*

But his wrist buzzed again, disturbing the moment and making him take a few steps back. He looked at the screen and muttered a curse.

"I'm going to need to do damage control for the evening, which will include meeting with several of my advisors from the various regions. Word is going to spread quickly of what you are to me, which I'd hoped to avoid. But my... *possessiveness*... overruled my strategic senses."

Possessiveness, I repeated to myself, considering the word. "Is that why you changed your mind?" I asked, genuinely curious.

"Yes. One of my men tried to attack you. I... reacted."

"And this?" I asked, gesturing at myself and the tree behind me. "Another possessive reaction?"

"Hearing you discuss another man's..." He trailed off, his gaze narrowing. "I don't share."

"As you've said." But I didn't bother pointing out that we didn't belong to each other yet because it clearly didn't matter to him. Despite fracturing the bond between us, he was still feeling very *possessive* over me as his mate.

And if I swapped our roles, I found myself understanding why.

Because if the elf had been naked in his room, I would not have been pleased. "Interesting," I murmured. "I don't believe I've ever felt this way before."

Just thinking about it had me wanting to shoot the elf myself.

Poor creature, I thought. "I wonder if he'll survive."

Vesperus arched a brow. "I suppose that depends on what type of elf he was."

I shrugged. "You would have to ask Lissa that. She wished for him."

"Hmm." He considered it for a moment. "You know, I think I'll give Kaspian that task since he seems so willing to take over my role in this territory."

"I wasn't taking over your role, just saving you from making an emotional decision," the male in question drawled as he appeared a few steps away. "But it seems I was too late for that, as word has already begun to spread about the goddess being your fated mate."

Vesperus clenched his jaw. "Raymond tried to shoot her. That's unacceptable."

"I agree," Kaspian replied without missing a beat. "But he had no idea who she was. All he saw was a powerful being in his mate's shop trying to seduce her with some naked elf. He reacted. I imagine it's similar to how you want to react now."

Vesperus's hands clenched into fists. "Just keep him away from me for a few days."

"Consider it done."

"I also need to gather the various leaders in the territory to tell them about Nyx."

"Cara is already working on that," Kaspian replied. "She'll have them here by tomorrow."

Vesperus nodded, his hand rubbing over his jaw. "I want to talk to them before I tell the other monarchs."

"Our territory is loyal. Word of your mating won't spread. But her power…"

"Was felt around the globe," Vesperus finished for him. "Yes, I know." He silenced yet another incoming call. "I'm going to be fielding complaints all night."

"Then perhaps draft a statement and send it to all of them at once," Kaspian suggested. "And handle your allies separately."

I glanced between them, curious about their dynamic.

It seemed clear that Vesperus considered Kaspian to be his advisor, and the way he nodded now told me that he often listened to the other man, too. Given the sound advice he'd just provided, I understood why. But it was refreshing to see a monarch actually listen to those around him and make joint decisions rather than individual ones.

He's definitely a good leader, I decided as he glanced at me.

"Have you eaten today?"

I blinked at him. "No."

"When was the last time you ate?"

"Um." Food wasn't something I often needed, so I hadn't really thought about it.

He faced me fully. "Nyx. When was the last time you had food?"

"It's been a while," I admitted, frowning. "My energy comes from the moon, not from sustenance. And it hasn't been very easy to find meals in this realm, given the way everyone reacts to me." I pinched my lips to the side and shrugged. "I'm fine, though."

His expression said otherwise. "I should have ensured breakfast was ready for you when you woke up."

"Among other things," Kaspian inserted, causing Vesperus to glare at him. Whatever he said, it wasn't out loud. And all it did was make the other man grin.

"I'll deal with you later," Vesperus said to him. Then he held out his hand for me. "Come on. We'll eat something. Then I'll start making calls."

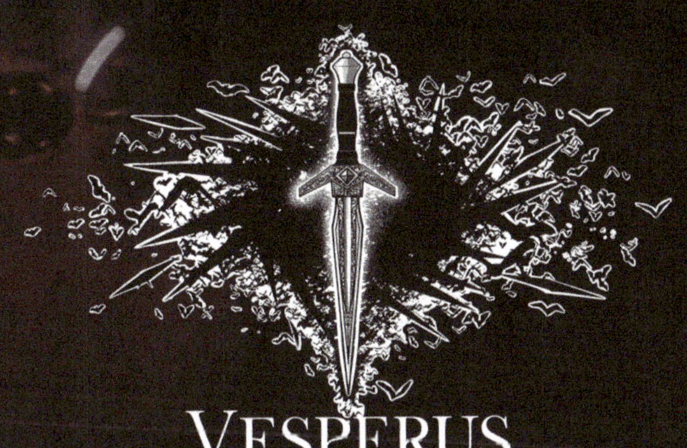

VESPERUS

I stared at the blank screen on my desk for a long moment, my exhaustion hitting me hard.

One pleading session with Cara.

Followed by three sternly worded messages.

And then five tense phone calls.

All after I'd introduced Nyx to the kitchen staff again, where I'd left her to eat. That'd been over three hours ago.

Fortunately, she hadn't left the palace, something I knew because I'd sent Cara to keep her company. Hence the *pleading* discussion we'd had earlier.

Cara must have gotten over my request because she'd texted me five minutes ago with a photo of the two of them lounging by my pool.

On the roof.

Nyx invited me up for a dip. I think I like her more than I like you now.

I read the message from Cara once more and snorted.

It was a much better note than the one I'd received before it from Empress Asbesta.

The House of Sea and Serpentine will not pay our part of the bounty while the entity roams free. It is causing distress in our water kingdom. Either remove it or find another way to fix it.

Prior to that message was one from Lady Gabriella reminding me to keep Sky apprised of *all* my updates.

And right before that had been a quick text from Volker saying, *Call me. Now.*

While I wasn't accustomed to taking orders from others, I'd phoned him back first. Mostly because he was a fae with abilities tied to the moon. Which meant he could feel Nyx more than most, something he'd admitted might have been causing some of his issues a few months ago.

But he was stable now, something I'd reminded him of when we spoke an hour ago.

I also reiterated my stance on killing an entity that hadn't done any true harm.

And when that hadn't been enough, I'd said, "She's my fated mate, Volker."

He'd find that out soon enough, so I'd figured it wouldn't hurt to inform him of the truth.

"I see," he'd replied. "That certainly complicates matters."

An understatement.

But it had calmed him down a little. Rather than demand again that I kill Nyx, he'd said to keep him informed.

"If you can't tame her power…" He'd trailed off, the rest of his sentence clear in my mind.

You'll either have to kill her or send her home.

Because that was what I'd tell him if the roles were reversed.

"I understand" was all I'd said back to him.

Our call had ended seconds later, the two of us on the same page. We weren't friends and we never would be. But a certain amount of respect existed between us, confirming he wouldn't act out against me unless absolutely necessary. It wasn't that he trusted me to handle this; he simply knew that I would.

Because I'd expect the same of him.

Elias Laskaris had been my second call.

He'd expressed his irritation at having been ignored for hours. However, he'd almost immediately added, "But I understand that you might be feeling a little distracted right now."

"So Kieran does gossip to you about our conversations," I'd drawled.

"Only the relevant ones," he'd replied vaguely.

With the secret having obviously been shared, I hadn't bothered to hold back from our frank conversation. Of course, I'd left out the bits about rejecting the bond and simply referred to Nyx as my fated mate.

"You're going to need to find a way to temper her power," he'd said. "The Houses won't accept her in raw form."

"I need time."

"You can't take too long. The others are already anxious, and once they realize she's your mate…"

He hadn't needed to finish that comment, as I'd already known.

"War," I'd stated simply.

"War," he'd echoed. I might have imagined the hint of pain in his voice, but I doubted it.

He'd lost a lot of important lives during The Great Sacrifice. We all had.

Our conversation had ended similarly to mine with Volker.

And I'd repeated the discussion a third time with Kieran, while also asking if there'd been any other incidents in his new territory.

"Nope," he'd said, his American accent coming through clearly in that single word.

Our call had been brief. Unlike the others, our talk had ended with me promising to look through some of the requests he'd forward to me from supernaturals switching allegiance to Death and Diamond.

My last two calls had been with Nolan and Slater, who were still pursuing leads. Slater had claimed the magical trace no longer existed. And Nolan had updated me on the remainder of his witness interviews.

No one knew anything.

Shocking, that.

I blew out a breath and shut down my screen. What I needed right now was sleep.

But I had a goddess to retrieve and a fae to kick off my roof.

I considered putting on my suit jacket but left it to hang on my door. I'd rolled my sleeves to the elbows hours ago, and I couldn't be bothered to put forth the effort of an elegant facade. This was my home. I chose to be comfortable in it.

Most of my staff were bustling about, the hours of our territory unique due to the long nights and vampire presence. But most chose a noon-to-midnight schedule, with shops opening around two or three in the afternoon and closing by nine or ten at night.

Which meant breakfast was typically around noon to three, lunch happened around six or seven, and dinner occurred by midnight.

The schedule worked for us, even when the days were long in the summer.

I'd shared the nuances with Nyx earlier. She hadn't seemed bothered by them, just intrigued. And she'd enjoyed making food requests in the kitchen.

When she hadn't been able to tell me the last time she'd eaten something, my heart had dropped. I'd not been properly caring for her, despite her *hospitality* comment last night.

Sure, she'd just become mine this week, but I felt like a failure for not even asking if she'd wanted to eat at the restaurant in Dublin. None of us had ordered food. However, that wasn't the point.

She was my mate—or sort of my rejected mate, anyway—and I needed to care for her.

I ran my hand over my face as I ascended the stairs and growled when my watch vibrated.

I'm done with political discussions, I thought at it. But when I saw that it was Kaspian, I answered it anyway.

"I'm exhausted," I told him. "Whatever it is, I trust you to handle it."

"I tried that earlier and it pissed you off," he remarked, the retort well earned.

And I was too tired to think up a witty comeback.

"What do you need, Kas?" I asked, continuing my climb up the stairs as a hologram of his face followed me.

"It's about Klas's burial," he said, diving straight to the point. "His body was claimed before Nolan could finish arranging a flight here. Apparently, Klas's mate decided to keep him in Ireland. She had him moved to another morgue earlier today. One that was closer to their home."

My steps slowed. "His mate?"

Kaspian hummed in confirmation.

My brow furrowed as I considered the transfer request I'd just signed off on the other day. "I didn't realize he had a mate." Had she been mentioned in the file? I'd reviewed so many that I couldn't quite remember.

"I didn't either," Kaspian admitted. "But I didn't know him well."

"Neither did I." A fact that left me feeling uneasy.

However, there were many members of my House that I didn't truly know. It was impossible to meet them all. That was why I had territory advisors, trusted members of my cabinet that I relied on to know the constituents within their jurisdiction.

"If his mate wants to bury him in Ireland, then we'll need to allow it," I finally said. "That's a family decision."

"I agree. I just wanted to let you know since you requested a warrior burial."

I nodded. "I did. But I didn't realize he was mated." Or I would have taken time to meet his mate in Dublin. "Can you send something? Not traditional flowers, but perhaps a fortune stone or something to commemorate Klas's service?"

Kaspian considered for a beat before dipping his chin. "I'll talk to Niamh about it."

Niamh was my sovereign in that region—one I was currently figuring out where to relocate now that Ireland was under Death and Diamond's control. "Is she coming in tomorrow for the meeting?"

"She is," he confirmed.

"Good." I needed to talk through some strategy with her. "Anything else?"

"Yeah, Cara keeps sending me photos of herself on your roof. Had I realized babysitting duties involved a swim in that pool of yours, I would have accepted the task."

I grunted, ending the call without replying. He wouldn't have expected one anyway.

Thoughts of tomorrow's meeting weighed heavily on my mind as I finished my trek up to the roof. Even if I wanted to sleep, I wouldn't be able to. Not until I sorted out what I wanted to say to my council.

Sighing, I used my thumbprint to access my sanctuary and stepped through the threshold. I'd asked Cara to take Nyx by security earlier, saying to grant her the same permissions as mine. And she'd obviously done that since she and Nyx were on my roof.

They were both in the pool, lounging near the streaming waterfall in the corner.

Both of them were naked, which could have aroused a thousand different scenarios in my head. But it was Nyx that captivated my attention, her long, dark hair resembling silk as it fell around her in damp waves.

She tilted her head back to stare up at the moon, that glittering substance dancing along her skin and disappearing into the water.

All thoughts of tomorrow fled as I began wondering how the fuck I was supposed to survive tonight with this seductress in my bed.

"Ah, there's our king," Cara murmured, her pale green eyes flashing with golden flakes as she grinned at me. "You've been holding out on us, *Your Majesty*."

"I pay you and your mate enough in magic to create your own oasis, Cara," I said, leaning against the wall beside the pool.

"Hmm." Her smile grew. "And speaking of Larus, I should like to return to him now."

She stood, completely unfazed by her nudity. She often used it as a weapon, luring in her prey with her looks before sinking a blade into their hearts.

I ignored her in favor of the goddess humming a soft goodbye from the water, her gaze still on the stars above.

"I hope you keep her," Cara informed me as she passed my leaning position. "She's fun."

"So you don't mind helping her shop for clothes tomorrow?" I asked, my attention still on the beauty in the water.

"I would consider it sexist that you're assigning a female to this task—particularly as Larus's taste in fashion is better than mine—but I'm going to accept the offer because it involves Nyx." She turned to give the goddess a little wave. "See you around three tomorrow, Twinkly."

"Twinkly?" I repeated.

"She's all twinkly like a star," Cara explained.

"Bye, Flower Fae," Nyx called after her, making Cara laugh out loud.

My brow furrowed. Cara wasn't a *flower fae* but a *deadly fae*. Although, she didn't appear all that lethal now as she giggled her way toward the door.

She grabbed a towel along the way and disappeared from sight.

"Flower Fae?" I echoed, feeling a bit like a bird repeating words.

"She thinks she's scary, but she's not," Nyx murmured, her eyes finally finding mine. "But her weaponry magic is fascinating."

"Did she try to attack you?" I wondered aloud, pushing off the wall.

"Not exactly. But she tested me."

I moved closer to her corner, skirting the edge of my pool along the way. "By sparring?"

"By displaying her marksmanship."

My lips curled down. "That sounds like she attacked you." Knowing Cara, it hadn't been a killing shot, or one even meant to wound, just a warning.

Nyx shrugged. "She was demonstrating her authority."

Those words confirmed my suspicions about Cara's motives, but I would need to have a discussion with her later about a more appropriate approach where my fated mate was concerned.

"It's all right, though," Nyx continued. "I returned the favor by turning her bullet into stardust."

I arched a brow. "Before she fired or after?"

Nyx's mouth twitched. "Before." The mirth in her golden irises suggested it'd been a humorous encounter. "The dust exploded all over her."

Amusement touched my chest. "I bet that pissed her off."

She shook her head. "No, she bent over laughing. Then I suggested we come up here to wash off."

"In my pool," I said, stopping beside where she sat in the water. "You realize that'll be hell on my filter, right?"

She shook her head again. "No, the magic dissolves and returns to the air." She lifted her arm to show me her glittering skin, then rinsed it again before pulling the stardust back to her being in the next moment. "See?"

I knelt on the side of the pool, my gaze running over every tantalizing inch of her, the water doing nothing to disguise my view. "Yes, Nyx. I *see*."

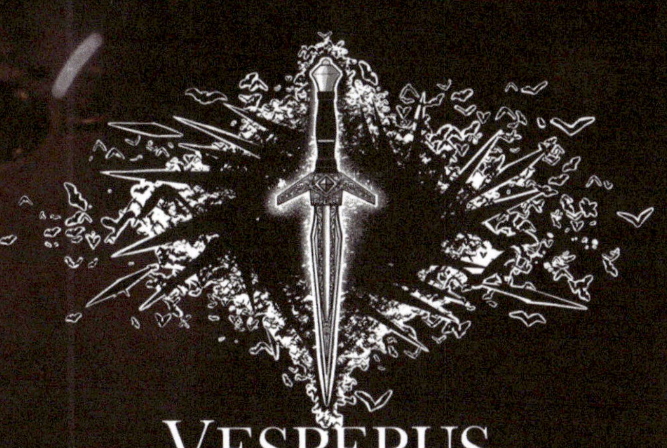

VESPERUS

Maybe it was my exhaustion.

Maybe it was the lingering impact of the fated-mate bond.

Maybe it was just *Nyx*.

But I didn't want to fight this connection or ignore the magic flourishing between us.

Which made being alone with her very dangerous.

I'd just spent several hours fielding messages and calls regarding her powerful existence, being told by nearly every monarch that Nyx was a problem that needed to be removed.

Taking her as my queen was going to create conflict. It could hurt my House. It might lead to war. I knew all that, and yet for once in my life, I wanted to be selfish. I wanted to do something for *me*—without thought of anyone else.

And for that reason alone, I pulled away.

Because I couldn't allow this intoxicating need to derail everything I'd built. There were too many lives under my control— under my *protection*—to give in to a selfish notion.

But that didn't mean I was ready to give up on a future with Nyx.

There had to be a way to make this work.

I stood and slowly unfastened my shirt while Nyx observed, her alluring eyes tracking over my movements in a predatory manner.

When I reached the bottom, I folded the fabric and set it on a nearby bench, then tugged my undershirt off over my head.

"I see you, too," Nyx murmured, causing my lips to curl as I bent to pull off my dress shoes and socks. "Mm-hmm."

Her forward approach was different from so many other women of my past, her appraisal one of truth and conviction, and not at all laced with malevolence. Or not any I could sense, anyway.

Of course, I still wasn't clear on the full extent of her powers. She could be similar to Cara—a black widow hidden in plain sight.

However, somehow, I doubted that.

All of Nyx's actions had suggested genuine intrigue, each choice almost innocent in nature. She could have severely hurt my people today, but rather than fight them, she'd created a magical barrier.

Perhaps it was all a ruse, a way to tempt me into bed and fuck up my carefully controlled world.

I could play the what-if game all damn night.

But what I really wanted to do was talk to Nyx, read her, and see if we couldn't come up with a solution to this issue—*together*.

This female could be my future queen. Why not treat her like one?

"You are not disappointing my imagination," she told me as I lost my pants. "Does this mean I get to lick you now?"

I faced her in nothing but my boxers. "No. We need to talk first." Which was why I left the last shred of my clothing on—we clearly needed a barrier here—before diving into the water.

It wasn't deep, so I kept my movements shallow, aware of the bottom and every corner of this pool.

I surfaced several meters away from Nyx, yet it felt like I'd come up right next to her. Her open interest warmed the air around me, filling my lungs with her seductive scent and drawing me back to where she sat in the corner.

Like a siren, I mused, swimming toward her. *Only, she doesn't need to sing to seize my attention.*

Her irises swirled with hypnotic desire as I grabbed the marbled edges on either side of her head, my body only a few inches from hers now. "You tempt my control, Goddess."

"Do I?" she replied, her eyes searching mine. "It's not intentional."

"Hmm." I wasn't sure I believed that. "Is seduction one of your godly gifts?"

She considered for a moment, her hands lifting from the water to swirl golden magic in the air beside us.

"I think power can be naturally seductive in nature," she whispered, the strand of shimmering energy dancing along my arm and leaving a hum behind in its wake. "I'm not sure if that's a gift or just a fact of life."

"Perhaps both," I told her.

"Perhaps both," she echoed with a soft nod. "I find your power seductive, which is interesting because you and Kaspian are very similar, yet I don't want to taste him. I only want to taste you."

"That's the fated-mate bond."

"Yet we rejected it," she mused. "So perhaps it's simply *you*, King of Vampires."

My gaze fell to her alluring mouth, the concaves of her full lips teasing the final vestiges of my control.

"Perhaps it's us," I said softly. "Regardless of the reason, I want you. But the monarchs of my world are not going to let me have you." Not like this, anyway.

Her fingertips skimmed my arm as she trailed a path up to my shoulder. "They want you to kill me." Not a question, but a statement.

"Yes and no. They fear what they don't understand, but there are other gods and goddesses who live freely in this world. Which tells me we have a chance to make this work."

"You want to make this work?" she asked, her fingers drifting up into my hair.

"I want to find a way for you to have the option to stay," I admitted. "And my reason for doing so is purely selfish."

"Is it?" Her nails combed through my damp hair, all the way to my nape. "Tell me your reason."

"I think that should be obvious, Goddess." My words were a whisper in the air, my lips nearly tasting hers.

"Tell me anyway." There was a slight quiver in her voice, a subtle sound that revealed her aroused state.

Not that I needed the verbal confirmation.

I could *smell* her interest, the predator inside me growling in approval at having baited and cornered its desired prey.

But I couldn't have her yet. Not like this. Not when everything hung so tenuously in the balance.

I ran my nose along her cheekbone, inhaling her addictive fragrance as I went, and pressed my lips to her ear. "I want you, Nyx. But I won't indulge in this craving until we've determined a path forward."

I lowered my mouth to her throbbing pulse, the sensual beat an invitation my fangs longed to accept.

But I pulled away instead and stepped beneath the waterfall, needing to clear my head.

Nyx joined me, her palm skating along my abdomen as she pushed me back into the wall behind the flowing water. I opened my eyes to stare down at her, my hands finding her hips to take control of her movements.

I'd intended to push her away.

Only to end up pulling her closer as her breasts met my chest.

She wrapped her arms around my neck, her pupils flaring with power.

"You mentioned that other gods and goddesses live in this realm. Do you mean gods like the one you call Odin?" Her words were just loud enough for me to hear over the water pouring down behind her.

"Yes, gods like Odin. He leads Spirit and Sapphire with Lady Gabriella. And no one questions or threatens his ability to reign despite his ample power."

Which suggested Nyx could potentially maneuver herself into a similar position in Gold and Garnet. We just needed to determine *how.*

I drew my thumb along her hip bone as I added, "The monarchs just need to better understand your abilities. And they need to believe that you don't mean our world harm."

They would also require assurances that she didn't intend to overthrow any of them, which would be the hardest battle to fight.

The Great Sacrifice had ended in peace, but it hadn't erased the ongoing power struggle that existed between the Houses. We were just quieter now about our conflicts.

"It won't be an easy feat," I concluded. "I'm not even sure you'll want to stay. But we can try to make it possible."

She hummed, her gaze searching mine. "I'm not sure I'll want to stay either," she murmured. "But my magic seems to want me to."

I frowned, my thumb still against her hip. "What do you mean?"

"My magic sort of attacked me earlier." Her nose scrunched a little. "Or it felt like it did, anyway. Like it was telling me not to retaliate against your people… maybe because they'll someday be my people?"

"Is it common for your magic to… attack you?" I asked, wary at the prospect. Because it suggested that she couldn't control her powers.

Which would make it impossible to convince the monarchs to accept her by my side.

"No." Her lips twisted a little. "It was my medallion that did it, which isn't technically mine so much as an enchantment tied to me. But like any energy source, it has a personality of its own."

"A personality of its own," I repeated slowly, not fully following what she meant. "How…?"

"Hmm." She twirled a piece of my hair around her finger at my nape, her gaze drifting to the side as she lost herself to her thoughts.

I waited, hoping this silence would lead to an explanation.

Because as far as I was concerned, energy was often controlled by the being that had created it. Yet she'd made it sound like her medallion enchantment possessed a mind of its own.

"My medallion is autonomous. I suppose you could even say it's sentient in a way, as it can resemble different forms, and it certainly has its own free will. But it's strongly associated with me and my fate."

"So it's an enchantment… with a conscience."

"Yes."

"And you created it?"

Her eyes returned to mine. "I wished for it. And while I could wish for another enchantment, I'm rather fond of the first one. So I'm hunting it because that's what it wants me to do."

She took one of her hands away from my nape to pool stardust in her palm.

"You see, I come from the time of creation, which means…" She tossed the sand-like magic into the air and smiled as snowflakes appeared. "I create."

One of the crystals touched my skin, the icy texture immediately melting into lukewarm water.

"That's how Lissa could wish for a real-life elf," I realized. "Your magic creates life."

She nodded. "And life typically has a conscience." She shrugged. "So my medallion does as well, and it's misbehaving because I think it wants to stay here."

"I see." I moved my hands to her lower back, holding her just a little closer. "Then you agree that we should find a way to make that possible."

"I agree that it's a direction I'm willing to explore," she replied, her free hand returning to my nape. "But I'm not sure how to win your monarchs over. You mentioned that gods and goddesses live among you, but I haven't seen any yet."

"They're rare, but Odin is one," I told her. "And he's a House leader."

"That imposter?" she snorted. "He's not Odin."

"He is in this reality," I assured her.

She appeared to be ready to argue that but paused with a frown. "Does that mean your reality has another version of me? More creation era gods?"

"If we do, I've never met them. And I've been on this earth for over fifteen hundred years."

"Oh." She considered me. "Where were you before that? Another realm?"

"Not alive," I told her. "Vampires are all born or created in this world, not another. At least… not in my reality."

Which was a weird thing to say because I couldn't fathom another version of this existence.

However, this being before me obviously could.

"I see," she murmured, her gaze going to my mouth. "Yet you seem to be the only one I want to taste, so there is clearly something special about you."

"Fate magic," I reminded her.

"Maybe." Her golden irises swirled with intrigue as she looked up again. "I think it might just be your power, though, King."

She pressed her lips to my neck, her blunt teeth skimming my pulse in a teasing bite.

My hands returned to her hips, holding her. "Nyx…"

She hummed in response, then went to her toes to press her lips to my ear. "I'm going to lick you, Vesperus. Maybe not tonight. But soon."

She nipped my ear and started to pull away, but I tightened my grip and lifted her off the pool floor.

Nyx giggled as I switched our positions, pressing her up against the wall and sliding my thigh between hers.

"I fully intend to lick you, too," I promised against her mouth. "Thoroughly."

I drew my hands up her sides, allowing her body to slide down mine as her feet returned to the floor.

"Completely."

I flexed my thigh between hers and slowly lifted it upward.

"Right here," I told her, my leg meeting her bare pussy. "Until you beg me to stop."

"Never going to happen," she said, her fingers in my hair again, her mouth whispering across mine. "I'll beg you to keep going." She nibbled my lower lip and pressed herself against my thigh. "I'll test your stamina, King."

I smiled against her mouth, my fingers trailing along the underside of her breasts. "That's only fair," I agreed, my palm drifting up to circle her throat. "Because I fully intend to test your stamina as well, Goddess. Just in a very different way."

I squeezed, indicating what I meant.

How long can you hold your breath? I whispered into her mind. *How much can you swallow?*

But I didn't give her a chance to reply.

I kissed her instead. It was a temptation I should have resisted, an allure I should have avoided.

However, I couldn't.

Not with her tight, sexy body pressed up against mine, all hot and aroused and *wet*.

I could feel her throbbing against my thigh, feel her pulse raging against my thumb, and sense her taut nipples against my chest.

It was too much to deny myself this introduction to her kiss. To her power. To her *skill*.

Knowing this beautiful being desired me was an ego stroke unlike any other.

Because Nyx radiated power. I could taste it with every inhale, feel it brushing my fingertips, and sense the stroke of it against my very spirit.

Yet she wanted me. Perhaps because of a magical pull. Maybe for nefarious means.

But at this point, I no longer cared about the reason.

I just accepted it as fate.

And embraced it with my tongue.

Devouring her. Learning her. *Mastering* her with dominant strokes while holding her captive by the throat.

Oh, but she didn't just stand there and accept it.

She fought back, her tongue dueling mine in an intimate dance of carnal anticipation.

She owned me and mastered me just as much as I did her.

And not once did she fight my hold. She simply dug her nails into my scalp and rode my thigh, claiming me in a savagely beautiful sort of way.

I palmed her breast with my free hand, needing to feel that perfect fit.

It's like you were made for me to worship you, I told her, my mental voice soft. *Fuck, Nyx.*

I deepened our kiss, needing more of her, and pressed my thigh even more harshly against her. She arched into me in response, riding my leg and clutching my hair while I squeezed her tit and pinched her tight nipple.

She could barely breathe from my grip around her throat, but she didn't seem to care. If anything, it seemed to turn her on more. Perhaps it was the threat of violence that did it for her. Or simply the show of a worthy power that drove her to new heights.

She scraped her teeth along my lip, biting down to make me bleed.

I growled and returned the favor, our kiss turning feral in an instant, which had her riding my thigh even more fiercely.

She was on the verge of shattering. I could taste that precipice on my tongue as though I were licking her right between her thighs.

You're going to come for me, aren't you, sweet goddess? I murmured. *Give me a taunting memory to take back to my shower tonight. A seductive sound to imagine while I pump my cock to thoughts of you and this beautiful fucking mouth.*

Her nails scraped my scalp, making me hiss against her mouth.

Then she sucked my lower lip between her teeth and bit me again.

So fucking feral, I growled, cutting off her oxygen flow for a brief moment before feeding her my blood with my tongue.

She moaned, her movements almost manic against my thigh now, rubbing that needy little clit against me with abandon.

I tweaked her nipple once more, driving her over the edge in a climax that had her screaming against my mouth.

But I swallowed the sound, keeping it for myself, for my memories, for my *dreams.*

I could push my boxers down, wrap her pale hand around my hard shaft, and beg her to finish me.

However, that wasn't the point of this introduction.

I merely wanted a taste. And my beautiful goddess had more than delivered.

I opened my eyes to find her golden irises swirling with hot power, her expression one of startled wonder, like I'd just blown her mind.

You're the most beautiful woman I've ever seen, I confided softly, brushing my lips against hers. *Nyx, Goddess of Night. It's an honor to be your rejected mate.*

NYX

I woke up alone.

Again.

For the eighth morning in a row.

My gaze narrowed at Vesperus's side of the bed, his blankets perfectly creased as they were every time I opened my eyes.

It was almost as though our evening ritual was an illusion—him finding me on the roof, indulging in intimate conversation beneath the moon, making me see the stars without *really* touching me, and leading me back to his room, where he showered alone before tucking himself in beside me.

We'd repeated that pattern for the last seven nights, never deviating, never going further than some groping and a kiss, and always waking up to the pristinely pressed sheets and comforter on his side of the bed.

I sat up. "Not today," I decided out loud.

While I didn't mind our evening routine, I did mind our morning one.

Well, mostly.

The notes he left on his pillow for me every morning were kind of fun.

I picked up today's paper with the masculine script on it.

Don't forget to eat breakfast, Nyx.

—V

P.S. I spiked your orange juice. ;-)

My eyebrows lifted as a laugh escaped me. I'd avoided eating every morning this week, preferring to find Cara and go exploring.

I wasn't naïve. I knew she'd been assigned to watch me, but I didn't mind. Mostly because I liked the fae female. She didn't mince words and spoke her mind, which was something I appreciated.

What I didn't appreciate was Vesperus running away every morning. I wasn't even sure if the damn male slept.

Maybe he just needs an orgasm, I thought. If he would let me reciprocate and lick him, I could give him one. But no. He seemed content to kiss me and pet me instead.

Which I admittedly enjoyed, particularly as we spent most nights learning about each other.

Such as last night when I'd discovered he could speak over a dozen languages.

And the night before when he'd admitted to having a medical degree.

"Why?" I'd asked him. "What made you study medicine?"

He'd shrugged. "Unlimited access to blood."

I'd thought he was joking.

He hadn't been.

"But it's also useful to know how human bodies work. Vampires have similar anatomy. It's come in handy a few times," he'd added.

"To save someone?"

He'd shaken his head. "No, to kill them."

"Definitely not a hero, then."

"Not to humans," he'd agreed. "My devotion is to my House. I'd do anything for them."

Including not mating me if I can't conform to this world, I'd thought, the same words repeating in my mind now.

It was a pragmatic stance, one that explained his reluctance to do more than kiss me at night. He was maintaining control.

As much as I wanted to push the boundaries and experience more of what he had to offer, I wouldn't. Because I respected his choice.

Just as he respected mine—which had included me continuing my hunt for my magic.

I could sense it lingering nearby, remaining just out of reach.

It was the first time in months that I'd been able to truly sense the familiar energy, with the first burst of it having been in Dublin.

Now it was hiding around me, confirming that it had wanted me in Iceland all along.

I just didn't fully comprehend why.

To mate Vesperus?

To make this place my home?

To complete some other task before allowing me to leave this realm?

What…?

What do you want from me, medallion?

All questions I would ask the sentient strand when it returned.

Alas, it continued to remain elusive, simply pulsing somewhere close to me without revealing itself.

I'll find you, I promised it as I rolled out of the bed. *But I'm going to indulge Vesperus in breakfast first.*

Because he'd *spiked* my juice. And I knew he wasn't talking about alcohol.

I showered and dressed in my new wardrobe—another black gown, but this one had slits up the sides and a modest neckline. No back, though. So I used my stardust to add a gold chain down my spine that met the dress just above my rump. Then I put on my crescent necklace again, the gold still stained with my blood.

And now Vesperus's, I thought, eyeing the charm in the mirror. He'd added a drop of his own essence the other night, deciding it would help mark me as *his*, and not just a temporary member of Gold and Garnet.

No one had given me any issues since the storekeeper incident, but the people here hadn't been all that willing to talk with me either.

Maybe I'd ask Cara if we could try visiting a pub today for a drink. Perhaps that sort of activity would be seen as normal enough to make me approachable.

Decided, I laced up my sandals—which Cara gawked at every time she saw me, saying something about it being beach appropriate, not Iceland appropriate—and shadowed into the kitchens.

"Oh!" Chef Betty exclaimed, dropping a pan and making me wince. "Nyx!"

I winced again. "Sorry."

"You have got to stop doing that," she scolded me, the witch one of the few who didn't seem to fear me. Probably because this was her space as head of the kitchen.

"To be fair, it was only the second time," I told her. Because I'd skipped breakfast every other day this week.

Hence Vesperus's reminder this morning.

"Well, maybe if the breakfast was spiked with your blood, I would remember to eat it," I'd told him last night. He'd remarked on my penchant for skipping meals, and I'd bluntly responded.

"Vesperus mentioned orange juice," I said now, smiling hopefully at Betty.

She rolled her almond-shaped eyes at me and stalked over to an industrial-sized oven with a heat rack on top. "Crepes, too," she told me, grabbing a plate with an oven mitt before continuing on toward one of the room's many fridges. "And yes, he made you orange juice. Freshly squeezed, too."

There seemed to be a pun in that last sentence, one that made me grin.

She set me up in the dining room that was closest to her kitchen, which I didn't really need, but I'd learned early on that disagreeing with Betty earned me nothing. I'd still end up at this table, eating whatever food she desired.

As she was a rather skilled chef, I truly didn't mind.

Thus, I settled into my chair and enjoyed the crepes before

treating myself to Vesperus's *freshly squeezed orange juice.*

So good. And definitely not alcohol.

His blood was as decadent as any dessert, yet not exactly a chocolate flavor like his scent. More of a sweet ambrosia that I could drink for days.

Unfortunately, it didn't seem to give me any of his abilities. Otherwise, I would have used telepathy to thank him for the delicious drink.

"There you are," Cara said, entering the dining hall with a huff. "You're supposed to call me when you leave your room. Remember?"

She'd given me a phone the other day for that purpose. However… "I left it on the nightstand."

"I know," she deadpanned, sliding the device across the wood.

I stared at it. "My dress doesn't have pockets."

"So wish for some," she countered.

My lips pursed. *Pockets will really ruin my gown.*

I studied the phone, searching for a solution, then sprinkled some stardust over it as I wished for it to turn into a bracelet.

My lips curled as the metal morphed into a golden cuff with a moon etched into the center. "That's so much more fashionable," I told Cara.

She glared at me, her expression suggesting she was about to lecture me on something unhelpful.

So I ignored her, slipped on the bracelet, and pressed the moon. Magic created a screen that allowed me to send her a text.

I'm in the dining room drinking blood-spiked orange juice. I won't be sharing.

Cara's glare melted into laugh lines as she shook her head. "You're a brat."

"I'm a goddess," I corrected her, closing the screen. "And I don't need a babysitter, nor do I need to eat breakfast. But the orange juice put me in a good mood, so I'm willing to overlook the insults of being treated like a five-year-old."

I set my napkin to the side and stood.

"Where can I go to appear natural in this territory?" I asked

Cara. "I would like to make friends." It would help me decide if I wanted to remain here.

Cara covered her heart and feigned injury. "Ouch."

I frowned. "What?"

"And here I thought you and I were friends," she continued, her voice overly dramatic and filled with false sadness.

"Are we friends?" I asked curiously.

She straightened and gave me a look. "I've hung out with you every day this week, Nyx. Pretty sure that makes us friends."

"We both know I'm an assignment," I told her.

"Yes, but you're an enjoyable one." She shrugged. "Beats the hell out of paperwork."

"I'm not sure if that's flattering or sad," I deadpanned.

"Definitely the latter. This whole territory shift has Vesperus drowning in relocation requests. He's been working with Niamh most of the week on it."

"That's one of his territory advisors, right?" He'd mentioned a few of them by name, telling me a bit about each of them. "The one from Ireland?"

Cara nodded. "Yeah, but we call them sovereigns. And she's been here since their meeting last week. He's working on her reassignment."

"Because he doesn't need an advisor in that part of the world since it's no longer his territory." Yes, he'd spoken about that as well. "I'm glad she can help with the paperwork."

"Have you met her yet?"

"No. She's not been staying here, and Vesperus tends to keep me away from his work." I looked Cara over. "He gave me a babysitter as a distraction."

She laughed. "I'm not a distraction. If you want to see him, we can do that before you change clothes."

My brow furrowed. "Change clothes?"

"Yes," she confirmed. "You said you wanted to go somewhere and appear natural in this territory. To do that, you need to dress for the climate." She made a show of gesturing to her sweater and jeans.

"Hmm." I no longer liked my plans for today. If I had to dress to impress, then I wasn't sure I wanted new friends.

"Come on," she encouraged. "We'll go check on Vesperus and his mountain of paperwork. If Niamh's there, you can make a new friend. Then I'll try to help you find more in the city."

I could hear the teasing in her words, but I shrugged, agreeing to her plan.

It meant more exploring in the end, which could help me try to pinpoint my errant magic while continuing to evaluate the territory.

"All right." I started toward Vesperus's office, aware of its location, when a tingling sensation shot down my arm.

I frowned, pausing midstep, and glanced at the goose bumps pebbling along my skin.

Have you decided to return to me? I thought at my errant magic, my gaze searching for the source.

But my medallion wasn't in the palace, just nearby.

Close. Very close.

I shifted directions, heading toward the back of the house through the kitchens and out the doors to the park area.

"Nyx?" Cara's voice reminded me that I wasn't alone. The other woman stood just a few steps behind me on the patio that wrapped around the back of the estate.

"Oh." I blinked at her. "My magic is calling for me. This way."

I didn't explain more beyond that, too eager to follow the familiar strand.

"Calling for you?" Cara repeated as she fell into step beside me on the path.

I showed her the bumps along my arm. "Yes." I picked up the pace as the enchantment tugged on my spirit, the urgency seeming to increase.

What's wrong? I asked it. *Why are you yanking on me like a leash?*

It responded by sending another jolt of electricity across my being. The panic in that stroke had me hurrying, my feet moving across the stone path at a jog that Cara easily maintained alongside me.

When we reached the back gate, I phased through it. Then I

paused to wait for more directions from my magic while the metal clinked behind me.

Cara joined me on the path, her expression curious. "Well?"

"I'm listening," I murmured, hushing her.

I closed my eyes and shivered when the magical essence touched my senses again.

It took me right, reminding me of my first day here.

Only, I didn't go to Lissa's shop this time, but two blocks beyond it.

Where my energy disappeared.

My gaze narrowed. "This game of hide-and-seek is growing tire—"

The enchantment pierced my heart, causing my knees to buckle and drawing a gasp from my throat.

I clutched my chest as glass exploded behind me, the sensations confusing and making the world spin deliriously around me.

Cara screamed my name, but I couldn't look at her. I was too stunned. Too… too *overwhelmed*.

What's… what's happening? Why did you…? I blinked several times. *Why did you shock me?*

The magic hummed urgently in response, drawing my focus to a woman nearby, her vibrant green eyes sparkling with power.

A witch? I guessed, confused by her aura. *So dark. Fractured. A soul… divided.*

I could feel her pain, almost taste it on my tongue. My enchantment whirled around her in desperation, trying futilely to reach her shattered spirit. To… to fix her.

I stared, not fully discerning the scene before me.

Wind rippled around her in the darkness, the nearby building seeming to disguise her presence.

Or is she shadowing? I marveled. *Who are you?* What *are you?*

Cara shouted my name again as glass continued to shatter, flames billowing in the air.

I tried to move, to stand, to *see*.

My legs shook as I forced myself upright, the shock of my power having rendered me temporarily useless.

But the street was beginning to clear, the chaos swirling around me becoming evident.

Another explosion.

I gaped at the destruction, startled by its sudden presence.

I took a step forward, my instincts firing as I searched for any auras that might need to be saved.

But my attention went right back to the inky presence nearby, that woman with the fragmented spirit.

I locked gazes with her and gasped as a bolt of pure fire pierced my sternum.

No. Not fire.

A bullet.

I belatedly heard the crack of it in the air, the scene shifting around me so brokenly that I hadn't… I hadn't sensed it properly.

And now…

I glanced down, noticing the blood on my fingertips.

I…

My knees buckled again, sending me to the ground. I caught myself on one palm, then fell sideways to curl into a ball.

This… this is no ordinary… bullet.

I could feel it… *shredding* me.

No.

Burning me.

Like poison. Like… like *acid.*

A scream left my lips, the sound one of agony and fear and *anger.*

I tried to claw at the sensation, to pull the source of it out of me. But the world… the world was… blackening.

My enchantment touched my skin, the sentient energy concerned.

I tried to grasp it, to… to pull it to… into me.

Only, I couldn't.

I couldn't… I couldn't do anything.

I could barely even… *breathe.*

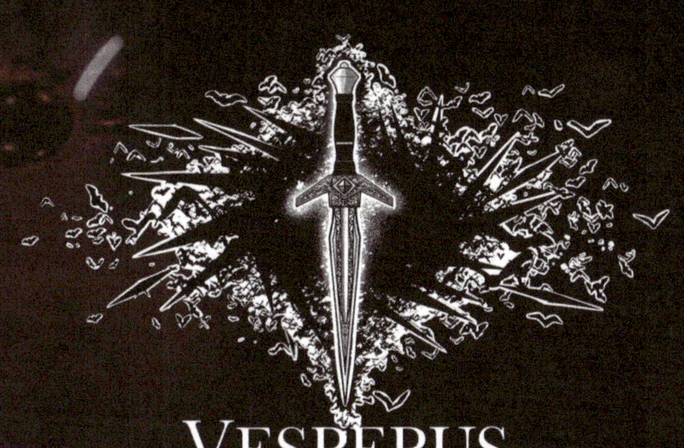

VESPERUS

"Hmm, it sounds like Sabrina approved the liaison role," I said, my eyes on the email I'd just read from Kieran. "So if you want to stay in Ireland, you can. But they may eventually ask you to relocate to Scotland."

Niamh nodded, her focus on the relocation reports in front of her. "I'll think about it, but that sounds like the best route to take, as Zabra isn't very interested in relocating. She prefers the seas around Dublin, as do I."

"Less icy," I agreed. I wasn't a sea dragon shifter like Niamh or her mate, Zabra, but I imagined the waters off the Irish coast were more accommodating than the frigid waters in Iceland.

Not that Ireland didn't experience the cold—it definitely did. Just on a less severe scale than we did up here.

"Perhaps you can take over training Bane and Nox, too," I suggested, thinking of other tasks Niamh could do in her new role. "The phantoms may feel more comfortable near their home soil as they go through their trials."

"I'm not sure Kaspian will want to give them up." Her turquoise eyes flashed with amusement as she glanced up at me, the color a vibrant contrast to her dark skin and black hair. "He seems to have taken to them."

I snorted. "He's been beating them up all week."

"Isn't that his version of flirting?" she asked, her lips curling a little. "Just yesterday, he had Nox pinned beneath him out in the training yard. I could swear I heard growling."

"Talking about me again, darling?" Kaspian drawled from the doorway. "See something you might want to experiment with later?"

Niamh smirked up at him. "Zabra doesn't invite cocks into our nest."

"Pity," he murmured, taking a seat across from her. "But she's right. I'm keeping Nox and Bane."

I arched a brow. "Here in Iceland?"

He dipped his chin. "They need a stern hand."

Niamh laughed, but he ignored her.

"They were trained by pacifists," he added. "I have a lot of bad habits to break."

"Such as mercy and compassion?" I guessed.

"Exactly that."

"Hmm," I hummed. "Just don't turn them into monsters, Kas. Not all of us crave blood the way you do."

"Someone has to be harsh around here, what with our leader handing out temporary asylums to our bounties," he shot back.

I rolled my eyes. "She's my fated mate, Kas."

"What an excuse," he scoffed.

"Don't listen to him, Ves," Niamh murmured. "He's just jealous that he hasn't found someone who will put up with his shit yet. Let alone someone who can tolerate him for eternity." She visibly shuddered at the prospect.

Kaspian chuckled and shook his head. "I'm good."

"Are you, though?" she asked, arching a sculpted black brow.

"Didn't realize you cared so much about me, Niamh," he returned, flashing her an easy smile. "You sure you and Zabra don't want to invite me over for a visit?"

I shook my head, ignoring their easy banter, and started typing a reply to Kieran.

Niamh wants a few days to—

My finger slipped to the Enter key as a jolt of power sliced through my sternum, stealing the breath from my lungs.

"Ves?" Kaspian asked, at my side in a blink.

I palmed my chest, my heart squeezing painfully and causing my head to fall to my keyboard.

Fuck.

Fuck!

I groaned, my insides *burning* from something intense, something impactful, something… something *lethal.*

Kaspian and Niamh started speaking in another language, the two of them making no sense.

All I could feel was *pain.*

Excruciating, agonizing torment.

I fell from my chair, hitting the ground as I tried to push through whatever the fuck was attacking my insides.

Only for it all to go dark.

And then light.

With a blaring alarm echoing throughout my office.

What the fuck is happening? I grabbed my head, my other hand on my heart. *What is this? A spell? A curse?*

"I don't know!" Cara's familiar voice filtered through my thoughts, the panic in those three words forcing my eyes to open. "She was shot. And now she's not moving."

Shot? I repeated. *Who? Where?*

That last question was repeated by Kaspian out loud, whether as a result of me pushing it to his mind or him just knowing what to ask, I wasn't sure. I didn't fucking care about the source. I just wanted answers.

Cara listed a street name and started talking about explosions.

"How many others are injured?" Kaspian demanded.

"I don't know ye—" The line went dead, making Kaspian curse.

"Call Larus," he said, taking immediate command of the situation. "I want Manx and Langly, too."

"On it," Paxton replied, the male's voice gruff and unexpected.

When did the warlock arrive? He usually stayed in Kaspian's quarters, serving as his personal assistant.

"Let's go, Veritas," Kaspian demanded, his use of my last name making me look at him. "Your mate's been shot, but not you. So get the fuck up."

What? I gaped at him, then palmed my chest again, realizing that was what I'd felt. *Nyx!*

I tried to pull myself upright, but the world spun from the effort, my vision blackening again. *Fuck.* It felt like I'd been shot, not her. *How is this even possible?* We'd rejected the bond. I shouldn't... I shouldn't feel anything.

And yet...

Kaspian grabbed my arm. "Snap out of it."

The order had me gritting my teeth.

Not out of annoyance at my second-in-command, but at myself.

He was right.

We needed to *go*.

I pictured the street Cara had mentioned on the phone and told my legs to start moving.

Except the world shifted around me instead, dark shadows stealing my vision and casting me into a sea of darkness.

Only for the street I'd just envisioned to appear in a blink.

My eyes widened, then immediately watered as a cloud of smoke infiltrated my being. Coughing, I ran out of it and found Cara shouting orders in the middle of the road.

Mercenaries were responding and jumping into fiery buildings, pulling out unconscious bodies.

But there was only one figure that held me captive.

Nyx.

I ran to her, my legs suddenly remembering how to move properly.

"Thank fuck!" Cara shouted upon seeing me, but I blew past her in favor of my unconscious goddess.

"Nyx..."

She wasn't breathing.

Her skin lacked her usual golden glow, too. It was pale, almost ghostly.

I went to my knees beside her, a sense of loss hitting me right in the chest. Right where our bond should exist. Right where I'd felt her that moment we'd first met.

Right where she should still be now.

What…?

"Vesperus." Cara's voice barely registered, and it was almost immediately drowned out by Kaspian taking over at the scene.

"Where the fuck is Astrella?" he demanded. "We need water!"

"She's putting the fire out over there," Cara told him, her presence fading away from my back as the two of them began to work in tandem.

This was an event we'd spent years training for, one I'd never thought we'd actually experience. Because my territory always came first. My people were my life.

But I couldn't… I couldn't focus. It felt like my soul had been removed from my body and pinned to the ground before me, dying right alongside Nyx. *My mate. My future.*

I barely knew her. However, my spirit… my spirit already worshipped her.

How is this even possible? I marveled, my hands fluttering uselessly over her. "What can I do?" She was a goddess. She couldn't truly die. She'd already told me that.

"If you somehow manage to destroy my corporeal form, my spirit will just go back to Khaos to be reborn again."

But how long would that take?

And would it feel like I'd lost her for good? Would it dismantle the fated-mate magic?

Was this sense of loss I felt a result of losing the other half of my soul?

I'd already speculated that her leaving the realm might feel as though she were dead. And so we'd rejected the bonds to avoid this sensation.

However, I… I felt fucking useless.

Alone.

Shattered.

Like I'd taken the bullet, not her.

My gaze went to her wound and the blood pooling around it. "I don't understand," I said, shaking my head. It was a simple gunshot to the sternum. Those hurt like a son of a bitch, but they weren't life-threatening.

I could survive several of these and remain awake for the agony of healing.

Nyx shouldn't have been taken out by a single bullet.

I checked her head and neck—two of the only true vulnerable locations on an immortal—and found nothing.

This didn't make any sense.

Kaspian reached my side, his hand on my shoulder. "I don't see a head injury. Spinal cord is intact, too," he said, speaking my assessment out loud. "Why is she still bleeding?"

I shook my head. "I don't know." The wound on her chest should be healing. But it wasn't. "Help me move her. Maybe the bullet is still inside her?" That shouldn't be possible either. My body always rejected foreign objects, pushing them out to heal. And quickly, too, as I was a master vampire. Same with Kaspian.

He helped me move her to check her back.

More blood.

"It went clean through," I said, shaking my head again. "She should be healing."

"Was the bullet laced with something?" Kaspian speculated. "A spell of some kind?" He assisted me in rolling her back to the ground as he yelled for Paxton.

We only had a handful of witches and warlocks in this territory, primarily because Gold and Garnet wasn't very close with Spirit and Sapphire—a House notoriously full of magic dwellers.

I ran my fingers through Nyx's hair, noting the dry texture of her strands. "She feels like death," I whispered, my heart in my throat. "It's like she's human." A startling discovery that made me realize just how petite Nyx truly was.

Her power made her appear so much grander, her svelte form strong and athletic and *unbreakable*.

But now... like this... she appeared mortal. Small. *So fucking fragile.*

"What are we looking at, Cara?" Kaspian asked as she joined us on the ground.

"Everyone will live," she said. "But we're going to need to find temporary housing for over a dozen families."

Kaspian cursed. "This was methodical, hitting in the residential district. But who?"

"I didn't see anyone," Cara said, sounding frustrated. "I was too distracted by the gunshots."

My brow furrowed. "Gunshots?"

"Yeah, someone tried to shoot Nyx three times. She ducked the first two. However, the third one…" She trailed off, her lips flattening. "I shouted a warning at her, but she was, like, entranced by something. She fucking stood up and practically accepted the shot into her chest."

That didn't sound like Nyx at all. Just the other day, she'd created a shield to protect herself. *What were you doing?* I wondered at her.

"What were you two doing out here?" Kaspian asked, his question similar to my thought but an entirely different sort of inquiry.

"She felt her magic again and was following it. Then…" She gestured around us. "The gunshots came first, followed by the explosions. I don't know if it was related, but the timing was… convenient."

I frowned. "Are you suggesting she did this?" The words sounded defensive to my ears, but I couldn't help the incredulity in my tone. *Why would she attack us and herself? That makes absolutely no sense.*

"I'm suggesting her power is linked to it," Cara said. "But I don't think any of this was intentional on her part."

I shook my head, denying that line of thought. "Her power didn't do this."

Nyx was all about stardust and wishes and creating life, not destroying it. We might have only spent a little over a week together, but I'd gathered that much about her character.

I read people well.

I followed my instincts.

And right now, my instincts told me she was innocent.

"Sorry, I came as quickly as I could," Paxton said, panting as he reached us. He knelt beside Kaspian, his midnight gaze sweeping over Nyx as a frown tugged at his features. "Why isn't she healing?"

"That's what we want to know," Kaspian told him. "Can you sense any magic on her? A spell? Something that's preventing her immortal abilities?"

"Something that's making her resemble death," I added, my voice low as I stroked her hair again.

That twist in my gut wouldn't abate. It kept telling me something was very wrong, that I had to do something to fix it. I just had no idea what.

Paxton cleared his throat, his brow crinkling as he evaluated Nyx. "May I touch her?"

The question was for me, and I found it alarmingly difficult to answer him. So I nodded instead of speaking, the motion unnatural.

Because I didn't want him to touch her at all.

I wanted to bundle her into my arms and disappear. Keep her safe. Ensure no one could ever hurt her again.

What the fuck is wrong with me?

I forced myself to release her hair, my heart splintering in my chest. These foreign needs were going to drive me mad.

Maybe she is really dying, I marveled. *And I'm already going insane from losing my fated mate.*

But that shouldn't be possible.

We rejected the bond!

I stole a deep breath through my nose, commanding myself to calm the fuck down. This anxiety, this need to *shred* Paxton for touching Nyx, and this desire to snatch up my goddess and disappear with her were all unhelpful cravings. They weren't going to fix anything.

But I really did want to know who shot my fated mate.

Because I was going to rip that being apart and feast on its blood.

My hands curled into fists, my fury mounting with each passing second.

I finally took in the carnage around us, the burn marks, the destroyed buildings, the huddles of supernaturals helping one another heal.

Cara had said there were no casualties, and the scene around us proved Nyx had been the most hurt of everyone here. *Because of a bullet. How the fuck did this happen?*

"I can't sense any magic," Paxton said slowly. "At least not an active spell. Do you know which way the bullet went?"

My brow tugged down. "You think the bullet might have been spelled?"

"Maybe." He didn't sound very sure. "I want to check it."

Cara blew out a breath. "That might be hard. It's somewhere in there." She pointed at one of the nearby houses that had been taken down by the explosions.

Paxton stood, evaluating the mess. "We'll need to dig." His eyes met mine. "In the interim, I suggest you treat her like you would a mortal."

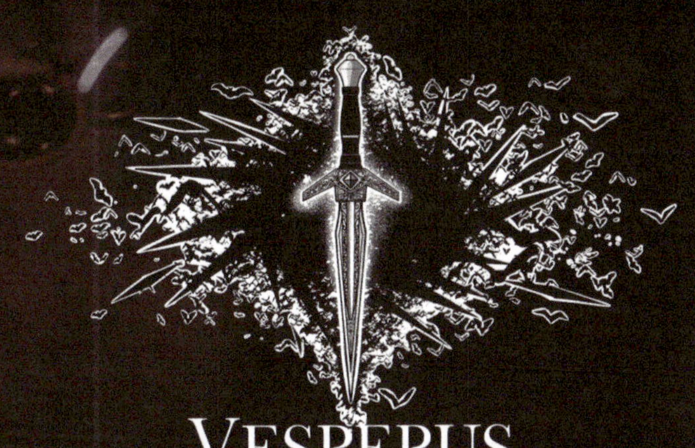

VESPERUS

A MORTAL.

I cursed.

Because it was similar to what I'd already thought about with Nyx's state, but I hadn't considered *treating* her as one.

"She's lost a lot of blood," I said, thinking out loud. "She… she needs…" My brow furrowed, another thought occurring to me. "She needs blood."

My blood.

I bit my wrist—*hard*—creating what would have been a fatal wound on a human. But I needed this to remain open long enough to *bleed*.

Rather than bring my wrist to her mouth, I pressed it to her sternum, willing my blood to mingle with hers.

The moment I felt my skin stitching back together, I bit my other wrist and repeated the action.

All while Kaspian watched.

"Do you want me to add mine?" he asked when nothing seemed to happen.

My jaw clenched, the notion of another being's essence inside my mate making me want to commit murder. But if it saved her, then so be—

A flutter in the air caught my attention, the glimmer so light and airy that I almost missed it throughout all the surrounding smoke. I blinked at it, not quite sure it was actually there. But it shimmered, dancing closer to me.

Is this…?

No.

I had to be seeing things.

This couldn't be Nyx's soul, right?

That… that wouldn't…

No. Her heart is still slowly beating.

So what is it?

"Ves?" Kaspian pressed. "Do you—"

"Hold on," I whispered, lifting my hand toward the golden sheen dancing toward me.

I could feel Kaspian gaping at me, because yeah, I was acting fucking nuts, but something about that energy strand felt right.

It continued gliding in the air, trickling toward me as though it were cautious of my existence. My conversation with Nyx regarding her sentient medallion came back to me, making me wonder if this hint of magic was linked to her creation.

Or this could be because of the explosion, I thought, pulling my hand back a little.

Cara had mentioned that Nyx had been entranced.

Because of something like this? I wondered.

The magic seemed to pause, the golden flare vibrating as though huffing at me in annoyance.

How bizarre.

"What are you looking at?" Kaspian whispered.

I swallowed. "I don't know." It could all easily be in my head. Or… or it could be something that might help Nyx.

Or it could be a trap.

I narrowed my gaze at the energy strand and lifted my hand again. "Keep watch," I told Kaspian, devoting my focus to this foreign spell. "And knock me out if I do anything weird."

"Like holding your arm up in the air while focusing on some sort of figment?" Kaspian muttered.

I ignored him, instead coaxing the energy closer. "You want me? Come get me," I dared it.

The substance seemed to shimmer as though puffing out its chest.

Then it came right at my palm, coiling tightly together into…

A pile of stardust.

"Holy fuck," Kaspian breathed.

"No," I replied. "Holy goddess."

"So not only can you teleport now, but you can also create fairy dust," he said, sounding impressed.

"Stardust," I corrected him as I ran my thumb over the soft substance, my gaze returning to Nyx's ashen features.

She'd explained enough for me to understand how this worked—I needed to make a wish.

Gods, I feel like I'm five fucking years old and wishing on a star, I marveled, shaking my head in astonishment.

This sweet goddess creature was dismantling every facet of my life. And despite sitting in the middle of chaos, I couldn't fault her for any of it.

All right, Goddess, I thought at her, holding my hand over her still-bleeding wound. *I wish for you to heal.* I released the stardust over her sternum and watched as it began to trickle over her, each speck dissolving on impact.

Kaspian whistled, drawing my attention to his gaze—which was on Nyx's arm.

Where a golden hue had blossomed on her fingertips. My lips parted as the color began to spread, inch by inch, up her hand to her wrist and gradually up her arm, chasing away the ashen quality of her skin and leaving behind a healthy glow.

"Holy goddess indeed," Kaspian whispered.

It turned out that Paxton had been wrong—I didn't need to treat Nyx like a mortal. I needed to remember that she was a fucking goddess.

A blood sacrifice, I thought, staring down at my healed wrists before glancing at her sternum. The wound hadn't closed, but she was no longer bleeding.

Because she's finally healing.

I pressed my forehead to hers, a breath escaping me on a

relieved sigh I hadn't exactly meant to reveal, but it felt as though a weight had been lifted off my heart.

And my soul, I thought, inhaling her scent and noting the underlying hint of orange lingering on her lips.

If it were any other moment, I might have smiled. But I couldn't. I was too exhausted to function, too beaten down to do anything other than hold her.

"I need to take her back to my room," I told Kaspian, my eyes having fallen closed. "Can you handle everything here?"

He didn't answer, making me frown.

"Kaspian?" I asked, forcing myself to sit up and meet his gaze.

Only, he wasn't there.

Because Nyx and I were no longer on the street, but on the floor of my bathroom.

"Did I…?" I trailed off, looking down at the resting goddess. "Or did you?" It came out on a slow exhale, one that sounded tired to my ears.

I'd barely slept in over a week.

And now this… I was at the end of my rope.

However, I couldn't leave Nyx in this state. Her skin was finally beginning to mend, but there was blood—both from me and from her—all over her chest and her dress.

Her skin was still regaining color, too.

She needed to be bathed. Cherished. Brought back to life.

I swallowed, my forehead touching hers once more. "I don't know what this was, but it had better not happen again."

At least I knew how I'd feel without her.

Even with the rejection in place, I was still somehow bound to her.

Is it because we keep drinking from each other? I wondered, at a loss for any other explanation. *That's not how fate bonds work.*

But maybe… maybe that was how they worked for her kind?

Except she'd said fated mates didn't happen in her realm.

So what is this, then? I wanted to demand. *Why am I so connected to you?*

It went beyond lust. I'd felt her loss in my fucking heart as though I'd been the one to take that hit to the chest. Some fate beyond anything I could even begin to understand had brought us together, and it surpassed all the logic of my world… and maybe even hers.

Regardless of the reason, we were together now.

Which meant we needed to find a path forward—one where we moved as one, not as two separate entities.

Because it seemed fairly clear to me that we couldn't just reject this.

The only way out is death.

And if today's demonstration was anything to go by—*death* would apply to both of us.

I ran my hand over my face and blew out a breath. "Right." I could dwell on this all afternoon and evening, and it wouldn't fix a damn thing.

But I could help her right now, right here, by ensuring she woke up warm and comfortable.

I stood and turned on the bath, finding the right temperature, and let the tub pool with water. Then I removed my soiled clothes and tossed them into the corner to be burned. They weren't too bloody, as my sleeves had already been rolled to my elbows, but they reeked of death.

Of Nyx's death.

And smoke.

And carnage.

And destruction.

Just like her dress, which I carefully removed, along with her sandals.

I put everything in the same pile to be dealt with later.

Then I checked Nyx's sternum and back, noting the fresh layers of skin covering her previous injury. Her unconscious state told me she was still healing her insides, but externally, she appeared healthy again.

Minus the blood hardening on her skin.

I considered the bath, noting the low water level, and decided to pull her into the shower first. Otherwise, we'd just be sitting in our filth.

Laying her on the bench, I turned on the various showerheads and grabbed a removable one to begin washing her off. She didn't wake, but her skin turned a rosy shade beneath the warm spray.

The blood and grime swirled around the drain, followed by soap as I cleaned us both.

By the time I finished, the bath was ready, the faucet having automatically turned off when it'd reached the appropriate level.

I added some citrusy scents to the water, then returned to grab Nyx from the shower.

And found her sitting on the bench, observing me with a curious expression.

I froze, her golden irises making me forget how to breathe.

Because she was staring at me like I was *prey*.

"You're naked," she said, those alluring eyes tracking downward. "And *wet*." She canted her head, her gaze on my groin.

Which had started to react to her perusal.

Because she was naked, too.

And looking very hungry.

She licked her lips. "Hmm, *that* was worth the wait."

I lifted my brows. "You didn't have to nearly die to see me naked, Nyx." I would have gladly stripped for her and done anything else she'd desired if it had meant never having to see her wounded and dying in the street.

"Die?" she repeated, her gaze returning to mine. "What do you mean?" She glanced around. "Is that… is that why I can't remember how or when we ended up here?" Some of her hunger seemed to subside as she sat up a little straighter.

The action made her wince, her hand coming up to touch her sternum.

"Oh," she breathed, massaging her breastbone. "I don't…" She frowned. "I don't remember anything."

"What's the last thing you do remember?" I asked, walking slowly toward her in the shower.

She shook her head. "Everything… everything feels fuzzy. But I think…" She touched her lips. "Was there orange juice?"

I squatted before her, my hands on her knees, and nodded. "I spiked your orange juice today. I wanted to make sure you ate something." Because she kept skipping meals. And while I understood that she didn't *need* food, some instinctual part of me wanted her to eat anyway.

She lifted her hands to rest them over mine, her fingertips cooler than they should be. But the color of her skin was right, her golden hue healthy and glowing.

"How are you feeling?" I asked her softly.

She shook her head again. "Confused." Her eyes searched my face. "What happened?"

"Cara said you were tracking your magic when someone shot you." I looked at her sternum. "There."

"Shot by what?" she asked. "Something large?"

"No. A bullet."

She stilled. "A bullet? As in… only one?"

"Yes."

"But that… that shouldn't…"

"That shouldn't have been able to almost kill you?" I suggested, finishing the sentence for her. "Yes, I agree. But I had to use stardust to bring you back."

"Stardust?" she repeated, her nose scrunching. "But how did you…?" She trailed off on a shiver, her skin cooling even more against my skin.

Her body was clearly still healing and reallocating energy as needed.

"I think your magic helped me," I admitted, frowning. "It… it sort of appeared and then pooled into a pile of dust in my hand." I squeezed her thighs. "So I wished for you to heal."

She blinked at me. "You had to wish for me to heal?"

"Yes. You were bleeding out."

"That's impossible."

"I would normally agree, but it's what happened," I told her, standing again. "Let's finish this conversation in the bath. It'll help keep you warm." And her fingertips were beginning to feel like ice.

Rather than help her stand, I bent and scooped her up off the bench. She didn't complain, just stared at me as I carried her over to the stairs that led to the whirling pool of warm water. The jets had turned on when the water had shut off.

Nyx still felt utterly weightless in my arms, her size and stature so much clearer to me now that I'd seen her in such a fragile state.

She'd always been smaller than me; I just hadn't realized how much smaller until today.

However, I had no doubt she could handle my power.

So long as she wasn't shot, anyway.

"Paxton thinks it might have been an enchanted bullet," I told her as I sat on one of the benches with her in my lap. "They're looking for the fragments to confirm."

"An enchanted bullet," she echoed, still studying me. "One that kept me from healing?"

I nodded. "That's our best guess at the moment."

"And who... who is Paxton?"

"Kaspian's assistant," I explained. "He's a warlock."

"I see." Her brow furrowed a little, her gaze drifting away from my face to stare at the water for a minute. Then she shook her head. "I don't remember anything."

"You're still healing, Nyx," I murmured, running my hand along her thigh. "Give it time. Your mind will catch up."

She swallowed, her head bobbing a little. "But I'm healing very slowly."

"Because of whatever tried to kill you," I reminded her.

"Yes, I understand that. But even with the stardust..." Her eyes returned to mine. "You made a wish for me to heal, right?"

"I did."

"Then I should be healed already," she replied. "That's... that's how it works. It's not gradual. It's immediate."

I frowned. "Did I do it wrong?" *Or maybe...* "Is it because I sort of conjured the stardust, and not you?"

"No, I don't think so." She considered me for a moment, then lifted her hands to reveal the ashen color returning to her fingertips. "I… I think I need more energy. Maybe from the moon?"

I swallowed and shook my head. "It's… it's not up yet." It was only midday in Iceland, the sun still in the sky.

"Then I need something… else."

"Blood?" I offered.

"Maybe," she whispered, her hand returning to the water. "I don't feel… *complete*."

I understood that sensation because I felt it, too. Almost as though that hollowness in my chest hadn't yet abated.

Because of our missing link.

Except it wasn't missing. That much had been proved over the last few hours.

"Maybe I need sleep," she added, yawning as her body twisted over my lap so she could rest her head on my shoulder.

However, the movement had her stilling again.

"Or maybe…" She shifted just her head until her lips were near my throat. "Maybe I need you."

NYX

Everything felt so heavy. *Weak.* Lethargic, even.

Except… except this forbidden craving inside me. This need to touch Vesperus. To truly taste him. To *embrace* him.

I'd woken up to the sight of his beautiful, firm ass and those long, muscular legs. Then he'd stood upright to reveal his toned back and that full head of thick, dark hair.

It'd felt like a dream, one I wanted to lose myself in and never wake up from.

I licked his throat, chasing an errant droplet with my tongue, and moaned at the taste of his skin.

Pure decadence.

I was ravenous for Vesperus. Hungry in a way I'd never been before. *Dying* for a piece of him. Anything to ground me, to make me feel whole.

Shadowing wasn't an option, my soul too weak to take me to a darker part of the world.

I needed energy now, but in a different way.

And my spirit was telling me to take it from Vesperus. To absorb him. To *join* him.

He'd been able to call some of my stardust to him. That had to mean something.

Then he'd used it to bring me back. And he'd wished for me to *heal.*

It had worked, but only on the surface. Because some part of my soul still ached for him.

"I need you," I repeated, more certain now. "I... I can feel the pull inside me demanding that I join you. It's this intense craving that I can't explain. I just..."

"Feel it," he finished for me. "I know. I sense it, too."

"You do?" I whispered, my mouth against his neck.

"I felt you dying, Nyx." His fingers wove through my hair as he cradled the back of my head. "I felt it as though I was dying right along with you."

I pulled away to meet his gaze. "But we rejected the bond."

"We did," he agreed, his dark irises flickering with power. *My* power. Because the irises were inverted again, giving his eyes that eclipse-like appearance.

So beautiful.

So enchanting.

So... *inviting.*

"We shouldn't be connected at all," he added. "But we very much are."

"We are," I echoed, sensing the thrumming pulse of that connection in my chest. "Is it the blood?"

"I don't know. You said your kind don't have fated mates."

"We don't." But that didn't mean my own magic hadn't evolved to accept the potential for one.

I was a being of creation. Everything about me and my power constantly evolved to manifest more life. More experiences. More enchantments.

Perhaps I'd been hunting for more than just a home. Perhaps I'd been in search of a new purpose.

Of a mate.

That could be why my medallion chose this reality—to pair me with the most ideal match.

Which meant our rejection hadn't been enough to dispel the bond. Because I was a being who existed *beyond* the magic.

I was the source.

"You've been inheriting my powers," I whispered, searching Vesperus's features. "My blood is making you evolve." I'd never seen that happen before, but those who had bitten me in the past hadn't been able to handle a single drop of my essence.

However, Vesperus had indulged in me as though I were a fine wine.

And I'd done the same to him.

"We're mates," I breathed. "We're linked beyond your world's magic."

He swallowed. "I think you might be right."

"That's why I'm craving more," I told him, my hand curling around his nape. "You're my other half. And *I need you*."

The dull tones on my fingertips had spread to my wrists, erasing my golden flare entirely and confirming my depleted energy.

I'd never experienced anything like it—the need to be healed or this gray coloring.

Normally, my skin paled during the day, then rejoiced in the evening as I replenished my spirit with stardust from the night sky.

But this ash-like quality—

Vesperus pressed his lips to mine, silencing my thoughts and bringing me back to him in a strong sweep of his tongue.

I moaned, my nails biting into his nape as I demanded more.

He responded by sinking his fangs into my lower lip. Then he licked away the pain while urging me to return the favor.

It was a violent approach. Almost feral in nature.

Yet it was exactly what I needed—a reminder that I wasn't broken or lost, but his equal in every way.

I was just a little bruised.

And he was offering me what I needed to thrive. To survive. To *revitalize.*

But I didn't want blood from his mouth. I wanted it from his pulse. *From his neck.* A true taste, one I hadn't indulged in yet.

I didn't warn him.

I simply *bit* him.

His grip in my hair tightened as he hissed in response to my sharp movements and feral decision. But he didn't try to pull me away.

No.

He held me *closer.* Urging me to drink. Daring me to swallow as much as I could, just as he'd promised he would.

Only he'd been talking about a different part of him when he'd voiced that statement about stamina.

The part of him that's beneath me. Hard. Ready. Pulsing with want.

It matched the savage racing of my heart, the intense yearning clawing at my insides and demanding to be sated.

This was downright animalistic.

A craving born of voracious intent. Whatever magic existed between us was taking on a new form of life, *creating* a new way to thrive, and mandating our union of souls.

His blood wasn't enough.

His kiss wasn't enough.

His *touch* wasn't enough.

I grabbed his shoulders and straddled him, noting the ashen quality of my skin and how it was slowly inching upward to my elbows. *Depleting my energy. Making me resemble the palest of moons. A starless night. A corpse without light.*

I shivered, the deathlike appearance startling my mind and momentarily shocking me out of the moment.

Only for Vesperus to arch up into me with a reminder of what was beneath me, *who* I'd just settled on top of, and *what* he was offering me.

Energy. Worship. A connection frayed by false rejections.

There was no time for foreplay or preparing our bodies for their joining.

I needed him. And I needed him *now.*

"Complete me," I begged him, my lips near his once more. "Please, Vesperus."

He grabbed my throat, his intense eyes meeting mine. "Wrap your legs around me, Goddess."

I obeyed, my limbs shaking with frailty, my soul screaming for the moon, the night, *anything* to ground me.

And then I felt *him* against my aching heat, his intimate touch sending a bolt of electricity through my spirit and reviving my bruised heart.

The eclipses in his irises pulsed, drawing me in, ensnaring me, and anchoring me to this reality as he thrust upward and connected us in the way we'd always been meant to connect.

This was what we should have done from that very first meeting.

This was the future we'd always been meant to embrace.

Our existence surpassed the rules and expectations of typical courting. We were two passing stars meant to collide, a fated meeting in the night, twin powers determined to find one another during an exploration of realms.

I felt it now, the truth of our destinies beating through my very being as I accepted him inside me.

"Fuck," he breathed, his lips against my neck, his palm still around my throat. "I feel…"

"Alive," I finished for him, my body still acclimating to his size. "Electric. *Complete.*" I started to move against him, needing to experience every inch, to embrace this moment, this joining, *him.*

My mate, I marveled. *He's my mate.*

His palm slid to the back of my neck, his opposite hand clamping down on my hip as he moved me where he wanted me.

I barely felt the water around us. Didn't care that it was moving with us, embracing our connection, and keeping us warm. Because I was too lost to the sensation of Vesperus, of his power, of each upward flex of his hips.

Of his eyes.

They were burning now, that eclipse so bright and vivid that I could feel him searing my being, claiming me entirely, and branding my soul as his.

"Kiss me," I begged. "Kiss me, Vesperus."

His lips immediately found mine, his hand on my hip moving to my lower back to hold me impossibly closer, ensuring our bodies were connected in every way.

Before taking control of my mouth with his tongue.

I gave myself to him entirely, trusting him to see us through to the end, unleashing the last vestiges of control I owned and bowing to his masculine grace.

He was strength personified, his body a gift from the heavens, and he filled me so completely, so *beautifully*, that I could barely breathe.

But it didn't matter because I had his mouth to guide me. His touch to ground me. And his soul to energize me.

I could feel our link reviving my being with each shift of our hips.

This wasn't purely about pleasure. This was about mating. About joining. About being one with each other.

I clung to him, tears leaking from my eyes as the moon kissed my spirit, securing me to this male, to this mate, to this *future*. I didn't know what it would mean tomorrow, or even later today.

But in this moment, it was right.

"Nyx." He tugged on my lower lip, his hand moving along my spine. "I want to feel you come while I'm deep inside you. Experience the sensations of you clenching around me with that sweet pussy of yours as you scream my name."

I shuddered, his words setting my blood on fire. I'd been chasing our joined energy, reveling in our bond, and he was reminding me that this was about so much more than that.

This was about *us*.

Our animalistic need.

Our savage embrace.

My desire to *taste* him. To know what he looked like when he climaxed. To memorize his growls and groans and learn every way to make him re-create those sounds.

Yes, yes.

I slowed my pace against him, going for long, languid strokes that caused my clit to rub against him. Delirious waves of enticement rippled up my spine in response, my abdomen tightening with each… sensual… gyration… of our hips.

Gods, he was stroking me so deeply.

So *thoroughly.*

I hadn't fully realized his girth or his length before, too caught up in the need to *join.* I really should have let him prepare me.

Oh, but it felt so, so *good.* Because I could truly sense every inch of him, his brand resolute and complete and *perfect.*

I panted against his mouth, his name taunting my tongue.

"That's it, gorgeous," he whispered, the endearment making my heart soar. "Show me what it feels like to be inside you when you come."

Gods, the things we were going to do to each other. We'd been slowly learning each other, playing in the shallow part of the pool, just to dive straight into the deep end.

And I couldn't think of a better progression.

Because I was all in now, embracing this new beginning and indulging in our fate.

My heart soared with the knowledge of it, my thighs clamping down around him, my insides squeezing. *So close. So, so, so close.*

"Fuck, Nyx," he breathed, slamming up into me in a sudden flex of his hips that tipped me right over the edge and drew a shocked gasp from my throat.

I wasn't sure how he knew I was about… to… *fly.*

But… but I didn't mind.

Because that thrust hit the spot inside me few others had ever been able to find, and had me drowning beneath a tidal wave of ecstasy.

One that kept rolling.

And rolling.

And rolling.

Pummeling my being, drawing out aftershocks and screams and crippling me with euphoric sensations.

The world dimmed, blackening my vision as trembles overwhelmed me from head to toe.

And then Vesperus's tongue brought me back to him again, his mouth providing the oxygen I needed beneath my sea of dark bliss.

His arm acted as a band around my back, his opposite hand on my nape as he lifted me from the water. I tightened my legs around him, clinging to him as we moved, our bodies still joined.

He hadn't exploded inside me, his need a palpable presence on my tongue, one that had me gasping as my back hit his mattress.

There were no towels. No moments of drying off. Just Vesperus coming over me and demanding that I hold on to him.

I dug my nails into his nape again, my other hand against his upper back, reveling in his power as he finally gave in to his need to fuck me.

It was as though he'd released a beast, his vampiric side taking over and sending us both into a rut.

I cried out as I came again, his prowess and positioning driving me into an oblivion with several swift pumps of his hips.

Only this time he finally joined me, his growl an alluring sound that vibrated my chest and had me wanting to force that sound from him every day for eternity.

Multiple times a day, I thought. *Every hour. Yes, yes.*

He kissed me again, our shared blood a defining flavor on our tongues, creating a dessert I longed to enjoy for the rest of my life.

Not chocolate. Not truly definable. Just… *ambrosia.*

Our breaths mingled as we finally came down from our high, our hearts beating the same rhythm in our chests as he stared down at me with those stunning irises. "Hold on to the headboard."

I blinked, startled by his request.

But I lifted my arms—which had regained their golden shine—and grabbed the wood above me.

"Don't let go until you want me to stop," he said, his words holding a sinful promise that had my cheeks warming in anticipation. "Stamina, remember?" He winked and started kissing a path down my body, pausing for a moment to worship my breasts, and moved to the apex between my thighs.

To lick me clean.

Starsssss, I hissed, arching into him, enthralled by his decadent choice yet jealous at the same time.

He must have known because he crawled back up my body to feed me some of our joint essence with his tongue, allowing me to finally taste him in the way I'd truly desired and teasing me into wanting to return the favor.

But he wasn't done.

He went back to his task, his tongue licking me from opening to clit, where he proceeded to destroy me with his talented mouth.

Over and over again.

I chanted his name, my grip on the headboard nearly crushing the wood. I couldn't tell if he was worshipping me or if I was worshipping him.

I eventually begged him to stop, just as he'd promised I would.

Then he fucked me again, this time slower, his mouth cherishing mine in a way that brought tears to my eyes again.

I desperately wanted to taste him, to return the favor and prove my own stamina, but he'd exhausted me entirely.

His lips feathered over mine as I lounged against him, several hours later, my moon finally appearing in the beautiful sky.

But it wasn't just me it blessed with stardust tonight.

It was Vesperus, too.

As my mate.

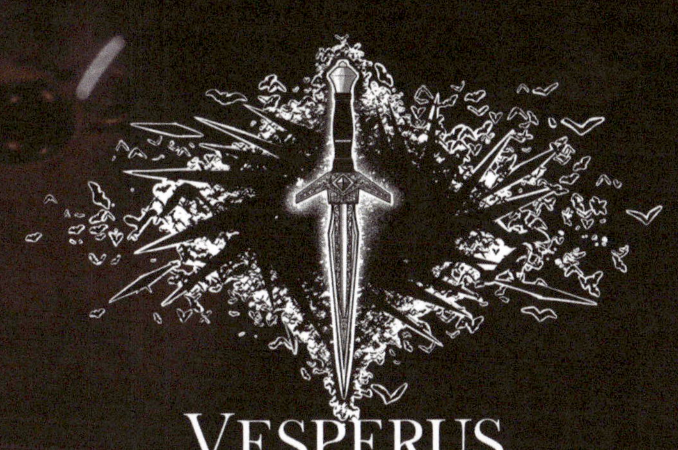

VESPERUS

I ran my fingers through Nyx's silky hair, pleased with the rejuvenated health of her thick black strands.

She was glowing again, her skin holding that luminous golden sheen.

As is mine, I marveled, studying the glittering texture. *I suppose there's no going back now.*

No harsh emotions accompanied that thought. No sense of guilt or doubt or unease, just acceptance.

Because it had already been clear to me that our souls were forever tied after I'd felt her dying.

Whatever laws or magical rules that I used to live by had changed with Nyx's arrival. Perhaps even because of it.

I'd felt her enter our realm, that subtle shift a catalyst that had prompted me into taking the bounty to find her. I might not have hunted her myself, but my House had.

And while Slater might have been the one to locate her whereabouts, I'd been the one to ensnare her.

Or, more accurately, she'd ensnared me.

Now… now we'd ensnared each other.

I pressed a kiss to her forehead, my lips curling at her citrusy taste. Her blood possessed a similar flavor, the sweetness holding a bite to it that was all Nyx.

Powerful. Beautiful. Independent.

A born leader. The question became—could we lead Gold and Garnet together? Or would we be forced to flee?

I pondered that query while I held Nyx, my gaze flitting between her and the moon outside my open balcony windows.

It was freezing outside, but I didn't feel it, my body hot from Nyx's touch. I fully intended to fuck her again as soon as she woke up.

Or perhaps I'd eat her for breakfast first.

While her blood resembled an intoxicating mix of zesty power and refreshing citrus, her arousal was pure decadence. Like the finest wine, aged to perfection.

I could indulge in her all day, every day, for the rest of my life and never tire of her flavor.

Which I supposed was a good thing, as it did seem we would be tied to one another for eternity.

Assuming no one shoots her again, I thought, frowning.

I shifted my wrist to check my watch, searching for any updates that had come in throughout the last few hours.

Nothing. My eyes narrowed. *That can't be right.*

Nyx nuzzled into my chest and released a content sound before sliding her leg over my thigh. She was still very much asleep and using one of my arms as her pillow. Fortunately, it was the arm I did not need.

With a slight rotation of my wrist, I pulled up a dark screen— the magic automatically put it in night mode—to send Kaspian a message. *Have they found the bullet yet?*

I kissed Nyx's head again while I waited for a response.

It didn't buzz my wrist, the watch aware of the late hour. Not that it mattered—I often stayed up all night to work. I was a vampire. The night was easier on my senses.

Although, the sun hadn't bothered me as much lately. I hadn't even needed sunglasses the other day.

A result of Nyx's powers mingling with mine? I wondered.

That would also explain why I'd only desired blood a few days this week. I wasn't even sure I'd required as much as I'd imbibed. But I'd chalked it up to my evenings of playing with Nyx.

Now I understood that it had been related to her, just not in the way I'd originally thought. Because her blood had been doing a lot more than just satisfying my hunger.

I checked my screen to see if Kaspian had replied and scowled at his single-word reply of, *Yes.*

And? I demanded via text and a mental note into his mind.

We should talk, was his response on the screen. *I'm in your office, but I can come up to you, if you'd prefer.*

You're in my office? I said to him mentally, surprised.

That could only mean that he'd found something important and was currently acting as the House's primary leader while allowing me my private moments with Nyx.

Kaspian really was a good friend and an even better leader.

If you don't mind coming up here, that would be preferable, I finally replied. Not with a text, just a thought to his mind.

I'm on my way up, he told me via text. *Cara is coming with me.*

It took considerable effort to pull away from Nyx, but I wanted to know what Kaspian and the others had found, as well as what they were currently doing in my office.

I kissed the top of Nyx's head as I settled her in my bed. She released a small sound of discontentment before burying her head against my pillow.

My lips curled when she sighed, her irritation melting away as she absorbed my scent.

Chocolate, she'd told me. *You remind me of a decadent sundae drizzled in hot fudge.*

Her own personal dessert.

I pulled the blankets up to keep her warm, thinking about my own preferred dessert that existed between her thighs. *I'll be back to wake you up for breakfast,* I mused at her, careful to not accidentally speak into her mind.

It was a simple switch for me. I merely had to consider the person I wished to speak to, and I shifted my thought to broadcast to them.

The ability was one I'd been born with and had mastered at a young age. Same with my talent for detecting lies.

But now I had a new skill at my fingertips, one I felt humming along my spine and daring me to try using it again.

I considered my closet and told my body to phase there.

The room melted around me and re-formed as a row of suits. I grinned and turned to open one of my closet dressers, preferring something more comfortable, as I didn't plan to remain clothed for long.

I pulled on a pair of gray lounge pants and a white T-shirt, then envisioned the hallway outside my room.

Where I found Cara and Kaspian waiting near the doors to my rooms.

Cara's eyebrows shot upward upon seeing me, her lips parting a little. "Fuck. You're glowing."

I smirked at her cliché expression, aware that she'd meant the words literally, and yet finding humor in the phrase as well. "Thank you."

Kaspian didn't appear amused at all, his gaze tracking over me with a touch of concern in his features. "I think it's safe to assume you're fully mated now."

"We are," I confirmed.

He nodded. "Then you're going to want to know what we found on the bullets."

My humor died. "Tell me."

Cara slipped her hand into her leather jacket pocket and pulled out a bag with several metal fragments. "From what we can tell, it wasn't a spell but a toxin."

My brow furrowed. "A toxin?"

"Some sort of lethal agent that causes erosion and decay." Kaspian glared at the metallic shards. "Paxton says that if it was created by a spell, it's not one he's ever seen. It's more likely chemicals."

"I see." I stared at the bag for a long moment, thinking about how it had destroyed Nyx's energy levels and made it impossible for her to heal. Even after she'd brought herself back to full health, the toxin had started weakening her again.

By making her skin dry out and turn gray.

Similar to decay, I supposed.

"That's new," I added, still frowning. "I've never heard of anything like it."

"Neither have I," Kaspian agreed. "But we recently acquired two phantoms who might know something about it."

"Noxious," I said, meeting his gaze as a bolt of adrenaline spiked my blood. "Do you think he did this?" He'd admitted to his penchant for chemicals and weapons, which was why he'd chosen his own name.

And Bane had stated his own talents for using Noxious's creations.

It made sense. They were both new to our territory. "But what's his motive?" I pondered aloud before Kaspian could respond to my first inquiry. "Why would he—or potentially *they*—do this?"

"There's only one way to find out," Kaspian replied, a dark emotion lurking in his tone.

If Bane and Noxious had betrayed us, Kaspian would be the one to handle their punishment. Because he'd been the one to take on the task of training them, and he would feel personally attacked if our suspicions ended up being true.

"We'll need to involve Kieran," I told him. "This sort of breach impacts his House—and potentially our relationship with that House." Because this could have been a ploy on behalf of Death and Diamond. Perhaps Bane and Noxious had been sent here to create chaos.

But I didn't know what Sabrina or Kieran would gain from that.

They had their hands full with the new territory assignments, and they'd been more than willing to work with Gold and Garnet to ensure a smooth transition. So why risk that by having Bane and Noxious cause strife near my headquarters?

Unless this wasn't about attacking my people at all, but about Nyx—the true victim of the attack.

Hmm, no, that didn't feel right either. Kieran had been particularly nonchalant about the whole thing.

However, he had told Elias. Which I'd expected him to do. But maybe my allies weren't as supportive as I'd hoped. Perhaps Noxious and Bane had been sent here to remove Nyx.

Except, no, that didn't make sense either. They'd arrived in Dublin *with* Kieran. And that was before any of them had even known I was fate-mated to the entity we'd been hunting all these months.

"Nothing about this makes sense," I finally said. "We definitely need Kieran here—if anything, so that I can try to get a better read on him." Taste his truths, determine his lies.

Kaspian nodded. "I'll call him."

"No, I'll talk to him," I said. "I need you to find Bane and Noxious."

"They're asleep in my house," Kaspian replied. "Paxton set up a barrier spell, so I'll know if they leave."

"Your house?" I asked, arching a brow. That was news to me.

"They have nowhere to live yet," he reminded me.

"We have local mercenary housing." Which I knew wasn't full because I'd spent the last few weeks evaluating all of the properties within our territory. And even with the new relocations necessitated by today's explosions, we still had plenty of space available.

He didn't say anything, just stared at me.

So I dropped it.

If my second-in-command wanted to play house with some phantoms, I wasn't going to begrudge him the experience. However, knowing he'd developed some sort of camaraderie with them had me hoping we were wrong about their involvement in this attack.

I didn't enjoy seeing anyone hurt, least of all my best friend.

"You can call Kieran," I told him, realizing he needed the distraction so that he didn't go home and potentially murder the phantoms before we had a chance to talk to them. He was masking his anger well, hiding his emotions behind a stoic shield, but he had to be fuming.

"Make sure you tell him that we don't know anything for sure yet," I added, my words more for Kaspian than for Kieran. However, I disguised them as a request. "We need to interrogate them first."

Kaspian's jaw ticked, but he nodded.

"Perhaps Kieran can bring another witch with him. While Paxton might not recognize any hint of a spell, someone else might," Cara suggested as she returned the bag to her pocket.

I dipped my chin in agreement. "That's a good point. Maybe he can bring Trixie, if she's still in his territory. And perhaps the supervisor Noxious and Bane had mentioned. Max, was it?"

Bane had said something about their former boss enjoying experiments. Perhaps he would recognize whatever agent had been used on the bullets.

"I'll talk to Kieran about it," Kaspian confirmed. "If I can convince him to fly out now, we could begin the interrogation in a few hours."

I glanced at my doors and then back at them. "I'm not sure Nyx will be awake by then." While I'd fully intended to worship her for hours—*days*—I recognized her need for rest after whatever had nearly killed her.

"I can stay with her," Cara offered. "If she's not awake by the time Kieran arrives, I mean."

"I would appreciate that," I admitted. "She has no memory of what happened, but I suspect that'll change when she wakes up again."

Or I hoped it would, anyway. She might be able to provide important details regarding the incident.

"I'll message you after I talk to Kieran," Kaspian told me. "We'll go from there."

"Yes," I said, agreeing to the plan as I turned off the sleep mode on my watch. I wanted to make sure I received Kaspian's updates in a timely manner.

I grabbed his arm as he tried to walk past me, his dark eyes holding a note of surprise as he glanced at me. "Thank you, Kaspian," I told him. "For everything."

He'd always had my back, no matter the situation. And I sensed this one would be the same. Even with the obvious changes to my appearance and powers, he would go down fighting at my side if that was what it came to.

I hoped it wouldn't. I hoped we could find a way to make this work.

But at least I knew that if something did happen—that if something or someone succeeded in removing me from my position as House King—Gold and Garnet would be in capable hands. *Kaspian's hands.*

We shared a long look, his expression telling me he understood everything I'd just thought. And he accepted the burden I was silently passing to him.

If something happens to me, you will lead. And you will do well. I didn't speak the words into his mind. I simply allowed him to see them in my eyes. *Because you already know how to be a king.*

He'd proved that countless times, including today.

He eventually gave me another nod. "You'll always be my king, Vesperus."

"I know," I replied. "But that doesn't mean you'll always be my second."

He considered me for a long moment, then clapped me on the shoulder. "Gold's a good color on you, mate. Matches the House. And your throne." With that cheeky commentary, he turned away and started walking again. "Text you in a bit."

Cara laughed in his wake. "He's right, though, Ves. Gold is a good color on you. So is Nyx." She winked as she passed me, then caught up to Kaspian and bumped his side. He wrapped his arm around her in a good-natured hug, one that would probably piss off Larus later.

That was likely the point.

Kaspian was a notorious flirt.

But he'd never make a real move on Cara. He respected the mate bonds, and while he joked about not searching for his own, I knew deep down that he desired someone to call his own. Man or woman, he wouldn't care. He just wanted someone to love.

I knew that truth now because I'd been just like him weeks ago, claiming not to have a desire to find a mate. And yet now that I had mine waiting for me in my bed, I realized how lonely I'd been. How much I'd longed for this connection. This… supernatural *bond.*

It wasn't love. Not quite. Or rather, not *yet*. It was more about being compatible and finding the other half of my soul.

My Goddess of Night.

She certainly wasn't what I'd anticipated in finding on the other half of the fated-mate magic. But I definitely wasn't disappointed.

I phased back into my room—*our* room now—and watched her sleep for several minutes before finally joining her in the bed again.

She immediately wrapped herself around me, her lips ghosting over my throat as though seeking my taste even in sleep.

I smiled and held her tightly, lending her whatever strength she needed through this enchanting connection, and closed my eyes while I waited for Kaspian to message me the details.

NYX

MMM, I HUMMED, INHALING THE SWEET SCENT OF HOT CHOCOLATE. The fragrance tickled my nose, the notes of caramel and marshmallow soon following.

I opened one eye to find the source of goodness sitting on the nightstand beside me in some sort of enchanted mug.

Along with a note.

Careful. It's spiked.

—V

I sat up, eager to try this decadent gift, and immediately picked up the tantalizing drink and took a sip.

"Stars," I moaned, in love with this amazingly crafted beverage. "It tastes like an orgasm in a cup."

"I can see that," a female voice drawled, snapping my attention to the woman standing in the doorway to the bedroom.

I'd been so focused on the aromatic breakfast gift that I hadn't even thought to evaluate my surroundings.

"Good morning, Twinkly," she greeted.

"Hello, Flower Fae," I murmured, relaxing against the headboard with my drink. "Back on babysitting duty again?"

"Not exactly," she said slowly, frowning a bit. "Do you remember anything that happened yesterday?"

I took another sip of my hot chocolate, my lips curling into a secret smile. "I certainly remember last night." And the beautiful connection Vesperus and I had created.

His spirit had energized mine, making me feel alive in a way I'd so badly needed.

I nearly sighed, pleased by our bond and the vivacious way it thrived between us.

Except the reason behind that stark need—the cause of my weak state—had my lips curling downward.

I'd nearly died. *Because of a single bullet.* I rubbed my sternum, the hint of yesterday's attack lingering in my mind.

"I was shot," I said slowly. "And… and there was a woman." I could picture her standing in the alleyway, surrounded by darkness, radiating her pain. "She was so broken." As though her soul had been ripped to pieces.

I set my mug down, the reminder of her presence sending a chill down my spine.

"A woman?" Cara repeated.

I nodded. "Hidden in the shadows."

"That's who shot you? It was a woman?"

My frown deepened as I shook my head. "No. I don't think so. She didn't have a gun. But my medallion was circling her frantically. I…"

I pictured the scene, trying to remember exactly what had happened.

"I was focused on her when something or someone shot me from another angle. It wasn't her." Yet she was involved somehow because she'd been there. "She watched it all happen." While cloaking herself in darkness.

Who are you? I wondered. *And why was my medallion magic swirling around you?*

Maybe Vesperus has a repository of images somewhere, something to help me find or locate the woman.

Or maybe I could go back to the same spot to find her.

But with some armor this time, I thought, my eyebrows pulling down. Because Cara's question about the woman told me they didn't know who had shot me. Or how it had nearly killed me.

I looked at Cara. "Where's Vesperus?"

"He's interrogating Nox and Bane," she replied. "He didn't want you to wake up alone, so that's why I'm here. Not to babysit, but to keep you informed and also find out if your memories have returned."

"They've returned," I confirmed, sliding out from under the covers. "And I need to talk to Vesperus." I started toward the bathroom area, then paused. "Wait. He's interrogating Nox and Bane?"

"The bullet fragments had some sort of toxin on them that promotes decay." Cara ran her light-colored eyes over me as though assessing the damage. "Or that's the theory, anyway. Paxton couldn't sense a spell, so we think it's a chemical of some kind."

"I see." I considered her words as I went in search of clothes. Rather than pick a dress, I chose a pair of black pants and a sweater, the outfit similar to Cara's in the other room. Maybe it would help me blend in better, something I'd prefer to do in case any of today's plans required me to leave the palace.

My dresses were my trademark. And if someone miraculously possessed the ability to kill me, then I wanted to be less obvious.

I pulled my hair back into a ponytail, my band the only gold trinket in my hair. Then I called for my crescent necklace and wore it on the outside of the black sweater.

And finished my wardrobe with a pair of socks and knee-high boots.

Cara actually gasped as I exited the bathroom. "Holy shit. You're wearing the outfit I picked out for you."

I curtsied. "I'm going for a more incognito look today."

Her lips twitched. "I don't know if that's possible, Twinkly."

I shrugged. "I'll wear a hood."

She laughed at that and shook her head. "I'm glad you're not dead, Nyx. You scared me for a minute."

"I would have come back," I told her. "I think." My soul should be indestructible as a being of creation, but the lingering energy deficiency inside me had me wondering if that was absolutely true.

Because I'd felt… *depleted*. And not just because of blood loss, but because of power loss. Like I'd been enchanted by death.

Can a toxin actually do that? I wondered. It seemed unlikely.

"I want to talk to Vesperus," I said, already walking toward the door. "I don't think Nox or Bane did this. But I would like to ask them a few questions." They were phantoms and therefore familiar with death. Perhaps they would have some insight into what had knocked me out so severely.

Cara took the lead, telling me Vesperus wasn't in his office but in another area of his estate, one I hadn't seen yet—the underground.

It wasn't a dungeon, necessarily. The lights were too bright for that, and the floors, ceilings, and walls were all in pleasant condition. They were just a little plain, and the lack of windows gave it a more serious effect.

There also weren't any cells or locked doors, something I remarked on to Cara.

"We don't hold our bounties here," she told me. "This is just a quiet area where Vesperus prefers to conduct his more private conversations."

When we reached a room at the end of the hall, I understood what she meant. Because there were only five beings inside—Vesperus, Kaspian, Kieran, and the two phantoms.

No one was chained up.

There were no bloody instruments.

Just a simple round table at which they were all seated.

However, Kaspian was noticeably closest to the door—and armed.

"I'm going to head back up to keep Larus company in your office," Cara said to Vesperus. "And by the way, she remembers everything."

With that parting comment, she left.

Vesperus stood, his eyes tracking over my outfit.

"I felt the need to blend in a little better today," I told him before he could ask.

He smiled, his palm cupping my cheek. "I don't think you could ever blend in, Goddess."

"That's what Cara said."

"She was right," he replied, leaning in to brush a kiss against my lips. "How are you feeling?"

His tenderness belied the tension in the room. However, he stared down at me as though I was the only one who mattered, like we didn't have an audience.

Because maybe to him, that was true. It was true for me, too.

"I woke up to an amazing hot chocolate," I told him. "It satisfied some of my craving, but I still want to lick you."

His lips curled. "We'll test your stamina after we're done here."

"Newly mated," Kaspian muttered.

"Yes, it's an amazing feeling, one I'm eager to return to myself," Kieran replied. "Vesperus?"

The Gold and Garnet King ignored him for a moment, his gaze still on mine. "What do you remember?"

I went through the events from yesterday in detail, telling him everything from when I'd sensed my medallion all the way through being shot.

"At first, I thought it was my energy attacking me again," I said, recalling how it'd sent me to my knees prior to that. "But now I realize it had been trying to protect me. Then it'd turned my attention to the woman in the shadows."

I described her fractured spirit and her other features—including her blondish-brown hair, piercing green eyes, and curvy stature.

"Do you know her?" I asked at the end. "Do you know what broke her?"

Vesperus considered me for a long moment before finally turning back to the table. "Kaspian?"

He shook his head. "I have no idea who she's talking about."

Vesperus focused on the other leader. "Any ideas?"

"You're asking me?" He chuckled a bit. "I don't know, Vesperus. This seems like a woman scorned. You piss anyone off lately?" He glanced around him to look at me. "Perhaps by taking a new mate?"

"No," Vesperus replied shortly.

"Our king has a thing about monogamy," Kaspian informed Kieran. "But it's a valid question, Ves. Can you think of anyone who might feel wronged by something? Maybe the Death and Diamond vote?"

Vesperus moved to my side, his palm going to my lower back as he considered the question. "All of the correspondence I've received has been mostly positive. The few complaints sent my way have all been dealt with, and everyone seems to be fairly understanding of the matter."

"It helps that yer offering those affected to choose a House and their territory," Bane commented, his dark eyes earnest as his Scottish accent came through in his words.

Whatever conversation had occurred prior to my arrival seemed to have put him and the other phantom at ease, which suggested they'd been absolved of their guilt. Otherwise, I suspected they wouldn't still be sitting cordially at this table.

While the tension remained thick in the air, it felt more residual than current. Or perhaps it was a result of the general topic.

"He's right," Nox agreed. "I haven't heard any complaints. Everyone has been appreciative of the collaboration between the two Houses."

"You hear that, *Ves*?" Kieran drawled. "They like that we're becoming friends."

"Really pleased by that, *Asp*," Vesperus responded, not sounding pleased at all. Apparently, he and the other leader weren't on the "Ves" level of friendship yet.

"Hmm." The vampire-fae hybrid evaluated him with his gray eyes. "Veritas?"

"Aspen?" Vesperus returned, telling me *Asp* had been short for Aspen. Which must have been Kieran's last name.

The other man nodded. "Agreed."

"Brilliant." Vesperus looked at Kaspian. "I'm at a loss. Can you think of anyone who might want to attack the House?"

"Or Nyx," Kieran added.

Vesperus glanced at him again, causing the other leader to lift his hands.

"She was attacked by a bespelled bullet that nearly killed her, Veritas. Seems rather pointed to me, considering everyone else was fine," he explained. "Almost like it was a revenge attack."

My brow furrowed. "Revenge for what?" I asked. "According to your laws, all I've done wrong is arrive via informal means."

"Illegal means," he corrected me. "And I'm not talking about revenge on you, but revenge on your mate. Hurting you hurts him. So I'll ask again—have you pissed anyone off lately, Veritas?"

"You can hear the truth in my words already, Aspen," Vesperus returned.

"That's not exactly how my power works. However, whether or not you're speaking the truth doesn't truly answer the question, does it?" he pressed. "Just because you can't think of something immediately doesn't mean your response is the truth."

I frowned. "He's a truth seeker, too?" I asked, glancing at the rare vampire-fae hybrid.

"Yes. Apparently, he was stabbed by a sword infused with a god's blood, and now he can compel others to speak the truth." Vesperus gave the male an appraising look before glancing at me. "It's what we were discussing when you arrived. Well, that and Kieran's claim that there hadn't been enough time for him to bring anyone other than himself today."

"Not a claim," the other leader interjected.

"You're right. It was a lie," Vesperus replied.

Kieran simply shrugged in response, not bothering to deny it.

"Sort of accelerates an interrogation when there are two literal lie detectors in the room," Kaspian murmured. "But at least we know the phantoms are innocent."

"Yes, the bullet fragments have magic on them, not toxins," Kieran replied. "Old magic. But I don't recognize it."

"You can sense it?" I asked, even more curious about him.

"I can sense the blood in it," he corrected. "*Ancient* blood." His attention shifted to Vesperus. "This has been a very interesting visit, my indebted friend. It seems I'm helping you solve all the riddles."

"And here I thought you didn't give a fuck about anyone other than yourself, Aspen."

He drummed his fingers against the table, his expression thoughtful. "I care about Sabrina. And she cares about Death and Diamond. So making good with the local monarch and his goddess mate seems like a practical move on my part."

His accent was decidedly not Scottish. Which I supposed made sense. From what I understood, he came from the House of Blood and Beryl, and they were located along the west coast of the former United States.

"We're losing sight of the discussion," Kaspian interjected. "We're looking for a female who might have a cause for revenge. And as she attacked Nyx, it seems rather personal to Vesperus."

"I don't think she's the one who attacked me," I said, frowning. "I think… I just think she's somehow involved." Because why else would she have been standing there? And why did my magic seem drawn to her?

"Which means we need to find whoever it is and ask some questions," Kaspian translated. "But I agree this is somehow linked to your recent ties to Nyx. This attack was meant to hurt you, perhaps to remove her as your fated mate. The question is, *why?*"

"You said she appeared broken?" Vesperus asked me. "Like her soul was fractured?"

I nodded. "Yes, like she was in a great deal of pain."

Vesperus considered that for a moment, his hand leaving my lower back. "Like her soul had been broken. Potentially by losing a fated mate." His gaze went to Kaspian as the other man clicked a button to drop a screen from the ceiling.

"I see where you're going with this, mate," he said, a keyboard seeming to appear out of thin air. "There's only one recent death that I'm aware of involving a fated mate."

"Who?" I asked.

"Fallon Doyle," he replied, typing in the name and hitting

Enter.

The woman's photo appeared, making me gasp. "Stars…" It was her. Yet not. She appeared a lot more vibrant in this picture, her lips curling into a pleasing smile, her green eyes radiant and alive. *Beautiful,* I thought. *Not broken.*

"Is that her?" Vesperus asked me.

I nodded mutely, still torn between the two images in my head—this female with the happy expression and the other one lurking in the darkness. "Yes," I finally whispered, swallowing. "But she… she doesn't look like this anymore."

She appeared to be destroyed. Annihilated. *Dead.*

"Did she…? She lost her mate?" I asked, seeing the details now below her photo. "Klas?"

"One of the mercenaries sent to track you," Vesperus murmured. "He died in the explosion."

"Which I'm guessing this woman thinks Nyx is responsible for," Kieran said, pushing away from the table to stand. "That still leaves the mystery of who attacked the bar, though. But I have faith you all will figure it out."

"Is that your way of saying you're out?" Kaspian asked him, a slight smile in his voice.

"Nah, I just don't want to get in your way," he returned. "Unless you think you need me to stay?"

Vesperus shook his head. "You've done enough. And we're officially in your debt. Again."

Kieran grinned. "Look at that. A friendship working in my favor. Elias will be proud."

"I'll trust you to keep him informed." Vesperus worded it as a statement but paired it with an arched brow.

The other leader simply shrugged. "Probably."

"Hmm." Vesperus looked him over. "You're not half bad, Aspen."

"Likewise, Veritas." He gestured to the screen with his chin. "Good luck with this." Then he looked at the phantoms. "If you decide you don't want them, send them back. Death and Diamond would be happy to keep them."

A layered comment, one meant to inform Bane and Nox that they had options should they need them. The fact that he provided them with that choice showed what kind of leader Kieran would become. He was saying rather bluntly that he still had their backs, if needed.

"Thank you," Nox replied, gratitude clear in his features. "But we're going to try to make this work."

Bane nodded. "They didn't imprison us and ask questions later. They were up front about their concerns, just as I imagined you would be."

"Eh, my father-in-law might have a few things to say about that," Kieran remarked, glancing at Vesperus. "Veritas."

"Aspen."

"I'll see myself out," the vampire-fae hybrid said. "Call me if you need more advice."

Vesperus grunted, the remark clearly one that held a touch of history between them. But I caught the small smile in Vesperus's gaze. At least until he looked at the screen again. "I want her found."

"I've already texted Slater," Kaspian replied. "He's our best tracker."

"He is," Vesperus agreed. "Maybe he'll recognize her magic as similar to the trace at the bar." He sat down again and pulled out Kieran's chair for me. "Let's review her file. And maybe bring Niamh down. She might have useful information since Fallon was a member of her territory."

"Will do," Kaspian agreed before glancing at the phantoms. "Do you want them excused?"

Vesperus considered the pair for a moment and shook his head. "No, I think it's safe to say they're involved now. I suppose this could be their first trial."

Bane and Nox leaned forward with interest as I finally took the chair beside Vesperus.

"Nothing like throwing them in headfirst," Kaspian mused, his lips curling. "Now let's learn more about Fallon Doyle."

NYX

Fallon Doyle was a witch.

But not a very powerful one, according to her records.

Niamh didn't know much about her, and the woman's record in the system didn't reveal much either. However, the witch ancestry had both Kaspian and Vesperus agreeing that she was responsible for the magic on the bullet.

"She might not have spelled it or fired it, but she'll know who did," Kaspian had said.

Vesperus had nodded, concurring with his second.

While I accepted their logic, I still wasn't sure about her guilt. Maybe it was the broken quality of her soul that held me back, but I couldn't forget the pain radiating from her spirit as though seeking an antidote and *begging* for help.

And my enchantment wouldn't seek to assist a cruel being.

Maybe that was really what held me back from believing she could be responsible for this.

Regardless, I listened while Vesperus and Kaspian strategized their next moves. They selected a handful of mercenaries, including Bane and Nox, to quietly search the city for Fallon.

"She may not know that we've identified her," Kaspian was saying. "We can use that to our advantage."

"She knows I saw her," I murmured from my position on Vesperus's couch.

We'd moved the meeting to his office, where Larus and Cara had been working. Niamh had joined us for a bit but had since left to make some personal calls to see if she could learn more about Fallon.

"But she doesn't know you're awake," Kaspian pointed out. "Only a handful of us are aware."

"Not true. The palace staff know," Cara said from her position on the floor. She'd scattered out some weapons that she appeared to be cleaning.

Larus sat beside her, helping with the task. His lips twitched as he added, "Which is why Cara and I spread the word that Nyx has no memory of the attack."

Kaspian and Vesperus shared a look that ended in approving grins.

"That's a good rumor to keep going," my mate agreed. "But I'm guessing she's hiding or using a potion to disguise herself."

"If she can do that, why not use the potion for herself originally?" I asked.

"You said she was wrapped up in darkness," he replied. "So maybe she doesn't need to disguise herself anyway."

"Because she's already hiding," I inferred, nodding. "That would explain why Cara didn't see her."

The female fae snorted but didn't further comment.

"So the scouts might be useless," Kaspian summarized. "But Slater is on his way with Nolan. I'll give them the bullet fragments and see if they can use the blood or the spell to track her."

"And if they can't?" Cara asked.

"We'll orchestrate a raid," Vesperus said, sounding tired. "The future Gold and Garnet Queen was nearly killed. The people will understand."

"Assuming they're willing to accept her as their queen." Kaspian's voice was soft, but his point settled heavily in the room.

Vesperus fell quiet for a long moment before saying, "You're right."

"They just need to get a chance to know her," Cara murmured. "Then they'll see how awesome Twinkly is. I mean, she fucking sparkles. She can star in her own disco party."

Larus chuckled, his dark hair waving with magic against his shoulders as he shook his head.

But Kaspian and Vesperus appeared less humored by her words, the two men sharing another one of those long looks.

After a beat, Kaspian cleared his throat and said, "You know what? I could use a nap. It's been a long twenty-four or thirty-six or however many fucking hours. Slater and Nolan won't be here until after midnight. We've already decided which mercenaries to send out to scout. I think we're done for now."

Vesperus gave him a thankful smile.

However, Cara appeared ready to argue. Only, Larus's hand on her nape stopped her before she could speak. He told her something with his silver-blue eyes, making her swallow and say, "Yeah, a nap is a good idea."

Kaspian nodded. "Excellent." He stood and grabbed the bag of metal fragments on Vesperus's desk. "I'll debrief Nolan and Slater when they arrive."

I arched a brow. *Before, during, or after your nap?* I wondered.

"Thank you," Vesperus said. "Let me know how it goes."

"I will." Kaspian angled his head toward the door. "Let's go, lovers."

Cara popped up and blew him a kiss that Larus immediately caught in the air. "No."

Kaspian chuckled, winking at the flirty fae female, and led them from Vesperus's office.

I waited for the door to close before saying, "Your leaders are not well versed in subtlety."

Vesperus laughed and pushed away from his desk to walk around it. "They're usually much better at it. But they clearly know that you and I need to discuss a few things. And I don't think they saw value in hiding that knowledge."

"So why not just say, 'Let's give Vesperus and his new mate a few private moments to talk about their future'? Instead of claiming a need for a 'nap.'"

Vesperus leaned against the edge of his desk and stretched out his legs to cross them at the ankles. "Not everyone is as forthcoming as you are, Nyx."

"A forthcoming approach is practical in most situations, King."

"I agree." His silver irises were normal again, but his pupils dilated as he ran his gaze over me. "Do you want to have this chat upstairs on the roof? Or here in my office?"

I glanced at the windows, noting the setting sun. "That is a very easy decision, King." I stood and pulled my sweater over my head, then kicked off my boots and bent to remove my socks.

"You're making me want to stay in my office," he deadpanned.

My lips curled. "You sure about that?" I phased up to the roof to continue disrobing.

He appeared a few seconds later with my boots and sweater in his hands. Rather than comment on his miraculous ability to borrow my shadowing, he simply set my shoes on the ground and folded my sweater onto a nearby bench.

"So you can phase now," I said conversationally.

"Apparently," he murmured. "Very useful trick. How far can I go?"

"Typically, it's about what you can envision more than distance," I told him as I finished removing my pants. "But the longer the phase, the more energy it requires."

He nodded as he began unbuttoning his dress shirt, his skin glimmering like mine. "Do you think this ability is linked to our connection or your blood?"

I considered it from the steps of his pool. "Perhaps both. But your irises don't resemble eclipses right now, like they usually do after drinking from me. So this could be a result of our mate bond."

"Eclipses?" he repeated, his undershirt joining his dress shirt on the bench.

"Your eyes resemble a total solar eclipse after you bite me." I smiled. "They're quite beautiful to behold."

"I could say the same about you," he returned, his gaze on my breasts.

"Your body has already provided me with the compliment," I told him, looking pointedly at his groin.

He didn't shy away from it, instead choosing to remove his trousers and boxers to give me a better view. But then he turned to fold the items like everything else before bending to pick up my discarded pants to add them to the pile.

"So prim and proper," I teased.

"My mother would be proud of that comment." He straightened and started toward me, his gorgeous body on full display. "Are you planning to stand here or join me in the water?" he asked, passing me on the stairs.

I admired the view for another moment before following him into the hot pool. "I'm starting to think water is our thing," I confided.

I supposed it could be considered appropriate, given my control over the tides. Although, that was more related to my relationship with the moon than the actual ocean.

"Water and truth," he marveled, kicking onto his back to scull a little. "Then I suppose we should discuss what being fated mates means for us, since there's no going back now."

"I think we both know what it means," I said, swimming toward him. "Our futures are tied whether we're ready or not."

"Indeed." He closed his eyes as the last rays of sunshine disappeared into the twilight. "The other leaders will not be pleased with my enhancements. I can phase. I can sort of call stardust. I no longer seem to need as much blood as I used to. And I find that the sun doesn't bother me at all now. Like I could stare at it and not feel the burn at all."

"Is that uncommon?" I asked, referring to the sun part. "Because I've seen plenty of vampires walking in the sun here."

"It doesn't hurt us. But our senses are refined with age, so I often find it bothersome. Or I did. Until today." He stopped sculling and moved forward, his legs bending under the water to put us at an even eye level.

I mimicked his stance, settling right in front of him. "So you're concerned the other monarchs won't accept these changes." It was a summary of what he'd already said, but I suspected that was the key point to this conversation.

"Yes." His gaze fell to my mouth before slowly returning to my eyes. "About fifty years ago, a portal opened in Portland, Oregon. It wasn't the first of its kind, but it was the first one that couldn't be hidden from humans. Because it opened in the center of a major highway."

"Oh." My eyes widened. "That must have been eventful."

"An understatement." His expression told me it wasn't a good kind of eventful, either. "The world changed drastically with magic more or less manifesting in humans, creating a variety of species and power levels, and causing general turmoil. All of which led to The Great Sacrifice."

"The genocide," I said, recalling our previous conversation. "The one that led to the truce between the Houses."

"Yes. It was a war, too. A mass culling. Because everyone fought for different reasons. But Gold and Garnet's purpose has always been about glory and honor. We protected our homes. And we profited on the blood of others."

"You did what you needed to do to survive," I translated.

"No, we did what we needed to do to *thrive*," he corrected. "We were better prepared than most, our skills already honed by our mercenary backgrounds. While we lost a great deal, we won a lot, too. Unity being one of those rewards."

I nodded, understanding what he meant. "Your men and women work well together."

"They do." He tilted his head back to look at the sky, his dark hair dipping into the water behind him.

I followed his lead, allowing the hot water to warm my head before righting myself and meeting his gaze once more.

"The Houses formed a truce after that fateful night," he told me. "That's why it's both a celebration to some and a memorial to others. Many lives were lost—*sacrificed*—that day. All in the name of a tenuous peace."

"Does Gold and Garnet celebrate or memorialize the day?" I wondered aloud.

"We might be mercenaries of death, but we never celebrate it," he replied. "We remember the fallen. And we honor them in our unity."

That matched everything I'd come to know about his territory and him as a leader. "You don't see that night as a victory."

"I don't," he admitted. "I see it as a turning point in our history, one we should learn from to avoid repeating."

"Which brings us back to your concern about the other leaders accepting your changing powers," I surmised.

"Which brings me back to the concern about the Houses allowing you and me to reign," he echoed, changing my words just a little bit. "But it's about more than that. It's about my people. Kaspian was right about whether or not they'll accept you. What he didn't add out loud was whether or not they'll accept the new me."

"If Gold and Garnet is all about glory and honor, then they'll respect your increase in power," I replied. "Right?"

"Yes, they will honor and respect it. But they'll know the rest of the world might not. And that insecurity will cause turmoil among the members of my House."

I swallowed, understanding what he meant. It was his job to protect his people, not their job to protect him. But they might be forced to if the other leaders didn't approve of his enhanced abilities.

"Your leadership will be putting them at risk," I said after a beat. "Assuming the other Houses won't approve of these changes."

"Yes." He stepped into me, his palm finding the back of my neck as he held me close to him.

"But you mentioned the fake Odin and how no one challenges his immense power," I reminded him. "So maybe what we need to do is prove to them all that we can lead in a similar fashion."

"First, he's not a fake Odin," Vesperus murmured, his silver eyes sparkling with mirth. "But I really hope to hear you say that to him one day."

"He's fake to me," I clarified. "Because I know the real Odin."

"Yes. From your world. I remember."

"My reality, yes."

"But in this one, he's very real. And you're right, he is well respected. Therefore, it's not impossible. However, my concern is in regard to how fast this has evolved. Many of the Houses will see it as a threat."

"What if we keep it quiet?" I suggested. "Ease them into it by demonstrating that we can control ourselves."

"Can we control ourselves?" he asked, his voice earnest as he searched my expression. "I think that's Kaspian's primary concern. And if I'm honest, it's mine, too."

"I can control my power," I told him, frowning. "I've done it for thousands of years."

"But your abilities far surpass everything known to this reality, Goddess," he whispered, his thumb tracing a line up my throat. "Control or not, your abilities are intimidating to those who don't understand them."

"That's because the beings of your world won't give me a chance to speak. They just want to shoot me."

"I know," he replied softly. "And that's what scares me most of all, Nyx. I know what it feels like to almost lose you now, and I am terrified of feeling that way again."

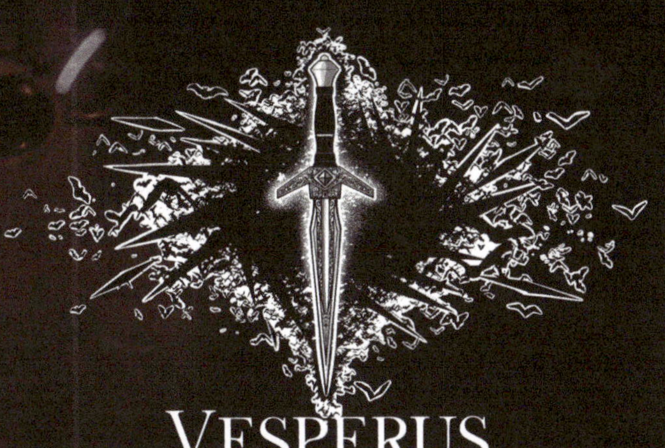

VESPERUS

It was a confession that came from my soul.

I'd felt her die. It'd taken a piece of me with her, making me realize just how linked our spirits were in this life. Even without the full impact of our bond in place.

And now… now we were fully mated.

Losing her would destroy me on a level that nothing else could. Which meant that for the first time in my existence, I had a true weakness.

Fortunately, she was a goddess and capable of taking care of herself.

Unfortunately, she was the target of the world leaders at present.

"Most of them have demanded your removal, whether by death or by sending you back to your realm," I told her. "If those are my only two options, I choose your realm. Only, I would need to go with you."

She studied me intently. "You would go with me?"

I nodded, having already made this decision. "Our souls are linked, for better or for worse, Nyx."

"What about your House? Your throne? Your life here?"

I stared down at her, my heart in my throat. "A good leader knows when to sacrifice himself for his people."

She blinked at me, the respect in her gaze telling me she understood what I meant.

"If this world won't let me have you, then we need to find one that will." It was our only choice. "If you leave, it will feel like you've died. And we've already established what that'll do to me. Hell, we're seeing it in Fallon's actions."

I grimaced thinking about the witch who was shattered over Klas's death. While I didn't condone her actions, I understood them to an extent.

Because for a few brief moments, I'd experienced that soul-crushing reaction to losing a mate. And she'd been enduring that for over a week.

That didn't excuse her behavior or her choices, but on some level, it explained the insanity of her choices.

"And even if I somehow survived you leaving, what kind of leader would I be?" I asked Nyx. "Being king means protecting my House, honoring my people, and keeping them safe. I can't do that if I'm broken."

It was precisely why I'd meant to avoid fully bonding Nyx. However, fate had made other plans for us. Plans that I'd accepted because there was nothing I could do to change them.

Plans I wasn't sure I would change, even if I could.

"I also can't protect my House if my increased powers create strife with the other leaders. My people will end up fighting battles for me, not the other way around, and I won't accept that fate for them or for myself. I won't put them at risk just to remain on my throne." It defeated the whole purpose of being a king.

Nyx pressed her palm to my breastbone, right over my heart. "You are a good leader, Vesperus Veritas. You're strong and wise, and I would be honored to be your queen. But I also accept that reigning in this reality might not be possible."

My lips curled a little. "Honored to be my queen, hmm? Even though I haven't officially asked?"

"You can't ask a goddess to reign, King. She does so naturally." Her words possessed a teasing lilt to them, but I caught the seriousness in her gaze.

This was a female who would never bow.

Not even to a king.

But she might kneel for me, if properly enticed.

I wrapped my arm around her lower back, my opposite palm still holding her nape. "What else do you *naturally* do, Goddess?" I asked, my lips a hairsbreadth from hers.

Her nails dug into my skin a little, her other hand going to my hip. "I do a lot of things naturally," she murmured, each word brushing my mouth. "I moan. I lick. I *suck*."

"Mmm." I gave in to the urge to taste her bottom lip before kissing a path to her ear. "But do you swallow?"

"Only when I like the taste," she whispered, her mouth finding my jaw. "And I just so happen to enjoy yours." Her teeth sank into my throat, her mouth working as she pulled my essence into her and *swallowed.*

That wasn't what I'd meant, something she absolutely knew, but I allowed it anyway. Because fuck, that felt good, feeling her mouth on me, her tongue teasing the wound to keep from closing as her endorphins shocked my bloodstream.

"Fuck, Nyx," I breathed, pressing my cock against her flat stomach.

I'd been bitten by vampires before, but none of them had felt like this. Her bite was an aphrodisiac to my senses, making me so damn hard that I almost felt ready to come.

But she gripped my base to stop the building sensation, her thumb tracing along the underside of my shaft before eventually reaching the tip.

Her mouth left my neck, her tongue tracing a path back to my lips.

And then she kissed me.

Not the other way around.

No, this was about a Goddess bringing a king to heel, which was the opposite of what I'd intended, and yet I was utterly lost to her mouth. Her touch. Her fucking divine essence.

My grasp on her nape tightened, my arm cementing around her as I returned her kiss with worshipping strokes of my tongue.

My Goddess. Mine.

Her nails in my chest told me she was saying something similar. *My King. Mine.*

"The moon is rising," she whispered, energy kissing her skin and mine. "Do you feel it?"

"Yes." I grazed her lower lip with my fangs. "I taste it, too." I bit her, needing her blood, and groaned when she squeezed my cock again.

"No. It's my turn to taste you, King." She started walking me backward, her golden irises reminding me of twin full moons. Glittering. Enticing. *All-consuming.*

I let her lead me, hypnotized by her hungry expression.

This female was my equal in every way. Maybe even my superior.

I'd been meant to hunt her. To tame her. To make her *obey*. But she had proved herself to be a predator, not prey.

And right now, I was her chosen meal.

I sat on the ledge as I reached it, reading the desire from her eyes, words no longer needed.

However, that didn't stop me from saying, "You'd better do more than taste me, Goddess. I want you to make me feel the stars."

"So demanding for a king," she mused, her hands on my thighs as she stepped between them to kiss me again.

This time it was softer, more of a tease than a proper embrace.

"That's what kings do naturally, Goddess. We demand. And everyone else bows."

"Except me," she whispered.

"Except you," I agreed.

She smiled against my mouth, then kissed my jaw and started licking a path down my body.

She didn't move quickly. She explored instead, her lips going to my pecs before venturing up to my shoulder and down my arm.

Her tongue traced my House tattoo, her eyes studying the golden sword dipped in blood.

She paused at the crown etched into the handle, then followed the chain link and blood drops to my palm.

Where she nibbled my flesh before taking one of my fingers into her mouth.

And sucking.

"Such a seductive moon nymph," I said, my hands grasping the edge of the pool beneath me and nearly cracking the marble tile in my grip.

"Goddess," she corrected.

"My fated queen," I countered.

Her irises glittered with approval as she kissed her way back up my arm and to my pec again. Only this time, she continued her path downward to the fine line of hair along my lower abdomen.

I released the edge of the pool to thread my fingers through her silky, wet hair. Her golden eyes flicked up to mine, a taunting smile in their depths as she moved lower. "I'm going to really lick you now," she said against the head of my cock.

My blood heated as she followed through on that promise, her velvety tongue driving me to madness with a single stroke. "You're killing me, Goddess."

"And yet, I've only just begun." Her lips whispered across my skin, memorizing my length and teasing my instincts.

I wanted to take charge, tell her how to please me, make her *swallow.*

But I didn't want to end this game too soon.

She wanted to master me, and I wanted to let her try. *Try and succeed,* I marveled, groaning as she finally wrapped her mouth around me. *So wet and perfect.* Just the right amount of suction.

And those eyes. *Fuck me, those eyes…*

She hadn't stopped watching me, her irises flaring with power.

This gorgeous creature was kneeling for me in her own way while ensuring I understood that we were still equals.

This was a gift.

And a stamina test she seemed hell-bent on passing. Something she proved by taking me deeper until I nudged the back of her throat.

"This visual of you is going to grace my dreams for eternity," I told her, my throat dry and making my voice rasp at the end.

She hummed in approval, her irises flashing.

Liquid gold.

Full lips.

Fucking amazing tongue.

Goddess, I'm going to lose my mind, I whispered to her mentally, fully embracing my downfall. *Keep doing that. Yes. Just like that.*

Her palms slid up my inner thighs, scattering goose bumps along my skin.

I cursed as she took me deep again, her tongue massaging the underside of my shaft and making my vision blacken in response.

Only to see her again, that sensuous smile in her eyes tempting me closer to the edge. "Take a breath, Goddess," I told her, my muscles straining. "Because I'm... about to *drown* you."

She shivered, her anticipation making my lower abdomen clench. My grip in her hair tightened, my body strung tight as I fought to indulge in a few more seconds of her glorious mouth.

But her tongue swept over my slit, her gaze demanding that I come.

"*Nyx.*" Her name left me on a hiss of sound as ripples of ecstasy trembled down my limbs, tightened my muscles, and forced me to explode in her mouth.

She swallowed around my head, drawing out the moment and stirring a quake along my spine. I held her gaze the whole time, let her see every damn thing she was doing to me, while she drank my pleasure down with greedy pulls of her mouth.

My climax felt unending, ecstasy warming every bit of my being.

But she didn't stop, determined to master me.

So I let her.

I gave in and let her win this round. Fuck, she'd destroyed me in the most glorious of ways. And I told her that with a few choice words to her mind.

By the time she finished, she was positively glowing. "Impressed?" she asked, waggling her brows.

"So much so that I might be in love," I admitted, using my hand in her hair to pull her up to me. "How did I taste?"

"Like ambrosia," she whispered against my mouth, her tongue dipping inside to give me a taste. "I think I'll lick you every day, King Veritas."

"Only if I'm allowed to return the favor, Goddess Nyx," I replied, grabbing her hips.

She squealed as I used my vampiric speed to shift our positions, laying her out on the side of the pool and spreading her thighs. But I didn't go straight for the heart of her. I went for her breasts first and sucked the stardust off her rosy nipples.

Her legs clamped around me in approval, her fingers in my hair as she guided my movements.

Nyx was the kind of woman to tell me what she wanted without words. But the direction wasn't needed. I already knew. And I proved that by anticipating each of her tugs and pulls, until finally I ventured downward to worship her properly.

Her nails bit into my scalp, urging me onward as she moaned my name.

How many times do you think I can make you come, Goddess? I asked. *I promised you would beg me to stop...* Which she'd technically done last night. But why not repeat the performance?

At least three, she replied, her voice warm and sensual and—

I paused, my mouth hovering over her clit as I lifted my gaze to hers. *I heard that in my mind.*

She blinked down at me. *You did?*

I did.

Her eyes widened. *Oh.*

My lips curled against her. *Oh, indeed.* Because that would make this so much more fun. Something I proceeded to prove by licking her deep and growling at the approval radiating from her mind. It was as though we'd created a new link, one that allowed us to *hear* each other, not just speak.

I tested the limits of it with my tongue and teeth, driving her to new heights before inserting two of my fingers into her slick channel.

She groaned, her hips bucking up against me, my name a chant in her thoughts.

She pulsed against me, her orgasm close and almost immediate. I licked her through it, loving the way she clenched tightly around me.

But she'd said three.

Which made me want to go for at least four.

Vesperus, she hissed, her legs trembling around me.

I skimmed my fang along her clit, easily taking her into a second explosion that had her screaming for the heavens to hear.

And giving me an idea on how to truly blow her mind.

Do you trust me, Nyx? I asked, purposely nibbling her sensitive nub.

She panted, her fingers fisting my hair even more tightly. *Yes.*

I could feel the truth of that in my blood, her body vibrating beneath my touch. She knew what I intended to do, and she was anticipating it.

I understand why fate tied us together, Goddess, I whispered to her. *We were fucking made for each other.*

She responded with an unintelligible noise that ended in a scream as I bit her. Right there. On the most sensitive part of her flesh.

And instantly sent her spiraling into a third climax.

The taste of her arousal mixed with her blood had me groaning, my inner predator reveling in her rewarding flavor.

It quickly became my new favorite drink, my tongue lapping at her, my fangs penetrating her, my fingers twisting inside her.

Her oblivion became my euphoria.

Until both of us were panting from our efforts, her cheeks flushed a beautiful shade of pink that spread all the way to her breasts, giving her a rose-gold color that had me wanting to fuck her all over again.

But that wasn't what this was about.

This was about our connection. Our bond. Our *future.*

So I pulled her off the ledge and into my arms, swimming with her until we were both in the center of the pool, and watched the moon climb in the sky.

It was red tonight.

A blood moon.

Which was strange. I hadn't known one was projected for tonight.

It's a blessing, Nyx whispered back to me. *The moon approves of our union.*

She nuzzled my throat as I considered the meaning of that. *Is this causing any mystical issues anywhere else in the world?*

She shook her head. *It's a projection, one I think only we can see. But it means change is on the horizon. And it's likely a message from Khaos as well.*

Khaos, I repeated. *Your creator.*

Yes. I suppose he's like my father. She smiled against me. *The red moon is his way of saying he approves, too.*

Her origin world was filled with wonder, creating a whole new universe for me to explore. A whole new life to potentially live.

It meant we had options.

Because if my world wouldn't accept her, it seemed her world would accept me. *Us.*

We'll handle this issue with Fallon, I thought both to her and to myself. *Then we'll proceed from there.*

I didn't want to leave my home or my people. But I also recognized that I'd served them for a very long time. I'd protected them. I'd groomed them. And I'd prepared them for a life without me in it.

That was what a good king did—he ensured his people were ready for the inevitable. Because while my kind could live forever, my position was one that possessed inherent risks, such as untimely death.

I'd survived a lot over my very long life.

If Nyx ended up being the catalyst for me losing my throne, I would accept that.

Because I accepted her.

My mate.

My future.

In a universe with a myriad of options and opportunities.

We can still try to convince them to let us stay, Nyx whispered. *I don't want to take you away from your people.*

I kissed her temple, holding her close. *As I already said, Goddess, a good leader knows when it's time to sacrifice himself for his people. And I can feel that time approaching. They need someone stable. Someone who can pick up my mantle and continue the journey forward.*

Someone like Kaspian, she replied.

Someone like Kaspian, I echoed. *He's already leading them. Maybe it's time he takes over my crown.*

Then I would become a retired king.

Destined to see the universe I'd never known existed.

With this beautiful goddess by my side.

That sounded like an appealing future to me.

But we would see if fate agreed.

NYX

Magic hummed across my arms, startling me from my sleep. It reminded me of the morning I'd met Vesperus, only this felt more urgent.

It scattered goose bumps along my arms and lifted the hair on the back of my neck. "Vesperus," I whispered, my hand on his shoulder. For once, he was actually in bed beside me, his eyes closed in a dream I couldn't seem to shake him from.

"Vesperus," I said, louder this time as my heart began to race.

Something was wrong.

He shouldn't be this hard to rouse from sleep.

And his skin was cool to the touch. "*Vesperus.*" I placed my palm on his chest. "Wake up."

Nothing.

No response.

Not even a change in breath.

It was like he was dead to the world.

And that enchantment continued to claw at me, prickling all my senses.

Deadly magic, I thought, shivering. *What is this web?* It reminded me of inky strands, crawling over my skin and leaving behind an unwanted residue.

I couldn't see it, just *felt* it. As well as my enchantment screaming at me to react. To do something. To *listen*.

It was humming madly in the air, battling the dark net of power creeping along my senses. I blinked, the world darkening. Then reappearing. Then darkening again.

What is this? I wondered, my limbs quivering uncontrollably.

Maybe...

Maybe I should...

I yawned, only to be zapped by the energy again, my eyes flying open again. "*What is this?*" I demanded, the stardust along my skin resembling ash instead of glitter. It was the same on Vesperus, his skin even cooler than before.

I forced myself off the bed, my legs shaking with the effort to stand. *I feel like death*, I marveled, shivering. *And Vesperus appears to be... No. He's breathing. But...*

He was turning gray.

Just like I did from the bullet, I thought, a tremble working its way down my spine. "What's causing this?" I slurred, my gaze finding the vibrating enchantment. It seemed to be at war with the darkness, and from what I could see... the darkness was winning.

Which meant I didn't have a lot of time before it overwhelmed me again.

I grabbed my clothes from last night—the ones Vesperus had brought back with us from the pool—and put them on. *Slowly. Far too slowly.*

Everything felt sluggish, like my body no longer had the energy it required to move. But I pushed through the thick haze of darkness, forcing my limbs to heed my demands, while my enchantment gradually dwindled in the distance.

What is this power that can so easily crush my creation?

Swallowing, I straightened my spine and reminded my legs how to function again.

The medallion magic swirled in a motion that seemed to say, *Hurry up!*

"I'm trying," I told it, my words measured and low. Because it took energy to speak. It took energy to walk, too.

I won't be able to phase like this, I thought, leaving the room. *I just need to find someone… anyone… who can help.*

My pace resembled a crawl as I moved down the hallway, my heart a slow beat in my chest. All the while, my magic danced around with hyper exclamation marks. It was either demanding that I move faster or cheering me on. I wasn't sure. But it was making me dizzy.

So tired.

So… so dark again.

Where's the light? Why is it so cold?

I shivered, my eyelashes parting in response and making me frown. *Did I just fall asleep on the stairs?*

Warmth hummed around me again, my enchantment's golden light edged with black. It was more sluggish than before, the sentient energy losing its flare.

Because of its battle with the darkness.

I tried to move faster, to pick up my pace, but the net felt so heavy. *Like trying to dig my way out of a grave,* I thought, my lungs barely functioning.

Black spots danced in my vision, the oxygen around me too thin.

But I refused to stop.

I refused to *sleep.*

The bottom floor finally appeared, but there wasn't a soul in sight. I tried to open my mouth, to call for someone. But I didn't have enough air.

Keep going, I told my legs.

Only they bent and sent me tumbling down the last few steps instead. Everything spun, my back and head aching from slamming against the ground.

Get up, I commanded myself. *Get up. Get up. Get up.*

The magic seemed to be saying the same, its dull light flashing, begging me not to let this be my end. Yet I could feel... *dirt...* weighing me down. *So heavy.*

What is happening to me?

I swallowed, the taste of earth in my mouth.

This can't be right.

Am I...?

I coughed, the sound foreign and unexpected and filled with... with...

I touched my lips, my fingers coming away with *ash.*

None of this made any sense. It was like a nightmare more than a reality. *Am I dreaming?*

I closed my eyes again, only to reopen them to darkness. All around me. The scent of fresh earth infiltrated my nose. And a flicker of energy blinked above me.

My dying magic. I lifted my hand to touch it, my ash-colored skin an alarming quality in the night. I was too pale. Like a dying moon.

Impossible.

I closed my eyes again, waking up in the palace once more. It was like I was in two places at once.

My head spun, my mouth dry. It took physical effort to look out the window and find the night sky.

Heal me, I begged. *Give me the strength to fix this.*

The moon was not in an optimal position, the sky dark but not dark enough.

I swallowed again, my hand stretching toward the window as a trickle of energy slithered through the air toward me. Just enough stardust for me to ignite my phasing ability.

Outside, I thought. *Take me outside.*

I pictured the park behind the estate.

But that wasn't what appeared around me.

A cemetery, I recognized almost immediately, the scents similar to the one in my dream. Or my reality. Or whatever that moment had been.

I ignored it all in favor of the moon, the hint of it still in the lingering night sky.

I inhaled, taking in as much energy as it could provide, and allowed it to chase the ice away from my limbs.

Except that weighted magic seemed to absorb it all in my next breath, that incessant energy sticking to my skin in invisible strands.

I growled, irritated by whatever enchantment had been woven over me. Over *us*. It was thick in the air, seeming to spread all over the city. But the source of its web was nearby.

I could taste the lethal magic.

My medallion appeared in its faded form, the trickle of remaining vitality waving in the distance. Floating. Pulsating. Spasming.

Above a grave.

I clawed at the earth as I forced myself onto my knees, my world rocking back and forth with the movement.

The moon tried to bolster me, the stardust fluttering around my being in useless golden waves. It could no longer break through the inky darkness that had covered my being.

Ice prickled my arms, digging into my flesh and infiltrating my blood.

But I kept crawling, forcing myself to see beyond the pain, to reach my medallion.

Worst case, I can jump realms, I thought. *But then… then I might not be able to come back.*

And what about Vesperus?

I couldn't leave him here. Not like this. Not knowing what it would do to him.

I don't… I don't want to leave him either.

He's mine.

I'm his.

Our souls are forever bound.

So, no. Jumping realms wasn't a worst-case scenario. It was an impossible one.

But maybe my medallion would give me the boost I needed to survive this, to *break* this. It was part of me. A sentient creation that just might be able to breach this thick, ash-like web.

The stardust continued to build around me as it tried to

penetrate the invisible magic suffocating my being. I couldn't actually see it, but I knew it was black.

Weighted down by death.

I pushed, and crawled, and pushed some more, and finally reached my withering medallion, the magic having reformed into its intended form. Only it was charred and decaying, the life dying with my corporeal form.

Maybe even my soul.

I could feel the frigid kiss of the afterlife beckoning me forward, seducing me with thoughts of giving in.

So strong. So enticing. So... so... wrong.

I shoved the yearning away, my focus on the solid metal in my hand. *My medallion.* It quivered against my fingers, stirring tears in my eyes.

I've failed you, I thought, holding it close. *But I'll bring you back. I promise.*

There was no other choice. I couldn't use it to jump realms. Not like this. Not when I didn't know if I could return. *I can't leave Vesperus. He's my other half. My soul.*

How has everything changed so quickly? I marveled, my gaze on the familiar token in my hand. *You knew, didn't you? You knew my heart existed in this realm, so you ensured I found him. And now...*

Now I had to reward it by killing the flicker of energy it had left.

By absorbing it back into me.

To fight... to fight what, exactly? This spell?

Would my medallion even be enough?

There was only one way to find out. *I'm sorry, old friend. You've been an... intriguing addition to my life. I... I wish there was another way.*

It trembled against my palm in response and dissolved into ash, just like it had on the beach months ago. Not by my own doing, but by its own choice.

Fleeing. Hiding. Confusing me all over again.

I don't... I trailed off as the energy sizzled along the ground below.

Fresh earth. The scent of it almost knocked me over, the sensory memory *strong.*

Dirt taunted my tongue again, my eyes darkening as I shifted positions… to beneath the surface.

I blinked and I was above ground again, my medallion's final strands of magic disappearing into the night.

My heart kick-started in my chest, my throat dry from the realization that it was gone. Dead. Having been killed by this intoxicating plague of madness.

All to show me… what rested beneath this freshly dug grave.

I didn't consider the hows or the whys; I simply started to dig. Because that had clearly been the sentient energy's dying wish—for me to unearth whatever existed below the ground.

Maybe this is all a dream, I marveled. But the dirt under my nails felt real. As did the cold noose around my neck. The ice coating my arms and legs. The stardust desperately trying to break through whatever inky veil threatened to destroy me.

I ignored it all, determined to dig up whatever secret lay waiting for me below.

Too much dirt. There's too much dirt!

I groaned in annoyance, needing a solution that wasn't just my hands. But the energy…

No. No failing now.

I was a goddess. A being of the night. And the dark sky was still mine. This *moon* belonged to me.

Closing my eyes, I fought for purpose, for something to hold on to, for some way to temporarily rid myself of this dreaded plague.

I need a closer moon.

It was the only way.

A slight tug.

But even that would alter the world, change the tides, and hurt innocents.

So I'll take something else, I thought, feeling out the stars and determining what could provide me with the strength to carry on. To accomplish my goal. To *defeat* this insanity.

I sat back on my haunches, my face tilted upward. *Help me,* I demanded. *Give me your darkness and help me break this curse.*

The stars twinkled in response. The moon glittering a little brighter. And a torrent of dust began to fall.

Covering me.

Covering the ground.

Covering everything in sight.

And still that invisible layer existed.

More stardust came, reminding me of snow, only gold instead of white. It pulsed with energy, demanding to be used, absorbed, *accepted.*

"Infect the soil," I told it through my teeth. "Unearth whatever it is that waits beneath the surface."

I shivered as the stars heeded my request, their power overwhelmingly beautiful and decidedly potent. Their glittering beads formed a violent blade, slicing through the dark magic to strike the earth below.

I rolled off the grave, giving it freedom to work.

The energy vibrated and pulsed, the stars battling the spell and demanding that the deadly shield *yield.* It was a devastating war, one I suspected could be felt all over the world as the night came to my aid, trying to fight through whatever dark web had tried to ensnare its queen.

But the ice continued to drizzle through my veins, freezing my limbs and making moving difficult.

I could barely even blink.

However, the ground was moving… the stars unearthing the mystery below the surface… and revealing what my medallion had been trying to show me.

It wasn't the other half of my soul, or even another part of myself. It was simply a woman with dirt-covered hair, ghostly white skin, and emerald eyes that no longer blazed or saw anything on this earth.

I recognized her face because of the pain etched into her still features.

My magic had been trying to lead me to…

Fallon Doyle.

NYX

I stared at the female beside me as the stardust floated back into the sky, my wish having been granted. But I didn't understand it. *How is she here? Why is she here?*

She wasn't truly dead. I could sense her lingering spirit. Which meant that she'd been put here, perhaps recently.

And buried several feet under the ground.

So that every time her immortality brought her back… she'd die again.

But for how long? And why?

I kept watching her, my body no longer able to move because of the lethal spell—the one turning me into a corpse.

I idly wondered if Fallon was impacted by it as well, when life returned to her irises, causing her to shudder madly as she began clawing at the air. In the next moment, she started hacking and vomiting up dirt, the sounds churning my stomach.

Yet I still couldn't move, or even react beyond shifting my eyes. Tracking her. Observing her. Wondering what she would do when she realized I was here.

She seemed to freeze then, perhaps sensing my gaze on her.

However, rather than look at me, she bowed her head to the ground and whispered, "I-I'm sorry. Please… please don't…"

She trembled, her words a rasp of air that I barely heard. But she sounded so broken and alone, her soul a tattered mess that I could sense more than see.

It took several moments of eerie silence before she moved again, her head barely tilting one way and then the other, her expression hidden from my vantage point. "Klas?" she whispered.

I frowned. *Is she calling for her dead mate?*

I couldn't respond, my lips frozen shut.

"Klas?" she repeated. "Are you…?" She braced as though anticipating a strike. But when no one responded, she sat up a little to glance around. And gasped upon seeing me behind her.

She scrambled to her feet and took several steps backward, her hand at her mouth. Then she looked at the ground and all around the cemetery.

"Oh, no…" She started shaking her head, tears piercing her green eyes.

Remorse over casting this spell? Or something else? I wondered.

Then it occurred to me that I might actually be able to *ask* her. *Because of Vesperus.*

Can you hear me? I asked her, curious as to whether or not that power was now mine to use.

She didn't respond, just continued to stare at me.

Maybe I'm doing it wrong. I tried to focus on her mind, on *her*, and asked again if she could hear me.

But she didn't react.

Vesperus? I tried, wondering if perhaps I could speak to him in this coma-like state.

Silence.

I longed to frown but couldn't. So instead I blinked, hoping the female would understand that I wasn't yet dead.

She gaped at me. "What are you?" she asked, searching my body for clues. "No, wait. I *know* you. From… from the street…" Her lips parted. "Klas shot you."

Klas? I repeated. *Your dead mate?*

"How are you...?" Her brow furrowed as she glanced over me. "How are you alive?"

Because I'm hard to kill, I wanted to tell her. *Although, your magic is doing one hell of a job holding me down.*

Or I assumed it was her magic, anyway.

I could see the power in her gaze as well as taste the darkness in her energy, and that fractured aura around her made me question her sanity.

She swallowed, her focus shifting to the cemetery and the trees beyond. "Gods, he did it, didn't he?" Her words were a whisper, her hands curling into fists at her sides as she shook her head sadly. "He finally did it."

Finally did what? I wanted to ask her. *And are we still talking about Klas?*

She fidgeted with a bracelet on her wrist, her gaze distant. "I tried to stop him. But... but I couldn't. He's... he's my mate." She shook her head, then frowned down at her hand. "My charm..."

Her attention went to the grave, her panic palpable as she ran back to her burial site and started digging frantically through the dirt.

"Where is it? Where are you?" She sounded manic. "Where are you?!" She was frantic now, her eyes overrun with tears as she started repeating, "No, no, no. Tell me he didn't take you. Tell me he didn't find you."

What are you looking for? I demanded, not understanding this woman's behavior.

She froze, her gaze slowly returning to me. "Did you just say something?"

Not aloud, I thought.

Her eyes widened. "How are you doing that?"

You can hear me? I countered.

"Of course I can hear you. You're in my mind." She palmed the sides of her head and began to shake. "I'm going crazy. He's finally done it. He's finally broken me entirely."

Who? I asked, rather than saying that she'd clearly passed crazy a few minutes ago.

"Klas," she hissed. "My fated mate."

She started pacing, her hands still on her head.

He's dead.

She snorted. "No. He's really not." She grimaced, then glanced at her grave again. "And he took my charm."

Your charm?

She nodded. "It gave me peace." She frowned. "It led me to you the other day, too. Whenever that was. Before… before Klas…" She swallowed, looking at me. "How did you survive that spell? It was intense decay magic." Her brow crumpled. "And how are you awake now?"

The night, I said, glancing at the still dark sky. *It's giving me what little it can… to keep me this way. But your spell is—*

"My spell?" Her eyes widened. "Oh, no. I didn't do this. I mean. I did. But… but I didn't."

I stared at her. *You did but you didn't?*

"Yes. It's my power, but… but I'm not the one using it." She glanced around, her voice lowering as she whispered, "He is."

He, as in Klas? I guessed, not fully following her logic.

"Yes," she repeated. "He drinks my blood and… and uses my magic." She sounded ashamed, her shoulders slumping as she curled her arms around herself. "I shouldn't have told you that."

What is your magic? I asked, ignoring that last part. *How are you… I mean, how is* he *using it to do this?*

"It's a form of necromancy." Her tone was low again, like she was afraid someone might overhear us. "Death magic."

Oh. That… that eerily made sense. It explained the sensations I was feeling, as well as how I'd nearly died.

Her gift was literally the opposite of mine—I created life. She controlled death.

And your mate has been using this gift, I said, thinking through what she'd told me. *With what purpose in mind?* He was one of Vesperus's mercenaries, right? Why would he use these powers to hurt Gold and Garnet?

"He wants to destroy—"

The ground began to shake around us, cutting off her explanation and sending her to her knees.

"Oh, no," she whispered. "He's initiating the next phase."

The next phase of what?

"Raising the dead," she said.

I frowned, but as the earth continued to move, I realized what she meant—the bodies in this cemetery. *Why?*

"To kill them all," she said, her eyes wide. "I should go."

No, I snapped, making her freeze. *You should help me so I can stop him.*

She stared at me. "I can't do that. If I counter the spell, he'll feel it."

So you're okay with everything he's doing? I asked, genuinely curious.

"N-no," she stammered. "But... but he's my mate."

I'm not following your logic.

"I can't... I can't tell him no. He's... he's my other half." She winced at the words, her eyes blazing with a fire that contradicted her words. "I have to help him." Her movements were stiff as she started to turn, almost as though part of her wanted to stay while the other half forced her to go.

Wait, I called. *Tell me about your charm. Tell me how it gave you peace.*

Because something she'd said about it leading her to me told me that charm hadn't been an ordinary piece of metal.

And the way she halted, like she was battling some sort of need to move versus stay, suggested that there was something else going on here. *Something that has to do with her fractured aura,* I realized, the words ones I kept to myself. Or I assumed I did, anyway. Because she didn't react to them.

Instead, she touched her wrist again. "It gave me peace," she whispered, her back to me. "I... I need to find it." She went back to her grave, searching for the token I knew she wouldn't be able to dig up. Because it was gone. And its last request had been for me to find her.

For whatever reason, my medallion had linked our fates. Perhaps because it had wanted me to fix her broken spirit. Or maybe it had seen something here that I couldn't.

Regardless, we were in this moment together now.

And I needed her to release me from this curse before the dead army around us rose.

Which seemed to be intermittent because the ground had stopped trembling, telling me whatever spell Klas had cast was settling into the graves around us.

Assuming it's him and not her, I thought. But no. I... I believed her. There was just something about the way she'd spoken and her demeanor that told me it was all true.

Another inherited gift from Vesperus, perhaps? I wondered, searching my link to him. He was still silent. But my soul could sense him, which brought me peace.

However, I suspected that peace would not last for long.

"Where is it?" Fallon demanded, her actions manic once more. "I need you. Please. You're the only thing that helps. I... I think clearly... with... with you..." She started to growl, her fury a palpable wave that struck my senses and had me widening my eyes.

Then she turned on me and hit me with a blast of power that had me gasping as the invisible net lifted from my spirit, freeing me from its deadly hold.

She stumbled back several paces and tripped into her grave. "Oh, no," she breathed. "Oh, no. Oh, no. Oh, no. Sh-shouldn't have done that," she told herself. "He'll be mad. We ... I... I support... I... Mated. We're mated. Mates support one another. Mates cherish one another. Mates *help* one another. Yes..."

Her voice had shifted from a scared tone to a chant of some kind, the words uttered aloud not sounding like her own.

But a spell, I realized.

She started to rise from her grave, her power licking over my being and filling me with a sense of dread.

I did not want to fight this woman. She had clearly been beaten down by her mate, and potentially even bespelled by him.

Or someone else, I thought as my body eagerly absorbed all the lingering stardust in the air.

"We must help him," she said, her voice still sounding distant and not her own. "That is my duty. That is my place. That is who I am in this world—Klas's mate."

Definitely a spell, I decided. *One I'm going to need a lot of power to break.*

Because I needed this witch on my side, not against me.

I could battle her deathly magic and try to take her down, but renewing her life would be a far easier task. Because I was one of creation. And mending a soul was well within my power to do.

The stardust pooled in my palm, preparing for my command, as her lips began to move in an ancient chant filled with dark tendrils of power.

"You don't want to hurt me," I told her softly. "This isn't you." Which I knew because I'd seen the real her in that fiery gaze, and in the blast of power that had released me from my ropes.

"This is my duty. This is my place. This is who I am in this world as Klas's mate," she said, uttering a different variation of her earlier chant.

"There is so much more in life than being someone's mate," I promised her. "It's a mate's duty to be a partner, not to bury you in the ground and abuse your powers. Your place isn't with him, Fallon Doyle. Your place is with *you*."

I blew the stardust in her direction, my wish for her to be whole, to be her own woman, to be *healed*, warming the golden crystals and showering her with renewed life.

She didn't react at first, her eyes rounding in confusion.

And then she screamed as a pulse of energy rippled out from her to the earth below.

It knocked me off my feet, but I phased to the other side of her, observing as her fragmented soul began to piece itself back together.

She fell to the ground, her knees coming to her chest as she shook violently in response to my power. I could almost see the spell breaking, whatever leash had been wrapped around her slithering away to die.

And leaving behind a furious female in its wake.

"Hello, Fallon," I said as I slowly walked around the witch to meet her burning gaze. "My name is Nyx. I believe we have some magic in common." I looked at her wrist. "Or we did until your mate killed it."

She stared up at me, her anger vibrating across her features. "He used an obedience spell on me," she bit out. "One that forced me to *worship* him."

Now *that* made a lot more sense to me. "Does that mean you'll help me stop him now?"

She growled. "I'll do you one better."

I arched a brow, waiting.

"I'll help you kill the bastard." She pushed herself off the ground, her limbs a little shaky, but that could have been from her residual rage.

"Where is he now?" I asked.

She shook her head. "Somewhere in the village. But I know how to draw him out."

I absorbed more of my stardust, needing it to bolster my spirit, and tried to push it to Vesperus through our bond. "I'm listening," I told her. "What do you suggest?"

"I suggest that I do this." She held her palms over the ground and blasted it with a wave of power that had me phasing again to keep from falling.

Then she screamed as she shattered the spell lingering in the air, releasing everything from death's touch all at once.

I could feel it leaving like a foreboding fog drifting into the distance, the power dissipating almost immediately.

She sent another blast into the ground, one I assumed was meant to stop whatever he'd been trying to do in the cemetery.

And then she looked at me. "Now we wait."

"For what?" I wondered.

"For him to come to us."

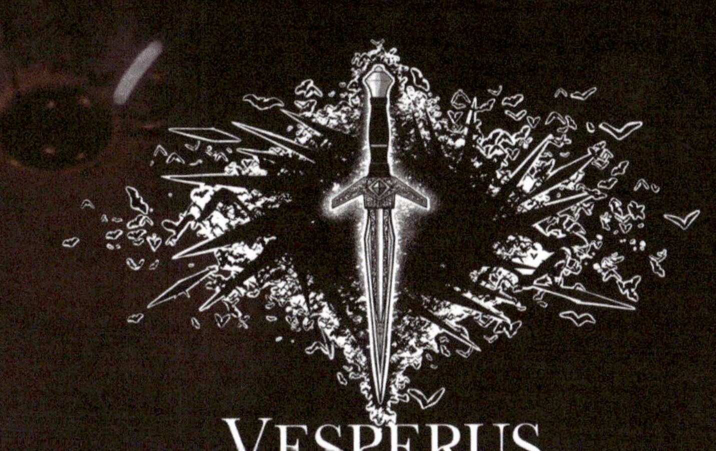

VESPERUS

"I told you not to underestimate her," a voice hissed nearby, luring me to awareness. "She's not of this earth."

"That's why we have our plan B," a male replied. "I learned long ago never to rely on a woman, let alone a *mate*." The venom in that word seemed to chill the air.

Except no, that wasn't what had caused the chill. It was something else. Something I felt deep in my bones, to my very soul. *Ice. Cold. Death.*

It reminded me of my first craving. While I'd been born a vampire, I hadn't been immortal until my mid to late twenties. Which had been when the bloodlust had hit me for the first time.

The world had been a very different place then.

And I'd killed without remorse, aware that blood was all I needed to survive.

But it had left me feeling so cold afterward, the tastes of their deaths a lingering flavor on my tongue. Similar to now, only this hadn't been caused by a bloodlust episode or a feeding frenzy. This lethal sensation was the result of a spell.

Nyx? I whispered, searching for her mind as I listened to the intruders in my room.

They were approaching my bed.

My limbs were too numb for me to react, my mind the only part of me that seemed to be alert. *Nyx?* I tried again.

Vesperus, she breathed. *You're awake.*

Not quite, I replied. *I'm… well, I'm not quite sure what I am.*

It's a necromancy spell, she told me. *Fallon has death magic. And her mate—Klas—imbibed it from her blood.*

Klas? I repeated.

"Hurry up," one of the voices said, my mind searching for the name of that familiar tone. "He's going to wake up soon."

"Fallon just broke the spell," the other one muttered. "We have time. Trust me."

I hadn't spoken to Klas enough to know if that was him or not. But… *Klas is dead.*

No, he's not. I haven't gotten that far with Fallon yet, but I am guessing he used her magic to fake his death. The truth of Nyx's words settled in my mind.

How do you know this? Where are you?

In a cemetery, she replied. *I woke up because of my medallion. But it's… it's gone now.*

Gone?

I'll explain later, she said in a hurry. *I need you. We're setting a trap for Klas.*

I don't think he's coming, I said as something pricked my arm. *He's… he's… here.*

What?

In… fuck, that burns. My entire body went up in flames, but I was imprisoned inside my mind, unable to react. *Fuck!*

Vesperus? Nyx asked. *Vesperus?!*

He's… here… Nyx. Rooms. Fuck, I felt… I felt… I swallowed. Or I tried to, anyway. Everything… everything was dark.

And silent.

Mysteriously so.

Too quiet.

Nyx…?

No reply.

Because there was no sound.

There was… nothing at all.

NYX

Vesperus! I shouted, my heart hammering in my chest.

No, no, no. Something is very wrong.

I could feel it creeping up my veins, searing my insides with *heat.* Scorching my soul. Setting me on fire from within. *Destroying* the magic inside my heart.

My Vesperus.

My mate.

"We need to go," I said to Fallon.

"No, we need to wait," she replied. "Trust me. He's coming here."

I shook my head. "No, he's not. He's with Vesperus. He's… he's done something to him." I palmed my chest as I felt the ache expanding. "We have to go to him."

"What?"

"We have to go to Vesperus," I told her, my voice a rasp of sound as my energy began to rapidly deplete. "N-now." I tried to phase, only to land maybe ten feet away.

Every part of me ached, our bond ripping apart... shredding me... *killing me.*

No, *killing him.*

Oh, stars... I found the moon in the sky, noting its twinkling departure. *Not now. Don't leave me now.*

I needed its strength. I needed the night. I needed *Vesperus.*

I gathered all my energy, every ounce I possessed, and demanded that my spirit phase to a part of the world with a high moon.

But a sprinkling of stardust was all I could produce.

This is bad. Very bad.

A hand grabbed my shoulder, pulling me up off the ground. I hadn't even realized I'd fallen, my legs weak. "What do you feel?" Fallon demanded.

"*Death,*" I told her, shivering. "But it's... it's hot. Like the bullet..."

She nodded. "He must have shot Vesperus before he could recover from the sleeping spell."

"Sleeping spell?" I repeated, my teeth chattering.

"Yes. That's what the spell he cast over the city does—it puts everyone in a deadly sleep. One they won't wake up from unless released. And only if released in time for them to recover." She looked at me. "That's the spell I broke on you and over the city just now."

This side of Fallon was very different from the one I'd unearthed. She was much more sure of herself now.

And she was staring at me with a grim expression.

"If he shot Vesperus..."

"Don't finish that," I said, my jaw clenching with the words. "We need... we need to go... to him." *And I need my moon,* I thought, staring at the night sky. I tried to phase again, but nothing happened, my soul denying my ability to properly move.

But Fallon helped me proceed forward, maneuvering us out of the cemetery and onto a nearby street.

I had no idea where we were, how far away we were, if we were still in Reykjavik, or if she was even directing me toward the palace.

However, I felt in my soul that I could trust her to help. It was an instinct, one I recognized as belonging to Vesperus more than me.

He reads people, I realized. *He read me.*

It was why he'd trusted me from the moment we'd met. Why he hadn't truly fought our connection.

Perhaps our rejection hadn't worked because neither of us had meant it. The snapping we'd felt had been a superficial break, one our minds had accepted, but not our souls.

Because I'm not a being of this world, I thought. *I'm something else. Something none of these supernaturals have ever seen.*

I'd played by their rules—mostly—and had been polite, harnessing my power and demonstrating my control without any of them truly realizing it.

But maybe it was time to just be me. And fuck the consequences.

Vesperus is worth it, I thought. *He's mine.* A simple declaration, one born of my soul. We were supposed to have eternity to figure this out, not mere weeks.

My medallion hadn't forced me to remain here for nothing. It had wanted me to save Fallon Doyle. And it had wanted me to find Vesperus Veritas.

"You're starting to glow," Fallon whispered.

"Because I'm pissed off," I declared, my eyes narrowing as I considered everything I'd been through in this realm. Everything I'd found. Everything I was about to lose.

And I didn't even know *why.*

"Why is he doing this?" I demanded, my ire increasing with each passing moment and filling me with a new kind of rage. A rage that required blood. A rage that made me want to slaughter *everything* in my path.

"The vote," Fallon muttered. "Vesperus voted in favor of Death and Diamond, so we lost our home in the process. Klas didn't take it well."

This is because of the vote? I thought.

"But he was already angry," she continued. "He's been a lower-level mercenary for decades and felt that he should be moving up faster. Then he found out Vesperus approved the vote, and it further proved to him that our king doesn't care about his well-being."

"So he took it personally."

"*Very* personally. But that's Klas. Everything is about him. If someone glances our way, they're obviously evaluating him. If someone cuts us off, it was intentional and meant to piss him off. If he was assigned a low-level mark, it was because Vesperus and the others undervalued him. He's..."

"A narcissist," I finished for her, unable to hide the hiss in my tone. All of this was because Klas felt left out of a decision that hadn't been his to make. A decision that had led to a mostly positive impact.

Kieran and Vesperus had offered everyone a choice. They were working together to ensure the comfort of those impacted, not to mention the long hours and careful evaluations of all the requests. I'd witnessed Vesperus's exhaustion firsthand. He genuinely cared about his people.

And this was how his mercenary chose to thank him? By creating chaos?

"Yes," she agreed after several minutes. "*Narcissist* is a good descriptor. When the vote happened, he was angry. So he decided to test Vesperus."

We turned onto a street I recognized, confirming we were still in Reykjavik. But it seemed we were several blocks from where I needed to be.

I glanced up at the waning night again, my heart in my throat. *Please don't let him die. Please let me make it in time.*

"He... he put in a request to transfer to Iceland, and when it wasn't immediately approved... he decided to take out some of his competition," Fallon continued, her words miraculously managing to reach me over the thunder in my ears. "In Dublin."

My brow furrowed, some of the roaring in my head quieting long enough for me to say, "He blew up the bar." I should have already guessed that. "To fake his own death." To cover his tracks and come here. *To hurt my mate.*

"He hired a witch to cast an explosion spell," she replied. "It was meant to take out Slater and Nolan. But you saved them. Which infuriated him. So then, yes, he faked his own death. And decided to come here for revenge."

I considered her words and the events in Dublin, how Vesperus had told me there were *three* dead bodies, not two.

Making Klas the third.

Stars, I thought. *Why didn't I ask more questions?*

Because I'd been too consumed by the fated-mate magic to focus.

Because I'd been too annoyed by the implication that I attacked the bar to question the body count.

I shook my head. It didn't matter now. All that mattered was reaching Vesperus and—

A gunshot cracked through the air, making me call on my ability to phase. Only it was still nonexistent. As was my ability to create a shield.

I ducked instead.

And somehow found myself under Fallon.

She felt heavy on top of me, which was strange because she wasn't very big. Curvy, yes. But short. I tried to maneuver out from under her, to see where the attack had come from. However, she wouldn't move.

She was dead weight on top of me.

A sickening feeling touched my gut as I realized why.

"Fallon," I whispered, something sticky touching my neck. I reached up to touch her shoulder and felt the source of it—*blood.*

From the gunshot.

Fallon had taken me down to protect me. She'd taken me down because… because… *because she's been shot.* And now she wasn't responding. *Is she…? Is she dead?*

I started to shake my head. *No. No, this is not happening. No.*

I was done with this bullshit.

Done with this world.

Done with people shooting first and asking questions later.

Done being benign and just watching it all happen.

Done feeling weak.

Done. Done. Done!

I closed my eyes as footsteps started toward me, the sounds of boots hitting the concrete a beat that matched my own heart. There were words. Voices. Someone saying my name.

But I wasn't focused on them.

I was talking to my moon.

To the night.

To my *birthright.*

Come to me, I whispered. *Come to me, dear moon. I need your power. And I'm done harnessing my strength.*

I'd tried to do this in a controlled manner. I'd tried to survive in this realm without exploiting my creation abilities.

And all it had done was end in deadly consequences.

Lethal spells. Narcissistic choices. Explosions. Unnecessary death. Pain.

The potential loss of my other half. Of my mate.

No more. No more kindness. No more gentle treatment.

No. More. Nice. Goddess.

I am the Mistress of the Moon, the Goddess of Night.

And. You. Will. Bow!

The ground rumbled beneath me as the moon heeded my call. This would have lasting impacts. It would change the predictions of all future sun and moon crossings.

But it wouldn't harm many.

Just create a few tides.

This world of magic users could handle it. They could protect their borders, use magic to fend off unwanted waves, and shield their below-sea-level cities.

It wouldn't impact them too much.

And even if it did, perhaps it was what they deserved.

"What the fuck is happening?" I heard someone demand, his voice close and yet not. Because I wasn't focused on him or the others who had approached.

My attention was on my moon.

I know it hurts, I whispered to it. *I'll soothe your inner burns. But I need you. I need you to bolster me, to shower me in your magic, and let me thrive. Let. Me. Reign.*

Because I was a goddess. And that was what we did—*we reigned.*

"Is that…?"

"Yeah…"

"Fuck."

"Yeah…"

I nearly hushed the male voices around me, not wanting their intrusion. But the moon did it for me by showering me with its glorious presence as it returned to the Iceland sky. It would be setting the orbit off by a week or so, giving me an unexpected full moon.

"Holy fuck…"

"It's… it's…"

"It's *burning*," I said, focusing on the three men who had joined us on the street. *Kaspian. Nox. Nolan.* "It's angry. It's *bleeding.* It's fire." I phased away from Fallon's body, landing easily on my feet several yards away. "You take the lives of innocents," I said to them, furious by their behavior. "*We needed her.*"

She was the antidote to all this madness, the only one capable of understanding and stopping her own power.

But not anymore.

Now this realm had me.

And my fiery blood moon.

This time it was real, not just a message from Khaos or a show of approval. This was a blood moon built of rage and flames and volcanic eruptions because its mistress had forced it forward by a week's distance along its twenty-eight-day path.

I would heal its wounds when I finished this fight.

But I needed to find Vesperus first.

"Klas has poisoned my mate. I don't know if he's still at the palace or not. But I am going to hunt him and kill him. And *you* are going to find a way to *fix her.*" I pointed at the witch on the ground. She'd survived being buried because of some sort of regeneration spell that had made her come back to life even after suffocating to death. Hopefully, that magic still applied and could work to heal gunshots, too.

Assuming I didn't break the rejuvenation spell when I pieced her spirit back together earlier.

I didn't wait for the others to agree with me. They were mine to command, and they would heel.

While I went in search of our king.

NYX

Vesperus wasn't in his room.

Or his office.

Or anywhere in his palace.

By the time I exited, it was to find Kaspian waiting for me, his expression wary. "You haven't found him." It was a statement, not a question, so I didn't bother replying to him.

Instead, I looked up at my angry moon, the fractures on the surface revealing fiery lines of erupted lava. For millions of years, those volcanoes had remained dormant. But my actions tonight had awoken the beast within, forcing the moon to pulse with the fury I felt in my heart.

"Show me where he is," I demanded. "Paint me a picture with stars."

Not even five minutes had passed from when I'd left Fallon's side, but it was enough for me to worry about where Vesperus had been taken. I could no longer feel him, my ire too great to sense anything other than *rage*.

This concept was new to me, this need to slaughter, to make

everyone bleed. But I would destroy this world if it meant finding my mate.

You've taken what is mine, Klas. You've hurt these people who should be mine, too. You will pay in blood.

"Get your hands off me," a female voice snapped, drawing my focus to a fuming Fallon. She appeared to be holding her arm but otherwise seemed fine.

I guess that healing spell still works. Or maybe she's just really hard to kill.

"Glad you're alive," I said.

She snorted and hooked her thumb at Nolan. "This idiot shot me in the shoulder."

"Because I wasn't trying to kill you," he muttered.

"And the impact knocked me out," she added. "Because my night hasn't been hell enough."

"You were dragging Nyx along beside you," Nox told her. "And our orders were to take you down."

"Actually, they had permission to shoot to kill," Kaspian clarified flatly. "You're lucky to be alive."

Fallon did not appear impressed or amused by their responses. "Fuck all of you." Her eyes flickered toward me. "Except you."

I returned my focus to the sky, waiting on my moon to draw me a path. I could feel the energy gathering, obeying my call as I held my moon captive in the sky via my link to its iron core.

It could move subtly to maintain its position along its path, but I refused to allow it to move forward until I was done. Until I found my other half.

"Show me," I said again. "Where is your new king?" Because that was who Vesperus had become as my mate—a God of Night. Perhaps not with all the same perks and abilities that I maintained, but given the abilities he'd already inherited, I suspected he would only continue to grow.

Because I will find you.

I will save you.

And I will claim you as mine again.

My other half. My fated mate. My future.

Energy hummed in the air, the moon answering my demand

with a flurry of stardust. I lifted my hand to catch the essence, allowing it to seep into my skin and fuel my being as I began the process of following the path.

"Should we…?" a male asked. Nolan, maybe. I didn't glance at him to check.

"Yes," Kaspian replied.

I assumed they were talking about coming with me. Since they'd obeyed my request to *fix Fallon*, I didn't stop them from trailing along behind me.

But if they stepped into my path, I would remove them from it.

Stardust continued to fall, the power soaking into my veins and revitalizing my spirit. I could feel it pulsing through my bond to Vesperus as well, ensuring he had energy to *fight*.

My mate. Mine.

"Slater," Kaspian called.

A flurry of feathers whispered through the air, the black wings blending in with the night as the raven shifter touched down a few feet away from us—and fortunately not in front of me. He stood off to the side, his slate-gray eyes observing the stardust as I collected it in my hand.

Vesperus was fond of this mercenary, stating he was his best tracker.

Which explained the male's uncanny awareness now, his wings nearly brushing my arm as he fell into step beside me. "We're tracking Vesperus," he said, not a question but a statement.

"We are," Kaspian confirmed. "He's been taken by Klas."

"Klas?" Slater repeated, his attention shifting to Fallon—who was walking on Kaspian's other side with Nolan and Nox right behind her.

I kept them all in my peripheral line of view while I focused on the stardust. It seemed to be leading us toward a residential area.

"He's alive," Nolan replied. "And according to her, he's been drinking her blood and using her powers."

"According to her," Fallon parroted at him. "Like I'm lying."

"You're not," I murmured. "Klas is responsible. Klas will die."

I glanced up at my moon, noting the fractures and fiery tears. *Yes, he will pay for making me hurt you,* I vowed. *He will bleed.*

The stardust hummed in response, the glitter continuing to soak into my being and rejuvenate my soul.

"What has it done to Vesperus?" Slater asked. "I can hardly sense his power."

"Death magic," I replied.

"It's a decaying spell. The same one used on the bullet that hit Nyx," Fallon added.

"What's the antidote?" Kaspian demanded.

"Me," I said simply. I would drown my mate in the power of the moon until he came back to me. There would be no choice. He would survive.

Right? I asked, looking up at the moon.

More stardust fell in response.

Right, I echoed.

Except the path suddenly stopped, causing me to pause and stare up at the sky while Fallon murmured something about a spell that could break the decaying magic.

Then she followed it up with, "But it's not guaranteed."

Kaspian started drilling her about her powers, demanding to know exactly what she could do and what had happened earlier tonight.

She explained the deadly sleeping magic to him before going into Klas's motives and plans.

All the while, I waited for my moon to continue guiding me.

But it didn't.

I looked around, trying to figure out why it had stopped. We were standing in the middle of a street. The closest building was almost a block away. Otherwise, we were surrounded by trees.

"Are you trying to tell me he's here?" I demanded. "Or... or have you lost him?"

The latter would not be acceptable.

And the former made absolutely no sense.

"I don't sense him here," Slater said quietly, his keen eyes searching the street. "This can't be right."

I agreed with him. "Where's my king?" I asked the moon.

Stardust fell on me in response, making me look down at the ground. The last time my magic did this, it wanted me to dig. And I found Fallon.

"Are there tunnels?" I asked, looking at Kaspian.

His brow furrowed. "Yes. But very few would know about them."

"Just like very few should have been able to find Vesperus's personal quarters as fast as Klas did," Nox added, making me frown.

That… was an interesting point.

From what I understood, Vesperus hadn't known Klas well, if at all. So how had he known where my mate slept?

His palace was huge. His rooms could have been anywhere. But to find him as quickly as he had after Fallon had broken the spell suggested he'd known exactly where to look.

"Maybe he used a locator spell?" Nolan suggested.

"Maybe," Kaspian said.

However, Fallon shook her head. "It's doubtful. He would have needed something of Vesperus's to properly craft the spell. And I don't think he thought that far ahead."

"Then how did he find Vesperus?" I pressed. "And how do we access the tunnels?" Because it seemed like my magic wanted me to go down again.

Kaspian canted his head toward the building ahead. "There's an access point in there."

I started toward it before he even finished, my boots moving quickly along the street. *I'm coming for you, Vesperus.*

"What about Paxton?" Nox asked quietly behind me.

"What about him?" That came from Kaspian.

The phantom seemed to hesitate before asking, "Would he know where Vesperus sleeps?"

"Of course he knows. He's my assistant and has access to almost everything." Kaspian sounded uneasy, but not necessarily annoyed or defensive. "Why?"

"Including the tunnels?" Nox pressed.

"Yes. Now tell me why you suspect him," Kaspian demanded.

"He's the one who said the bullet fragments weren't spelled but chemically enhanced." Nox paused for a beat. "It seems like a good way to derail an investigation, especially when you're a warlock who should be able to sense magic."

I'd almost reached the building ahead, but I paused at the door to look at Kaspian.

His midnight eyes resembled obsidian flames, his anger confirming that he understood and potentially agreed with Nox's suspicions. "He told us that while Vesperus was indisposed."

"Which means you have no way of knowing if he was lying or not," Nolan added.

"Can you track Paxton's magic?" I asked Slater, driving straight to the point. I wasn't going to play a game of speculation when we could confirm the truth with our natural resources.

"Yes, I'm already searching," the raven shifter confirmed.

"Then tell me if you sense it along this path," I said, entering the building. "Where am I going, Kaspian?"

He took the lead, taking us to a door with a security panel on it. *More proof that Klas has help.*

"How many people know this code?" I asked as he keyed it in.

"Maybe half a dozen," he admitted. "And Paxton is one of them."

"Have you ever met Paxton?" Nox asked Fallon.

"No. I've not heard the name before either. But Klas never let me meet any of his friends." It was a soft statement, one filled with loneliness and heartache.

"I sense him," Slater confirmed quietly from the top of the stairs, his black feathers ruffling in agitation. "And I can smell the death magic, too." His nose crinkled with the words, his gaze narrowing.

Kaspian entered first with Slater moving in behind him.

Which placed me behind his big black wings.

Well, mostly black. Three white feathers stood out among the sea of inky plumes, making me wonder if they served some sort of purpose or were a marker of some kind.

But I didn't ask.

Because the moment we reached the tunnel floor, I could *feel* Vesperus.

I phased ahead of the group, my night energy ready to *kill*.

I'd never been one for violence, but I would be tasting Klas's blood tonight.

Vesperus's aura called to me, his presence a beacon in my mind that I followed without looking back.

Mine, mine, mine, my heart beat.

Kill, kill, kill, my soul demanded.

I kept phasing forward, chasing Vesperus's essence, his chocolatey scent curling around me in warm welcome.

A bullet fired, one my stardust caught in an instant shield, my powers ready and alert and prepared to *annihilate*.

Someone cursed. I wasn't sure if it came from behind me or in front of me. I didn't care. I was singularly focused on finding Vesperus.

There, I thought, catching sight of his crumpled form and immediately hitting him with a blast of stardust.

More gunfire started to rain down upon me, along with someone whispering a chant.

I sent a tidal wave of power in their direction, the energy whistling like a whip and taking them all down.

Six men.

Three women.

I only recognized Paxton.

But they were all armed and shooting at me.

"I have had enough of your toys," I seethed, hitting them with another blast of my power. "All you beings have done since the moment I arrived is try to kill me. And you know what? I think it's time I return the favor."

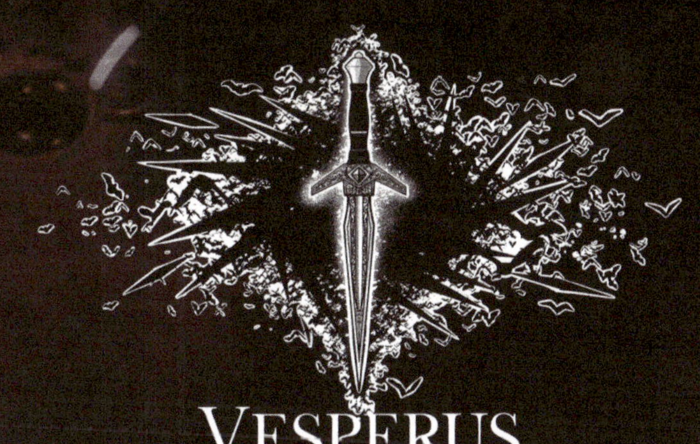

VESPERUS

Fire licked across my senses.

Hot. Intense. Flames.

It made my nose twitch, the scent intoxicating in nature.

Because it's underlined with a sweet, citrusy undertone, I marveled. *Nyx.*

Vesperus, she replied, the relieved quality of her voice making me frown.

Another blast of heat touched me, causing stars to dance across my vision.

No, not stars.

Nyx.

My lips parted as she lit up the dark space with a flash of golden magic, her fury wild and palpable and borderline terrifying.

A chill of power followed, the source coming from deeper in the tunnel. *How did I end up down here?* I marveled, my mind lacking the answer.

I was naked.

Weak.

And curled up on the dirty floor.

What the fuck happened?

Klas shot you with the same kind of bullet that he'd used on me, Nyx snarled. *And I am really tired of guns.*

Her golden magic flickered through the tunnel, followed by the sounds of metal bending and snapping.

No. More. Shooting. At. Me. The anger in her mental voice had my heart skipping several beats. It didn't sound like her at all. She sounded almost possessed. Borderline enraged.

And her snarl confirmed it.

She created a whip of power that sliced right through three of her attackers. Their heads fell to the floor in an anticlimactic thud, followed by their bodies.

But Nyx didn't even look at them, her focus on the others.

She started counting in her head as she dropped each one of them to the floor in a similar fashion until only two of them were left.

Paxton and Klas.

I frowned, the memory of hearing them in my room tickling my thoughts.

And something about an injection.

I don't think he shot me, I said slowly, my brow furrowing. *He… he injected me with something.*

Nyx didn't seem to hear me, her ferocity focused entirely on the two men.

"If you kill him, you'll hurt Fallon," someone said. *Nox.*

I frowned. *When did he get here?* I glanced around for him and gaped at the crowd behind Nyx. She'd brought an army down here, yet it seemed none of them were needed.

"It's okay," Fallon said, her gaze narrowed. "He deserves to die."

"It'll fracture your mate bond," Nox whispered.

"I would rather go insane than remain mated to him," she replied.

"You always were a cunt," Klas snapped.

"*Quiet.*" Nyx wrapped her golden whip around his neck with the word and squeezed.

The mercenary's eyes went wide, like he was shocked she wanted to kill him. Or perhaps that she even could. But she'd just slaughtered half a dozen people without blinking.

I need to know what he injected me with, I told her.

She still didn't seem to hear me, her ire overwhelming her instincts.

"Nyx," I said, my voice a rasp of sound. I could barely move, my limbs weighed down like lead blocks.

She growled, her eyes finally finding mine, and I stared at her red-tinted golden irises. They resembled blood moons.

Oh, shit. "You're experiencing blood rage." It was similar to bloodlust, only characterized by the need to fight, kill, or fuck.

And right now, she was possessed by the need to *kill*.

That was why she sounded different to me. This wasn't Nyx.

Well, it was her and all her glorious goddess power. But the furious need to slay wasn't her.

"I need to know what he injected me with," I told her in as soft a voice as I could manage. "It wasn't a bullet."

Klas's lips curled into a grin, the look one that reminded me a bit of a charming sociopath.

Plan B, he'd said.

What does that entail, Klas? I wondered. *Are you going to use this to negotiate?*

Nyx was still looking at me with the whip wrapped around his throat.

"What did you inject me with?" I asked, grimacing at my hoarse voice and the heaviness in my body.

The only reason I seemed to be awake was because of Nyx's energy blast. Perhaps she could cure me. But the crazed look in Klas's eyes suggested otherwise.

He's not going to tell us anything.

"Paxton?" I prompted, causing a growl to leave Kaspian.

"I don't know what was in it," Paxton replied, the truth in his words making me sigh.

Because that meant whatever this was, it had been Klas's plan.

I hadn't pieced it all together yet, but it seemed everything had been Klas's doing.

"We need him alive, Nyx," I told her. *At least until he talks.*

She hissed. "No. He *dies.*"

The whip began to tighten, her blood rage in full effect. *Fuck.*

I did the only thing I could think of and groaned, then I allowed her to hear my pain, the agony in my thoughts, my need for a cure, and in the next moment, she was on her knees beside me, her hands on my face as she pushed energy to me.

I leaned into her, desiring her touch and warmth and reveling in her stardust.

She blew some over me, her wish clear—she wanted me to heal. But I suspected we would experience something similar to her healing, where her body started to decay again because of the spell.

And mating wasn't going to fix it this time.

Kaspian started issuing orders in the background, his words quiet as though not to disturb Nyx, but she was too focused on me to notice him.

She kissed me, her tongue trying to coax mine into action. Then she bit herself to feed me her essence. I swallowed, her taste and blood a welcome antidote, even if it was temporary.

Take me back to my room, I told her, aware of what I needed to do to help her blood rage subside. *I want to be inside you.*

She released a primal sound and phased us back to my bedroom in a blink. But instead of straddling me or trying to fuck, she started checking me for wounds.

Her lips and hands were everywhere, ensuring I was still here, ensuring I existed, ensuring I belonged to her.

By the time she finished, I really was ready to be inside her because she'd aroused my need with her feral behavior. She'd been a gorgeous queen, riotous in her fury and stunning in her golden glimmer.

However, she made no move to take me.

Instead, she nuzzled into my neck and sighed. "Mine."

My lips curled. "Feeling possessive?"

Her eyes met mine, the reddish hue having dissipated and leaving behind her golden flecks.

Her blood rage is gone.

She'd cured it through worshipping me. That was definitely not a way I'd ever heard of placating a blood rage. But nothing about Nyx was normal or ordinary.

She was a goddess. *My goddess.*

"I need to heal the moon," she whispered, making me frown. "It's bleeding fiery tears."

I stared at her. "What?"

"I called it earlier, to replenish my powers. And I promised it Klas's blood as payment. I have to kill him." This wasn't the blood rage speaking, but a goddess speaking of sacrifices to her greater entity.

"You called the moon?"

She nodded. "I impacted the cycle… by about a week."

My eyebrows rose. "You're saying you pulled the moon out of orbit?"

"No. I kept it on its path. I just shifted the position on that path," she explained. "And now I owe it a tribute—Klas's blood."

"Fuck," I breathed. "Did it impact the world? *Our* world?"

"A little. It mainly impacted the tides. But the moon is hurting the most. I need to pay it in blood," she insisted.

"We need to know what he injected me with first." We also need to find out if there were others he was working with… like Paxton.

I want their motives and reasons for attacking Gold and Garnet, too.

And I needed to do a full assessment on what effect this might have on our House.

I ran my hand over my face, thinking about the paperwork and necessary interrogations. In addition to all the phone calls I was about to receive regarding Nyx.

You moved the moon, I whispered. *That's… a terrifying ability, Goddess.*

It's not one I've ever deployed before, she replied. *But I needed to find you, my king.*

My blood heated from those two words, which I suspected was the point.

However, I couldn't tear my mind away from the list of tasks forming in my thoughts—damage control being at the top of those items.

But I wasn't sure it would matter.

Nyx had moved the fucking moon… *for me.* To find me. To save me.

Talk about a seismic gesture, I marveled to myself. But I knew she'd heard it because her lips curled.

What am I going to do with you, Goddess? I thought, searching her gaze.

I have some ideas. But I think a shower might be a good place to start.

A shower did sound like a good way to loosen up my limbs now that I could move again. I just wondered how long it would last.

Perhaps indefinitely.

Perhaps not.

I grabbed my watch from the nightstand and sent Kaspian a list of items we needed to do.

Call Kieran. He can help force the truth out of Klas.

We need to draft a formal statement on what happened here, specifically in regard to Nyx's power.

We should probably add a formal mating announcement to it, since that's rather obvious now.

Don't kill Klas—Nyx needs his blood for the moon.

She said the moon is on fire… is that true?

The last item was more of a musing from me, as I couldn't see the moon from my position in the bedroom. But there was a strange orangish hue outside, reminding me of the sunrise. Yet it wasn't time for that yet.

"Shower?" Nyx prompted.

"Shower," I agreed as my watch buzzed with Kaspian's reply.

Kieran is already on his way.

Cara is almost finished working on a statement for both items.

We'll talk about that blood tribute more. Fallon deserves to be involved in that discussion.

See attached.

An image came through in the next second, causing me to gape at the screen. "This gives new meaning to a blood moon."

The moon was literally on fire with fissures of lava. There was no way the other leaders wouldn't notice this.

Fuck.

Nyx glanced at it and winced. "This is why I need the blood tribute." Her gaze met mine. "Klas needs to die."

"And he will," I vowed. "Just as soon as we gather the information we need from him." I cupped her jaw. "How about we take that shower and you tell me how you want to kill him?"

She considered it for a beat. "With a knife. But I'll tell you more under the water."

"It's a date," I joked.

She frowned, pondering the words. "I've never been on a real date, but I accept this proposal. Water, revenge, and orgasms."

Well, when she put it that way, it did sound intriguing. "I promise to deliver on all three."

"Good," she replied. "Because I have high standards."

"I'd expect nothing less from a goddess."

"Just as I'd expect everything from a king," she countered.

I grinned. "And everything, you shall have."

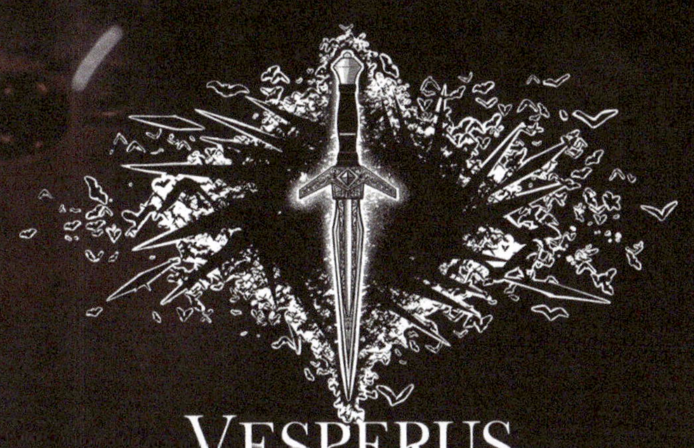

VESPERUS

KLAS HAD INJECTED ME WITH A COCKTAIL OF HIS BLOOD AND DEADLY potions.

It'd essentially been a decaying curse tied to his essence.

"He manufactured it as a way to keep himself alive," Kaspian summarized. "Because without regular doses of his blood, you'd die."

"Except he didn't anticipate there being an antidote," Nox added, showing me a vial. "Fallon helped create a counter to the curse, and she used her blood to counter her mate's."

Kaspian clasped his hands together. "We just need to inject it into your blood."

"I see." I glanced at Nyx beside me. We were seated on the couch in my office with Kaspian behind my desk and Nox standing beside him.

An ideal position, one that seemed to foreshadow Gold and Garnet's future, given the situations of late.

I'd spent most of the last two days in my rooms because every time I fully healed, I started to turn gray again. Just like Nyx had after being shot. She kept me alive and healthy with her stardust, but it was a temporary solution, not a permanent one.

Meanwhile, Kaspian had overseen Klas's and Paxton's interrogations. Kieran had visited again to assist, his ability to compel the truth out of others decidedly useful in this situation.

I'd only seen the other leader in passing, but he'd said something to me that sounded a lot like a goodbye.

"You're a good man, Veritas. I've enjoyed this friendship of ours. And I want you to know that your former territory is in good hands." He'd glanced at Kaspian as he'd added, "And I'm not just referring to those owned by Death and Diamond."

I'd nodded, reading between the lines of what he was telling me, and had simply replied, "I know."

Because Kaspian was going to make a fine king. He was already performing the role, and as he sat behind my desk now, it was clear that he was ready to own it, too.

Which was a good thing because the general consensus around the world was that Nyx could not stay here.

Empress Asbesta had been among the loudest to demand Nyx's extermination. My mate's manipulation of the moon had wreaked havoc on the tides, and while very few were injured, the Sea and Serpentine leader was furious. And I didn't anticipate her ever backing down.

She was actually more likely to go to war, something she'd more or less threatened in her message to me.

If you don't remove it, I will do it for you.

She hadn't even bothered with a formal address or signature.

Lady Gabriella had expressed a similar feeling on the matter, her stern words layered with threats.

We trusted you with this bounty, and you've failed. Your judgment is blinded by fated-mate magic. We will do what is necessary, Vesperus. Consider this your only warning.

I hadn't spoken to Sky Serpell, but Kaspian had. And he'd confirmed via a quick call with her that Spirit and Sapphire were already preparing for the inevitable.

I wasn't sure if Sky had bluntly told him that or if he'd simply interpreted it based on whatever she'd said.

However, the point was moot. What mattered was that at least two Houses were already preparing to invade.

And my allies would not be coming to my side.

Volker might even join in the resistance against me, a choice that was only fair, as I'd consider the same move if our positions were reversed.

Elias had expressed disappointment, saying he knew this would be a difficult decision. But in the end, he already knew what I would choose.

"You've been a good King, Vesperus," he'd said. "Kaspian has quite a journey ahead of him, but he was groomed by one of the best."

It'd felt a lot like goodbye, similar to my conversation with Kieran.

The other leaders of the world had been cordial, their warnings all politely worded.

However, it was clear that remaining here would drive the Houses to war. There would be no understanding or slow acceptance of Nyx's powers.

And this was without any of them realizing that her gifts had begun to affect me, too.

That detail would be the final nail in our House's coffin. And while my people might fight for me—for *us*—it was a position I would never put them in.

I focused on my second behind my desk. "Are you going to do the honors?" I asked him, referring to the antidote Nox held beside him.

"You're giving me an opportunity to stab you with something?" Kaspian asked, mirth playing in his dark eyes.

"Consider it a rite of passage," I replied. It was a token of trust between us. An intimate gesture of friendship.

I stood and removed my suit jacket, then unbuttoned my shirt and shrugged out of it to expose my arm.

"You're sure about this antidote?" Nyx asked, moving fluidly to my side in one of her trademark dresses.

"About ninety percent, give or take," Kaspian replied.

My mate narrowed her gaze. "That's not a hundred percent."

"He's lying," I murmured, sensing the joke in his words.

"Am I lying because it's actually more than ninety percent, or because it's less?" he mused.

"Just fucking stab me, Kas," I drawled.

He chuckled as he filled the syringe.

I'll be fine, I told Nyx.

Now who is lying?

Well, I'm ninety percent sure I'll be fine, I clarified, winking at her.

Kaspian grabbed my arm and searched for a vein before poking me with the needle. Nox took it from him and left the office, presumably to discard the syringe.

Nyx's gaze narrowed, stardust already piling in her palm.

You're sexy when you're protective, I told her.

She didn't reply, her eyes searching me for any sign of damage. When nothing happened after several minutes, she started to relax, but only a little.

"We'll know in a few hours if that worked," I declared, aware of my symptom cycle. Nyx had healed me right before this meeting had started, so I had at least sixty minutes before I started to turn gray again.

But I'd prefer to go several hours without symptoms before saying the antidote worked.

"Distract me with updates on everything else," I requested, my focus on Kaspian as I settled into my couch again. Nyx sat right beside me, her palm on my thigh, like she needed to be touching me to keep me safe.

I placed my hand over hers, giving it a squeeze. *I feel fine.*

For now, she returned.

For now, I agreed.

"Do you want to discuss what we learned from the rest of the interrogation or review the myriad of calls that I've received from pissed-off astronomers?"

I arched a brow. While the former was what I'd had in mind, I couldn't help repeating, "Pissed-off astronomers?"

"I moved the moon," Nyx murmured. "That impacts projections for all lunar-related events." Her nose scrunched. "But if I move the moon back, it'll hurt again. And I just started healing it."

She'd used a bucket of Klas's blood—which Fallon had brought to her after eviscerating the bastard—to perform a sacrifice ritual last night. The moon's glowing orange rivulets had slowly calmed, leaving it with a faint white glow.

She'd said the process would need to be repeated over the next six nights—with more blood.

"I could do this faster if you let me kill Klas, but after everything he's done, this does seem more fitting," she'd said.

"Yeah, well, maybe I'll let you talk to the next astronomer who calls," Kaspian muttered.

"There are still astronomers in this world?" I marveled. "I thought that was a human hobby."

"Magic might change our views of the world, but the fascination with the universe remains." Kaspian grimaced. "And they are a loud group of scientists."

Nox returned with Nolan and Slater, the three of them grinning as they entered.

"Did another stars enthusiast call?" Nolan asked.

Kaspian rolled his eyes. "You know what? I'm going to assign the three of you to all future calls. Let's see how much you enjoy being chastised about eclipse charts and the lunar calendar."

"I can talk to them," Nyx offered.

"That would probably make it worse," Kaspian admitted. "And it's not just astronomers, but also advisors from various Houses."

I nodded. "I've been reviewing the messages you've forwarded, and I've spoken to a few of them personally." Such as Volker and Elias, as well as Kieran during his visit. "Tell me more about what Klas has said."

I'd left Kaspian to manage it all, the task feeling like a final farewell in a way.

Or a graduation of sorts.

Because I hadn't involved myself personally. I'd simply allowed Kaspian to handle it as a king would.

Slater and Nolan took over the couch across from me, their expressions sobering.

While Nox went to stand behind Kaspian again, the symbology making me wonder if the phantom was vying for a protector sort of role. He seemed to care about Kaspian, which pleased me. Because I soon wouldn't be here to protect my old friend.

"Well, as I said, he admitted that the purpose of his 'plan B' was to tie himself to you. It was his way of saving his life without any regard for the others who had helped him. Most of whom came with him from Dublin. The others were members of Paxton's family from Ireland, which is why he betrayed us."

Yes, Kaspian had messaged me about that. He'd been beating himself up for not seeing it, but I'd told him it wasn't his fault that Paxton hadn't voiced his discontent.

Unfortunately, however… "This all tells me that we have some members of our House who are not pleased with my voting in favor of the creation of Death and Diamond."

"Yes. I'm working with Niamh on it. We're going to send out advisors to everyone impacted and provide a more personal touch for the decision process."

I nodded. "That's something I should have done initially."

"The way you and Kieran have handled the territory transition is better than most. You offered to financially cover relocation costs for anyone wishing to move into Gold and Garnet's territory. And you negotiated the option for them to stay."

"True, but it seems I should have met with our constituents to better understand their feelings. A lot of this could have been avoided."

"Yes and no," Kaspian replied. "Perhaps it would have kept Klas from reacting when he did, but I think he was a ticking time bomb waiting to explode."

"He's a fucking sociopath," Nox muttered. "The things he's done to Fallon…"

Kaspian's jaw ticked. "She's another matter entirely."

"Oh?" That sounded intriguing.

He grunted and shook his head, dismissing my intrigue. "I'm handling her for now. However, I have concerns about her powers." His gaze flicked to Nyx before returning to me, his message clear— his concerns were about the other territories reacting to Fallon's death magic.

I'd never met a witch with those sorts of abilities before. I would almost label her as a necromancer rather than a witch, but I wasn't sure if she could control the dead or not.

"What about those working with Klas?" Slater asked quietly. "Are there others?"

"Nyx handled the small following he'd obtained. None of them were mercenaries. They were desk job types, kind of like Paxton." Kaspian's teeth ground over the name, his irritation palpable. "So Niamh will be focusing on those with similar trades first."

"I don't understand why they would protest the territory shift—they could have remained in their profession and stayed in their homes, just under Death and Diamond's rule instead of Gold and Garnet's," Nyx murmured.

"It's the wealth and glory aspects of Gold and Garnet that they craved," Nolan told her. "While many of us are mercenaries who earn our glory through honor, our House also values wealth. And many of those tradesmen own profitable business ventures."

"Business ventures they don't want to move," I realized. "But they don't want to lose their House name either."

Nolan dipped his chin. "Exactly."

"Maybe I should pair you up with Niamh for this investigation," Kaspian said.

"You want to put me on interview duty?" the archangel drawled, his multicolored eyes flashing. "Are you sure about that?"

Kaspian smiled. "Sounds like a challenge."

Nolan folded his arms. "A challenge I likely wouldn't enjoy. Maybe give it to Slater instead. He likes tracking things. I'm sure he's good at paperwork as a result."

The raven shifter's eyes flashed, but he didn't issue a retort in the way he usually would. Instead, he remained thoughtful, causing my lips to curl down.

"What is it?" I asked him.

His slate-gray eyes met mine, the perpetual shadow of dark hair along his jaw thick again from a lack of shaving. "I'm thinking about the bar in Ireland, and the witch he hired to bespell it."

"He didn't know the witch's name," Kaspian added, clarifying

Slater's comment. "It was a witch for hire. Which he apparently has a penchant for doing because he also hired a witch to create that potion that removed Fallon's free will."

"Yes, it's common. Similar to Kieran hiring Trixie," Slater murmured.

"Have you spoken to her?" I asked him. "About the bar?"

"I haven't yet, but I know it wasn't her. The magic doesn't match. However, whoever it was… is someone I need to find."

I hadn't suspected the attack was Trixie's doing, just thought she might have been able to provide some helpful insight.

But I didn't comment on that.

Because the urgency in his tone at the end of his statement had me focusing on his comment about needing to find the witch responsible. "Why?"

His lips twisted as he considered how to reply. "Because I think I've been cursed."

Kaspian and I shared a look, but his lack of a reaction told me Slater had already shared this information with him. *Because Slater already sees Kaspian as his new king.*

My heart stuttered a little at the thought, but it almost immediately warmed again in its wake. Because *this* was what I wanted for my House—for them to not only accept Kaspian but also embrace him.

And seeing the structure play out in the room told me how far everyone had come in welcoming this fate.

"Cursed in what way?" Nyx asked, her palm still on my thigh.

He ran his fingers through his short black hair and blew out a breath. "Three of my feathers have turned white. And I haven't been feeling… right." He seemed perplexed by the comment, like he couldn't fully describe *why* he didn't feel right. He just knew that something was wrong.

"Is that what the witch meant about your darkness?" Nyx inquired. "The one from Dublin? The one who said you needed Triarchy-like power to cure you?"

Slater blinked at Nyx, his lips curling down. "I forgot about that. Her concerns had seemed so trivial at the time, but I completely disregarded her comments." His focus went to me and then to Kaspian. "Does either of you know what she meant by Triarchy-like power?"

I shook my head. "No, but I'm not familiar with the beings of Spirit and Sapphire." Which tended to recruit a lot of witches.

"I'm not either," Kaspian admitted. "But I'm willing to grant you a paid leave of absence while you pursue it. I just ask that you let me know if you find the witch responsible for that spell in Dublin."

Slater dipped his chin. "That's a given. I'll consider it a bounty."

"Good," Kaspian replied, his attention shifting to me. "Vesperus?"

I studied him for a long moment, my throat suddenly thick with emotion.

Because this was it.

This was the moment Kaspian needed. The moment our *House* needed.

The moment where I recognized formally that I was no longer their king.

Nyx squeezed my leg, clearly sensing the shift in my thoughts, or perhaps she felt the rightness of this instant as well.

Because it was time.

I'd made my decision the moment I'd woken up and learned that Nyx had moved the moon. I knew there would be no staying here.

To keep the tenuous balance intact between the Houses, we had to leave.

And I would leave knowing that I'd handed over the reins to the most capable of replacements.

"I think that's a fine plan," I started slowly. "King Antonik."

I dipped my head in a show of reverence, the room falling silent around me.

Kaspian cleared his throat after a minute, drawing my gaze to him. "You're still my king, Vesperus."

"Yes," I agreed. "But you're no longer my second, Kaspian."

He swallowed, his dark eyes taking on a sheen of emotion that was uncommon for my old friend. It disappeared in a blink, his head inclining in confirmation and acceptance of his fate.

"You're going to be a fine king, Kaspian," I told him. "Thank you for allowing me to leave with the knowledge that my House will continue to prosper long after I'm gone."

NYX

I painted the ground with the remainder of Klas's blood and sprinkled some of my stardust over the edges.

Vesperus sat beside me, observing as the magic vibrated like it had every night for the last week, and watched as the mixture of gold and blood disappeared into the wind, the night carrying it up to my moon to provide a final layer of healing.

It no longer cried fiery tears, the volcanoes having calmed once more.

"The blood debt is paid," I whispered, smiling as a warm hum of energy settled over me, the moon showing its gratitude.

It didn't matter what realm or reality I visited; the moon was always mine, our history one we shared in every version of the universe.

The iron inside the core linked to my soul, no matter the time or place.

"Do you still want to kill Klas?" Vesperus asked softly.

I considered it for a moment and shook my head. "I want him dead. But killing him is not an honor I can accept." That belonged to Fallon. And she seemed to be working toward that resolution on her own terms.

"That's what I said to Kaspian about Paxton," Vesperus murmured. "He betrayed me, yes. But it was Kaspian he'd betrayed most."

I nodded. "It's a need and a punishment, in a sense. One wants revenge, but to carry it out… hurts."

"Yes," he agreed. "But Kaspian will heal."

"He will," I agreed. "And he killed Paxton rather humanely, too." By slicing his head off with the Gold and Garnet House sword.

Vesperus stared up at the moon for a beat before meeting my gaze. "I suspect Klas won't die as quickly."

"No, I suspect he won't." Because Fallon was angry. Hurt. And deep down… scared. That male had broken her spirit with his potion—forcing her to obey him, to *help* him, to honor him.

And then killing her… while using potions to keep her alive…

I shuddered. "I hope she makes him suffer." *For a very, very long time.*

"Me, too," Vesperus agreed, his gaze on the stars now. "I wish I could say that healing the moon would earn your favor with the other Houses, but…"

"It won't," I said, leaning against him, my stare following his to the night sky. "I hurt their trust. However, they never really earned mine, either."

He hummed, the sound one of agreement.

We sat in silence for a long moment, enjoying the tranquil ambience of his roof as stardust fell over us from the sky.

"This world is too established," I told him, my voice quiet so as not to disturb the beauty of the evening. "I want a reality like this one, filled with magic where supernatural beings don't have to hide from humans. But I need it to be a world that respects me—respects *us*."

"A world where perhaps you've set the seeds for magic to grow into something that embraces you rather than rejects you," he surmised.

"Yes. A world where powerful beings walk the earth, but they don't fear the creator that moves among them."

"And where would we find that world?" he asked, his gaze meeting mine again. "Can you create a new medallion to take us there?"

"I can try," I replied, my lips twisting. "But it'll be a new sentient energy, not the one I lost. Which means it'll have a mind of its own. So I have no way of knowing what reality, or even time period, it'll take us to."

"Time period?" he repeated.

"Well, when I created my first medallion, it kept jumping realities and time." I canted my head. "Dinosaurs existed, by the way. In case you were wondering."

His eyebrows rose. "You time-traveled?"

"Sort of," I said slowly. "It took me to an ancient era, where I wandered for a bit. Then I slept… and woke up in the current time. So it fixed itself, but it wasn't immediate."

"I see." His silver-black eyes flickered. "That sounds dangerous."

"Creation magic is always a risk," I murmured, shrugging. "You can make something with good intentions, but you can't control what they actually do."

He considered that for a moment. "I understand that to an extent. It's just like leadership—you can provide counsel, but that doesn't mean your people will listen to you or follow your advice."

"Yes, exactly that. Creation magic works the same way. Just because I wish something into existence doesn't mean it'll do precisely what I desire. Like that elf the shopkeeper wanted. Had he survived, who knows what he would have done? She'd just wished for him to exist. He would have chosen the rest."

"Makes it rather disappointing that Raymond killed him, then."

"Yes and no. Yes, because he didn't deserve to die. No, because I don't think this world would have accepted him as my creation." Which was precisely why I needed to leave. This reality would not allow me to be myself.

And it wouldn't allow Vesperus to thrive either.

We hadn't formally discussed the decision to venture to a new realm. We both just sort of reached the conclusion on our own.

Which made it that much more powerful. Because we weren't leaving for each other—we were leaving *with* each other. An important distinction, at least to me.

I wanted Vesperus to be by my side because he wanted to be there, not because of a fated-mate spell or the fact that our destinies were forever bound. But because he actually desired *me*.

And he did.

I could hear it in his mind, feel it in his touch, and see it in his eyes.

"When my medallion brought me here, I'd been enthralled by the magic," I confided softly. "I'd thought this world might be my new home. But now I realize that it was never about finding a place to live. It was about finding the other half of my soul."

That was what had driven my need to explore the various realities and realms—my soul had desired its mate.

I hadn't realized how empty I'd felt until now.

I'd been wandering worlds for millennia, enjoying passing affairs and indulging in brief friendships. But none of it had left me feeling fulfilled... until Vesperus.

I stared at him and simply felt complete. Like I'd found a new purpose to my existence. A way to thrive and live. A reason for being.

"My medallion wasn't playing a game with me. It was searching for a new purpose. Because it knew I'd found what I was looking for in this realm. So it had left me to find another fractured spirit to mend, as my partial soul was about to become whole. With you."

Vesperus's silver eyes glittered. "Then I suppose we need to make a new medallion together, one that responds to our joined souls and takes us to a realm where we can make a home. Together."

"Yes," I agreed, my palm opening to collect the stardust freely falling from the sky. "A medallion that will take us to a new reality where we can plant the seeds of our own magic."

"Yes," he echoed. "A reality where you'll reign as a goddess, and I'll worship you as your chosen king."

"Only if the worshipping goes both ways," I told him. "I rather like licking you."

His lips curled. "You are welcome to lick me whenever you want, Nyx, Goddess of Night."

"And you are welcome to lick me whenever you want, Vesperus, King of Night."

"Mmm," he hummed. "A new title."

"Yes. It seemed fitting."

"Perhaps, but a beautiful woman once told me titles don't often mean much. And that they also fail to reflect true power."

"She sounds like a brilliant goddess," I replied, smiling. "One you should probably accept a title from, as it's likely not something she bestows often."

"True," he agreed, his arm encircling my lower back as his focus went to my palm. "Well, Goddess. Are you ready to make a new future?"

"I am," I whispered, the medallion already forming in my hand. "Are we done with our goodbyes in this realm?"

"We are," he confirmed. "Kaspian's ready. Cara and Larus will become his seconds-in-command. The House has been informed of his new reign. And the other leaders will soon learn of our disappearance."

"Without a trace." Because that was the only way for Gold and Garnet to be safe. We could no longer be affiliated with them or this world. To do otherwise could tip the scales and create strife among the Houses.

We were leaving to avoid that.

To keep Gold and Garnet safe.

And to find joy in our own world, one where we could live freely. Together. Forever.

I would miss the friends I'd made here. Especially Cara. But life was long for an immortal. She would move on, as would I. However, I would forever carry the memories of her in my heart.

Fallon, too. Even though our time together had been brief, my magic had connected us. I would never forget her.

I would never forget any of them.

A subtle weight rested against my palm, the medallion fully formed.

I stared into Vesperus's gaze, loving the way his silver irises glimmered beneath the moonlight. "Are you ready, King?"

"I am, Goddess," he confirmed.

I smiled. "Then let's go exploring."

The medallion hummed to life, the world around us melting away, leaving only our memories behind, as magic propelled us into a new reality.

Where we would create our own future.

Together.

With magic.

EPILOGUE

NYX

"Tell me your dream for a perfect world," Vesperus whispered against my ear. "Perhaps I can make all your wishes come true."

I giggled as I rolled into him, my limbs aching after too long of a sleep. "I wish for a world in a more current time period," I confided, aware of our game because we'd spent the last several years playing in the ancient history of multiple realms.

It seemed our medallion wanted us to start at the beginning of time.

Perhaps to spread the seeds of magic in an ancient population, rather than impact already evolved humans later in life.

So we'd finally given in, choosing twenty mortals to bless with stardust magic, and now we were waiting to see what they would do. How they would form. What they would come to be.

Vampires were likely, given Vesperus's heritage. Wolf shifters might occur as well because of my ties to the moon.

And some sort of fated bonds.

But with a choice.

Both Vesperus and I had felt that would be important for any mortals who suddenly found themselves as immortals—they needed a way to mate their fated other half.

"Hmm, a current time period," he mused. "What else, Goddess? What other wishes can I grant for you?"

"A world full of magic," I said, staring up into his eclipse-like eyes. The black had overwhelmed the silver again, telling me he was full of moon magic.

I nuzzled against him, my tongue tracing the column of his throat as I tasted his dessert-like flavor.

"A world where I can lick you however, wherever, and whenever I choose," I added, my leg coming over his to straddle him. "A world where you're mine to ride. Mine to please. Simply *mine*."

He slid into me with ease, his cock already hard and ready for me.

"What else?" he asked, his gaze darkening as I began to move.

Not quickly.

Just leisurely.

Enjoying him. Loving him. Indulging in him.

I sat up, my palms on his bare chest. "A world that respects us. A world that understands us. A world with a hot spring we can call our own."

His lips curled as he pushed himself upward, his palm wrapping around the back of my neck. "In that order, Goddess? Respect, understanding, and a hot spring?"

I shifted my legs around him, bringing us closer and taking him deeper. "I miss your roof pool."

"I do, too," he admitted, thrusting up into me. "Perhaps we can go build a new one."

I smiled. "Yes, when reality catches up with our timeline."

He nibbled my lower lip. "Hmm, is that another wish, sweet goddess of mine?"

"It is," I whispered. "But I think I already mentioned it."

"You did," he agreed, his arm banding around my lower back. "What else do you desire, Goddess?"

"Right now?" I breathed, my hips moving faster against his. "Pleasure. To see the stars. A dance with the moon."

He chuckled, the sound husky and low against my mouth. "Pleasure," he repeated, his hand slipping between us to stroke my clit. "Pleasure, I can give. But I think there's a reason you woke up needy, Goddess. Full of life. Ready to explode."

I hummed. "Because I woke up next to you, King." He constantly set my blood on fire, making me want to ravage him at all times of the day. "You're my favorite dessert."

"And you're my favorite breakfast," he returned. "All citrusy sweetness, a drink I adore first thing in the morning."

"Then fuck me and lick me clean," I told him.

"That sounded more like a demand, Goddess."

"Because it was, King."

He spun us until my back hit the mattress, his hands catching mine to raise them over my head as he began to show me his power.

I arched into him, losing myself to his touch, his existence, his *magic*. I could feel it everywhere, suffocating my insides, warming my blood, and drowning me in a sea of enticing enchantment.

It almost reminded me of his home realm, his energy intoxicating and stirring a thousand memories.

I scraped my nails down his back, needing more, needing to drown in the magnitude of his power, to revel in the bliss of his existence.

"Vesperus," I whispered, panting against him.

I wasn't sure how he was doing this, but I felt more alive than I ever had before, like he'd done something to bolster my existence, to make me feel even more complete.

"Scream for me, Goddess," he demanded. "Make them all hear their queen."

My blood pulsed with the power of his words, the moon bathing us both in unlimited stardust and energy. *I'm close,* I told him. *Oh, stars, I'm so close.*

And it felt massive.

Like I was going to set off for the heavens themselves, explode into a thousand lights, and join the moon in the sky.

So intense. So beautiful. So us.

I cried out on an eruption that sent lava flowing through my veins and twisted my abdomen into an exquisite agony of pleasure.

Vesperus soon followed, his mouth hot against mine, his seed warming my insides.

He released my hands to cup my cheeks, his thumbs wiping away the tears I'd magically shed. Because that... that had been... *mind-blowing.*

"How...?" I breathed, studying his features. He'd fucked me a thousand ways, bringing me to climax intensely and thoroughly, but this was different. It felt new. Renewed with life. *Full of vitality.*

"Don't you feel it?" he whispered, his body moving slowly against mine, both of us riding out the residual aftershocks. "Don't you feel the magic?"

I swallowed, nodding. "Yes. Have you manifested a new ability?"

He shook his head. "No, Nyx. I've simply helped you make your wishes come true."

My eyes searched his. "My wishes? My...?" I trailed off as understanding finally began to dawn on me. "My world..."

His lips curled against mine. "Your world."

I grabbed his shoulders. "Our timeline has caught up?"

"Our timeline has caught up," he echoed. "And your magic is definitely thriving."

"You went to look without me?" I asked, my tone revealing my hurt.

"No, Goddess. I can just feel it. Can't you?"

The gold stardust shimmered along my skin, confirming his claim and whispering words about my new reality. *It's time,* my medallion was saying. *It's time to see what you've created, Goddess.*

"I feel it," I whispered, my eyes widening. "We did it."

"We did it," he repeated, smiling at me. "You ready?"

"I am," I breathed.

"Then let's go see our utopia..."

USA Today Bestselling Author Lexi C. Foss loves to play in dark worlds, especially the ones that bite. She lives in Chapel Hill, North Carolina with her husband and their furry children. When not writing, she's busy crossing items off her travel bucket list, or chasing eclipses around the globe. She's quirky, consumes way too much coffee, and loves to swim.

Want access to the most up-to-date information for all of Lexi's books? Sign-up for her newsletter here.

Lexi also likes to hang out with readers on Facebook in her exclusive readers group - Join Here.

Where To Find Lexi:
www.LexiCFoss.com

ALSO BY LEXI C. FOSS

Blood Alliance Series - Dystopian Paranormal

Chastely Bitten

Royally Bitten

Regally Bitten

Rebel Bitten

Kingly Bitten

Cruelly Bitten

Blood Alliance Standalones - Dystopian Paranormal

Blood Day

Crave Me

Dark Provenance Series - Paranormal Romance

Heiress of Bael (FREE!)

Daughter of Death

Son of Chaos

Paramour of Sin

Princess of Bael

Captive of Hell

Elemental Fae Academy - Reverse Harem

Book One

Book Two

Book Three

Elemental Fae Queen

Winter Fae Queen

Hell Fae - Reverse Harem

Hell Fae Captive

Hell Fae Warden

Immortal Curse Series - Paranormal Romance

Book One: Blood Laws

Book Two: Forbidden Bonds

Book Three: Blood Heart

Book Four: Blood Bonds

Book Five: Angel Bonds

Book Six: Blood Seeker

Book Seven: Wicked Bonds

Book Eight: Blood King

Immortal Curse World - Short Stories & Bonus Fun

Elder Bonds

Blood Burden

Assassin Bonds

Mershano Empire Series - Contemporary Romance

Book One: The Prince's Game

Book Two: The Charmer's Gambit

Book Three: The Rebel's Redemption

Midnight Fae Academy - Reverse Harem

Ella's Masquerade

Book One

Book Two

Book Three

Book Four

Noir Reformatory - Ménage Paranormal Romance

The Beginning

First Offense

Second Offense

Third Offense

Fourth Offense

Underworld Royals Series - Dark Paranormal Romance

Happily Ever Crowned

Happily Ever Bitten

X-Clan Series - Dystopian Paranormal

Andorra Sector

X-Clan: The Experiment

Winter's Arrow

Bariloche Sector

V-Clan Series - Dystopian Paranormal

Blood Sector

Night Sector

Vampire Dynasty - Dark Paranormal

Violet Slays

Crossed Fates

Other Books

Scarlet Mark - Standalone Romantic Suspense

Rotanev - Standalone Poseidon Tale

Carnage Island - Standalone Reverse Harem Romance

www.ingramcontent.com/pod-product-compliance
Lightning Source LLC
Chambersburg PA
CBHW051127300726
48981CB00024B/583/J